BEYOND

THE

BOUNDS

OF

INFINITY

Beyond the Bounds of Infinity © 2024 by the authors

Published by Raw Dog Screaming Press
Bowie, MD
All rights reserved.
First Edition

Book design: Jennifer Barnes
Cover art copyright 2024 by Lynne Hansen
LynneHansenArt.com

Printed in the United States of America
ISBN: 978-1-947879-70-6 / 978-1-947879-71-3

Library of Congress Control Number: 2024932724

www.RawDogScreaming.com

BEYOND THE BOUNDS
OF INFINITY

An Anthology of Diverse Cosmic Horror

Edited by

Vaughn A. Jackson

Stephanie Pearre

Contents

Foreword

"Fear makes companions of us all."

Odd, I'm sure, to start the foreword to a horror anthology with a *Doctor Who* reference, but the second I sat down to write this, I knew it was perfect. See, at first glance it's simple, "we all have to live with fear," but in the context of the show, where a Companion is the title for the titular character's running mate, it starts to mean something more akin to, "fear makes us into Companions."

For who? Each other.

"Fear is like a companion. A constant companion, always there. But that's okay, because fear can bring us together." Sixty years, and a whole lot of time travel later, we get this expansion of the initial quote.

Fear is relational, it's a writhing knot of blackened veins that connects all of humanity, and horror as a genre is (or perhaps should be) a safe space to experience and understand fear. H.P. Lovecraft said, *"The oldest and strongest emotion of mankind is fear, and the oldest and strongest kind of fear is fear of the unknown."*

This isn't the first, or only, thing the man was wrong about in his life: the oldest and strongest kind of fear is the fear of being *alone*. When ancient humans were terrified of the unknown, they joined together—because even the unknown is less scary when you're facing it with other folks just as scared as you.

Sure, horror shines a light on the things we'd rather not acknowledge-- the darkness of our souls, the demons that torment us, and the hurts we can't quite snuff out. But through the emotional catharsis of being *seen*, horror is unifying. Trauma and pain are at their worst when you feel completely isolated by them, but seeing your experience understood, be it in a book or a film or another person lifts a bit of that weight from your shoulders, because suddenly you aren't alone.

Jordan Peele's *Get Out* was one of the first movies where the horrific aspects felt like they were catered towards me—I still shudder at the 'fist bump' scene—and it brought to my attention how little I related to characters in horror. It didn't take long for me to realize that if *I* felt this way about Black characters (I mean, who wants to relate to the guy who dies first) then surely other marginalized ethnicities and orientations—who are lucky to have characters in these stories at all—probably held similar feelings.

Thus, this idea began to form, and it wasn't until much later when I fully started grappling with the *ahem* problematic nature of a few of my favorite classic horror authors that I really put the pedal to metal.

As a fan of cosmic horror in particular, it grew hard for me to really prop the genre seeing how racist and intrinsically *other*-ing its origins (and to this day, a lot of its proponents) are. I got really tired of saying things like "Go check out this book, it's great, just remember, the fish people are a symbol for the horrors of mixed-race breeding so maybe…okay, yeah never mind, maybe just don't." And it wasn't until I read *The Ballad of Black Tom* and *The Worm and His Kings* by Victor LaValle and Hailey Piper, respectively, that I realized there were other people trying to rally against the negative stereotype. This got me wondering if maybe, just maybe, there were a lot more people out there trying to get their versions of cosmic horror told—to reclaim a great subgenre of horror and show how it could work without vilifying entire races! (You'd think, for a genre overflowing to the brim with tentacle monsters and things so horrifying the authors would run out of words in the dictionary to describe them, that maybe we wouldn't have to spend whole sections hating on Black people, or the Irish, or Jewish folks, right?)

I can't say I was surprised to find that there were, nor was I surprised to find that some of these people were having difficulty getting these stories out into the world, for whatever reason. My personal favorite is always: "People can't relate to this character/culture," meanwhile we are all supposed to be able to relate to the guy whose entire grasp on sanity is upended because immigrants started moving into Red Hook. But I digress, and it threatens to become a rant, so…

I was lucky enough to find a publisher, and a handful of authors who were of like mind on this topic. We put out the call and—somewhere close to 350 submissions later—we were well on our way. I point out the number we received not as a bragging point (though I feel like it is just a tad brag-worthy), but because such a large turnout for two first-time editors in myself and Stephanie was mind-boggling. The stories themselves proved our assumption that cosmic horror does not have to rely on fear or hatred of the other to work.

I'm beyond grateful to everyone who submitted, and flattered that people would trust their tales to me (if you were just trusting them to Stephanie, I understand, and don't blame you). You made the process incredibly difficult and if I thought a three-hundred story anthology was doable, well…there's a reason I'm just the editor, not the publisher.

At last, this is where we stand.

This collection houses nineteen phenomenal stories by a cast of authors new and known that will give you a healthy glimpse of just what the genre can be: from cozy to gothic, enraging to empowering, and so many kaleidoscopic ideas in between. By casting a wide net and seeking diversity in the authors we accepted, we created an anthology that is not only a stellar introduction to cosmic horror, but a variety pack showcasing all the different forms that cosmic horror can take when viewed through a different lens.

These are the voices of The Other that have been held in contempt for so long. Follow their whispers into the void—away from the trite and overwrought hatreds of the past—and step *Beyond the Bounds of Infinity*. With each of these stories, a new breed of fear is being born. Take our hand and know that even in a world that casts you as an outsider, you are not alone. You are *never* alone.

Necrophantasmically Yours,
Vaughn A. Jackson

The Birth of Sound

Timaeus Bloom

You've had a long night.

Whoever you are, whatever it is that filled your evening.

Perhaps it was work. A normal shift that tiptoed, and then sprinted, into the midnight hour.

Perhaps you landed after a long flight, that spreading cancer we call jetlag seeping into your mind, your bones…your soul.

You're exhausted, but the last thing you can do is sleep.

Or better yet, maybe tonight was a good night? A nightcap with a not so former lover.

Or no! You finally started that book of yours, the "Great American Novel" that this country so desperately needs. It's poignant, critical, truly a *tour de force*.

It's likely that's not it either.

Did you stay up late chatting with friends online? How fun. That one person is always so funny. He's a trip.

No matter what you did or didn't do, it left you exhausted, devoid of energy. Sleep would be a welcome gift, a blessing to combat this curse of unrelenting insomnia.

Are you in your car? Turn on the radio.

THE FREQUENCIES CRACKLE

Or perhaps you use your phone—open up an app and scroll through your list of tracks. You like music okay, but it's not your life. For ninety-nine cents a pop, you were quick to smack your thumb on the "buy" button for these songs. If it's got a good beat, and you can tap your feet to it, it's just fine by you. You don't know your jazz from your blues, your country from your folk, but they're hits for a reason, right?

Scratch that. You're a snob. You've got so many pieces of vinyl that those cheap IKEA shelves are buckling—leaning forward like your uncle when he's had more than his fill of the sauce. You own a high-dollar system that you're still slaving away on weekends to pay off. You wouldn't be caught dead listening to a CD or, God forbid, streaming a song. When you listen to the opening chords of Yes' "Roundabout," you want to hear Steve's strings ring.

What was it you said on that message board?

"Audio Files are like dipping a dead frog in formaldehyde. Kill it, but it lasts forever." You drop the needle, let that record ease you like Sunday morning, but you don't hear Lionel Richie. Whatever you click, swipe, or flip, it's all the same: a disquieting silence and a little bit of me…

THE FREQUENCIES CACKLE

I say the same old schlocky disc jockey tags that have been slopping out of speakers like curdled sweet milk for decades. Back in '27 when Thomas Edison told us for the first time that "Mary had a little lamb" on his phonograph, who'd have thought that I'd be easing people into Sunny D commercials by catching them "in the meantime, and in between time" in the era of Synthwave and whatever Bjork is.

To you, dear listener, my voice is in competition with the buzzing frequencies. The harsh, biting sound of electric waves, discombobulated and swarming, like ants under a demolished mound of dirt. And just as eerie as those creepy crawlers scurry every way and no way, so too do these echoes of communication.

White noise. So much white noise. But my dulcet tones break through, in spite of sound itself trying to silence me, forcing me out with its screeching cacophony.

It's here you've had enough of me, here any available extremity of yours reaches for the console to cut me off. This is worse than odd. It makes no sense. You don't hear music, unless you count the unvarying emissions of my piercing backbeat—and I do count it. Who is this voice you're hearing? What channel is this, what station, what dial? Scrolling across your dash or your phone, your mind, are my call letters: WZLG, the Hidden and Forbidden.

THE FREQUENCIES CRY

I think of better times…roads that led me here, things that were taken from me to elevate others, and let them ring from speakers and bow at the applause of thousands. I take a break. My voice quiets…the static lessens…clears… evaporates into quaint nothingness as music begins to play…

The echo of the last piano key drifts into space as the crackles re-emerge. While an assortment of inconsistent and disconnected songs played, there had been relief. The station would not fade away, turn off, or die, but at least *I* was not there. For a while, it seemed to you as if the nightmare was fading into the mundane, becoming something, if not exactly explainable, at least reconcilable. Weird things happen when your body sits, but your brain drifts. But I'm back, midnight rider, for you, for them, for everyone. You lie still. My tone wavers, as if making peace with something that I'd always known was coming.

Always the professional, I hit the post. "And that was Meat Loaf with 'Two Out of Three Ain't Bad.'"

You'll excuse me if I seem a bit out of sorts. I've been told this evening is to be my last show.

We had it all. Outside the banks of the Saint Francis River in Arkansas, I formed a band with my closest friends in Glenn's dinky little tin shed. And we had it, baby.

We had a nice groove, with a drummer so deep in the pocket that we had to pry him out with a crowbar after every set. Our singer, though, wasn't much to write home about, I will humbly admit. Where we wanted a James Brown or an Otis Redding, we had something more akin to a bleating lamb. But he had the look. We had a good swing, and that was more important in those days. If you had a groove, it didn't matter if Porky Pig—"That's all folks!"—gripped the mic. Our band was dynamite.

THE FREQUENCIES SING

That sound you're hearing under me, those chords that are making sweet love to your ears and tickling your loins—my mother always called that baby-making music—is one of our first recorded songs. Back when "funk" wasn't a good thing. When it was a pejorative, equated to mess, garbage.

My apologies, dear listener, I needed your full and undivided attention. You're wondering why you can't move. Your earlier attempts to shut me off were unsuccessful, but at least you maintained your mobility. At least you had control. I don't like to be interrupted—nor do I like to be ignored. You see, when you understand sound—forget the notion of music—it's all about sound. When you understand sound…what we hear, what our throats emit…when you learn to give into it, and let your body wade in its waters like an old country baptism, that's when you've got it. When you can be more than what labels society defines you by, more than a white picket fence, an HOA, or a W-9 form. When you are listless, unmotivated, exhausted…when your brain drifts into inactivity but refuses to let you sleep, that's when you are mine.

It's fine, relax. Weren't you tired?

Where was I? Right, my old band. We called ourselves the Jet-Sons with the general idea, cheesy though not uncommon, that our music was "out of this world"—that the lines we were laying down *had* to come from the future. But don't get me wrong, even that wisecracking Rosie the Robot may have looked sideways at what we were putting out.

With very little natural talent, but an understanding of wires and conduits, I played bass. My own creation, even. Helped put together by my dad. My old man was a good, if not aimless, man who made a living as one hell of an electrician, and I miss him.

Like many parents in those days, he had little respect for the "career path" I'd aggressively chosen for myself—but that just made my motivation cooler and worth pushing towards. So I spent nights alone, listening to old records, taking in the thumps and silences that forefathers like James Jamerson laid down on so many classic Motown tracks. If you can explain to me how it's possible to listen to him playing on Marvin Gaye's "What's Going On," and not feel like no other soul should touch that instrument, then I might just free you from the stupor you find yourself in.

Keyword: *might.*

THE FREQUENCIES BECOME ARGUMENTATIVE, INCREDULOUS

My voice cuts out as the static grows louder, angrier, vengeful. The static fights with me, binary competitors, disc jockey and radio waves, struggling for control. You hear me scream, you hear me rage. I told you I didn't like to be interrupted. But I don't blame *you.* This isn't *your* fault. I am fighting the tower, laying siege to the waves themselves. Sound crashes from your speakers—whatever device houses them—and crashes into you, colliding with your eardrums like darts on a checkerboard. The nodes of your brain flash and come alive, activity not spearheaded or condoned by you forced upon your neural network.

"Dear, listener…." I grunt, my voice wavering and coming in long, breathy pauses. "I'm in the fight of my life…but I will succeed. *How can you fire white noise?*"

Voices that do not belong to me push through this raucous battlefield of noise. They contrast mine. When things are good and swinging, my voice is all there ever is: pleasing and ever-relaxing. It was never meant to sing, but it could always soothe. But these are the voices of the others: the pencil-pushers, the program directors.

The prodigal enemies of creativity and art.

Music, my lambs, is not—nor has it ever been—*work*. Oh, yes, it's a billion dollar "industry" that has corroded ingenuity and deserved success, but this has never been natural.

THE FREQUENCIES COMPOSE THEMSELVES

In measured, artificial tones the electronic chorus addresses me and you, "Our apologies for the interruption. The station is now under new management. Despite these technical difficulties, we can assure you that in the coming days we will restructure ourselves to a more user-friendly, engaging station that offers the best of today's hits with entertaining personalities who, though edgy, present the best radio has to offer without crossing the line. Again, we apologize for any inconvenience tonight's broadcast may have caused."

I repeat, these voices do not soothe, calm, or decompress. They are innately untrustworthy and demanding. To suggest that they offer the best for their listeners is ridiculous, but they do offer control. For a few moments you are allowed to move. Your neurons fire in ways that you are accustomed to. You wiggle fingers, toes squint your eyes. Some of you, unfortunately, have soiled yourselves. Your waste drips down the cushions of your chairs, the stench of excrement permeates your abode. But you are free—in a sense.

Freedom is a fallacy.

There is much money to be gained—and it's always about money—in offering the customer the appearance of choice. What is it Burger King says: "Have it your way"? Yeah, it's your way alright, as long as you want heat-lamped patties, drooping lettuce, and coagulated cheese. The fixin's are all yours.

But time's a-wastin'. In those brief few moments, some of you were quick, sharp enough to turn me off. You are, "gone." But many of you remain. I never needed all of you. Whether I'm performing at Carnegie Hall or that quaint little dive bar Don't Tell Mama's, *I* always deliver.

The crunching, pulsating waves that have forever pervaded late night rides, or early-morning alarms continue with a fervor. The suits—the authority—are pissed. They cracked through, but it wasn't quite enough. I have to keep pushing. Next time, I won't be so lucky.

THE FREQUENCIES CACKLE

"Pardon the interruption." I'm rattled, but not deterred. "I had to take a quick pause for the cause."

They won that battle, but the war? The war is all mine. Those of you still left—and there are more than enough. You freeze once more. Locked in place—attentive. What is going on, you wonder?

You're easing back into comfort again.

I clear my throat. The mic is hot, and I don't like to do it on the air, but I'm recovering from what just happened, so I didn't think to press the cough button. That's okay, it's all smoke and mirrors.

We were fantastic. Once in a generation type stuff. We all know how the stories go. Bad management, crap contracts; we got taken for a ride, and that's fine. I've made my peace with it. But what I *do* regret is the music that never got out there. See, the band thought I was becoming too much, too involved. More "audiophile," than musician. Which is true. I love what we can do with just a piece of wood and an assortment of strings, plus a little amp. But what I really cared about was the sound. Reverberations, echoes, the weight of silence. So when I took our newest single, "Body Ride (I Love My)," the night before it was released and re-edited the production, I knew what I was doing was next level. Yeah, the unedited song was funky, but I didn't care about that anymore. There was a nice groove—a great one even—but it didn't play with sound. It didn't do anything.

So I fixed it.

I went into the studio after all the lights were out, when only the roaches and the rats had business to attend. The doors were locked tight, and the parking lot was as empty as the marriage bed of a cheating spouse. And I made *my* magnum opus. They should have been grateful—over the moon—for what I'd done for us. Maaan, this was out of sight, next level stuff. I gave them credit, of course, left them mixed in with the roaring waves and splintering sounds of cracking glass, birthing mothers, and other auditory ambrosia. Shelly's there, his snare tight as always, Glenn is too, that busted Les Paul crying for its life. And our singer? His squeals can be heard…if you have a keen ear. Telling his girl that her body is like a Cadillac, "Big in the back, and hot under the hood."

THE FREQUENCIES EASE, REMINISCING

Forgive my hubris, dear listener, but I have no doubt that the recording I produced that night is the closest thing our insignificant little ball of fledgling life will ever get to the Voice of God. That morning, as the Sun rose and calmly told the moon that it was overstaying its welcome, more than a few tears ran down my face. I remember the taste of those salty droplets as they slid into my yawning mouth, my lips wrinkled from a plastered smile that refused to fade.

Like any of those trendsetters before me: Noah, Gandhi, Dylan when he plugged in that Strat at the Newport Folk Festival in '65, I was—at best—met with cynicism. I was more than kicked out of the band, I was erased. They took the tapes from me. Allowed me to witness as they were burned and trampled. And then I was alone. But that's fine. I didn't need them, and they sure as hell didn't deserve me. Commercialized sellouts. What's their legacy now? A forgotten best of tape and a gig at the Hillside Peanut Festival in Alabama. I don't hate them for continuing on without me, absolutely not. But I'll never forgive them for the erasure. No, I don't think I'll ever live quite long enough for that. And trust you me, dear listener, I will live.

You've gone numb again. Even those sparks of life jumping within your cerebrum have slowed down. You may even begin to feel like you're growing tired now. This is a gift I give to you. You've listened to my little walk down memory lane. Now it's time to run. The road's been bumpy, but the way ahead is paved with care. The—

THE FREQUENCIES RAGE

Right on time, back for their last stand. I've gotta be fast now. My voice swiftens, though it still retains that nice, steady rhythm. I sound like a mixture of shuffling sand and an easy river. From my home within this cage, from which I seek to escape, I lay it all out:

"Now I don't claim to be Art Bell. But I have seen a thing or two that I would call abnormal. Nothing so standard as ghosts or anything. I've always found the concept of them funny. Is it that only the white ghosts can come back? I have a feeling if my ancestors rose from the grave, howling and shaking chains, they'd be breaking off their feet in every pale ass they came across. Nah, I like *Ghostbusters*, and that scene with Swayze, Demi Moore and the vase was alright—excellently highlighted by the Righteous Brothers' 'Unchained Melody'—but that's not what I'm talking about.

"The other day a listener called up, telling me about a campus he was meant to visit. Said people changed, bodies twisted and morphed until their flesh grew into identical jeans and sunglasses, shaking their hips like they were dancers on *Soul Train*. Everyone shimmying to their own careless whisper. We miss you, George. That's the kind of stuff I'm talking about. Or one time I went to the john to drain the lizard—I only had as long as a commercial break—and the 'door' was the outstretched face of, what was the cat's name? They say he's sleeping under Giants' Stadium? Hoff-somebody. Yeah. Well, he told me what happened to him that night. Damn near pissed myself I was so caught up in the tale."

THE FREQUENCIES GIGGLE

I have given you this backstory, this *Behind the Music* special which was only heightened by that earlier interruption, because this is the one instance I've felt it necessary to pull back the curtain. And when I'm done here, it'll be impossible to close it. In the old days it was always about the music. Sure, there were DJs like Casey Kasem, Wolfman Jack or The Nightbird who made names for themselves as personalities, but that's never really been my bag. Nothing I could ever say was better than what I could *play*.

What you're used to hearing, what you like—this "music" is only sound at its most artificial and botched, unnaturally twisted by the plucking of strings or the mashing of buttons. It's all bullshit! Excuse me, I should stay professional. But it's not real, it's not *true*. The buzz of this station, this chaotic static? It's older than me. It's older than you. It's older than babbling brooks or the whisper of the wind. Eggheads talk about a Big Bang that got everything in motion, about stars like sperm spreading out amidst the sky and fertilizing life. What you're hearing now—what we're listening to together—is the best we can get of that moment, from the dawn of creation. Aged and rusted, decayed and lost in translation, this buzz comes from that. From that laughing tongue to our inexperienced ears. We're all so quick to move on.

"Where's the music? I want to hear today's pop tune number three."

Sickening, dear listener, abhorrent even.

While I have lost what I created back in that studio so many years, days, hours ago—I cannot recollect—I have grown closer to the static. Everywhere I go, I hear it. I've not heard another sound in so long that I can only pray my words are being delivered to you coherently. I hear only what I gained the right to hear, the walls of this radio station.

THE FREQUENCIES CACKLE, A SCREAMING LAUGH

They *are* me. The antennas *are* me. Even the static will soon become me. You've helped my noble cause. As you laid—or stood or sat—in your forced stupors while the scatterings of your impulses and desires faded away, and the lonesome cries of these hungry signals oozed into your ears and laid snuggly within the crevices of your brain—I slid in. Do you hear it, too? Do you finally *hear* me?

THE FREQUENCIES SCREAM, BELCH, PUKE

That's it, you're losing yourself, you're...drifting. Don't worry about that pounding on the door you're hearing. They've finally wised up. They've found me. But it's too late now, isn't it? Far, far too late. I will give you all "music." I will instill within you the art of sound. You will hear nothing but the truth, the chorus of the redeemed. You fade and you fade, and when you awake:

THE FREQUENCIES NO LONGER SCREAM

THE FREQUENCIES ARE JUBILANT AND PLEASED WITH THEMSELVES

THE FREQUENCIES HAVE AN EVER-FAMILIAR VOICE, THAT ANDROGYNOUS, DULCET, AND RELIEVING TONE THAT SEEMS OH, SO FAMILIAR, BUT SOMEHOW NEW

You look at your listening device. Outside there is life, movement, things that should be offering sound. But you don't hear what once was. Just the noise of channels and connections and signals.

You open your mouth, but what comes out isn't you, though it certainly must be:

"See you on down the dial."

Fractures of Her Reflection

Amanda Headlee

"If I don't tap the inside of my bedroom door three times after waking up, the world will end."

Earl maintained a straight face for a moment before cracking a smile. "Dava, the world won't end if you don't tap your door."

Dava scraped the outer edge of her right thumbnail three times. Then she switched to her left thumb, performing the same scratches—back and forth. Her cheeks tingled, and the image of her face on the computer screen flushed. She hated virtual sessions with her therapist; so many words and images lost in translation over the Internet.

"It will," she whispered. "You don't understand."

Earl cleared his throat.

Heat flared in her head, trickled down her spine, and spread to the rest of her body. She'd never told anyone about what happened. The only ones who knew were those who visited her at the hospital afterward—her nan and Auntie Jenna. She'd moved in with them after the event and had lived with them ever since because her father didn't want her anymore. The accident was her fault, after all.

Earl's here to help you. You contacted him.

"It happened when I was eleven. Denny was one but managed to sleep through everything somehow. There was a lot of screaming and things crashing downstairs that night. Once it quieted, Mom came to my room and said we had to go. I think her head was bleeding. Dad was somewhere in the house too. We took nothing with us, and Mom said nothing as she backed out of the driveway. She didn't turn on the radio." Dava exhaled and bounced her foot as she pushed a fingernail deeper into the flesh of her thumb. "We always played music in the car. Mom would tap the palm of her hand on the door's armrest, her wedding ring tinged out the beat. I tried to mimic her, making our taps in sync. That night, Mom drove with both hands on the steering wheel, and she didn't have on her wedding ring. The car was steeped in silence.

"From what I was told, we were only about five miles from home. She'd forgotten to stop at an intersection, and we drove right into the path of a semi." Dava felt hollow; there was no more breath inside of her.

"I was the only one who survived." She stopped the story there. It wasn't the end, but it was all she wanted to tell Earl for now. Dava wasn't sure if he was ready to hear about her recurring dream, the one that began the night she woke up in the hospital after the accident.

Honestly, it wasn't as if she could explain it anyway. She never remembered anything about the dream except for a cryptic message, and the ominous feeling that something hid in the darkness watching her—something with three purple eyes.

The message seemed significant. It *needed* to be told, but a dilemma plagued her: Was she the recipient, or the deliverer?

Earl's lips drew in a tight line. "Why do you think tapping your door every morning keeps you—no, the world safe?"

Dava wiped her nose with the back of her hand, then picked up her pen and started doodling on a lavender sticky note. "We didn't tap to the beat of the music that time. It's the only time I remember not doing that. My whole world was in the car with me that night." She cringed. Speaking about the accident triggered her, rekindling the old pain. "By not tapping, I didn't keep the car safe."

"Was the car your safe place?" Earl asked, then looked down. Dava could hear a faint, rhythmic clicking through her computer speakers and knew he was typing notes about her.

"Yes," she whispered. "It got us away from Dad."

"Is your bedroom your safe place now?" he asked while continuing to type. "Yes."

Earl's arm appeared on the computer screen as he looked at his watch. "I'm sorry, Dava, that's all the time we have today, but I'd like another session in two days—this Wednesday. We made progress, but I feel we have a lot to unpack here."

Dava chewed the inside of her cheek.

"I would like for you to do something, think of it as a homework assignment. Try not to tap your door for the next two days. Metallica has a song that speaks about how feeding your compulsions once causes them to stay forever. Let's stop feeding them." His attempt at a sympathetic smile was lopsided and seemed forced.

Dava pinched her thumb hard, wanting to hide. "Bye."

She left the video call.

The comforter landed on the floor as Dava flung herself out of bed and raced to her bedroom door. The lavender sticky note hung to the right of her doorknob. On it, she'd drawn a pyramid with cat eyes located at each point. Dava didn't remember attaching it to the door before she went to bed.

Peeling the paper off the door, she tapped the wood beside the knob three times with her right index finger. Relief washed over her. Today would be a safe day. Earl's homework be damned.

The adhesive stuck to her fingertips as she crumpled the sticky note in her fist and tossed it into the waste bin before heading downstairs to make her breakfast of tea and buttered toast. She didn't want to look at the doodle of the eyes.

They'd appeared again during her dreams last night.

The rest of her morning ran like clockwork: iron clothes (shirt, then slacks, then socks), shower starting with the feet and working to the head, comb then dry hair, brush teeth, apply mascara, get dressed. Dava always finished by looking at herself in the bedroom mirror and mentally checked the order of completed tasks. If any were out of order, she'd have to restart the process again. And she loathed those days because they made her late for work. Her nan and Auntie wouldn't leave their rooms until she left the house. Over the years, they had learned not to interrupt her routine.

Donning a jacket, she paused before reaching for her bedroom doorknob.

You forgot to tap, her mind whispered.

"No, I didn't," she said aloud.

Are you sure? People will get hurt if you don't.

Dava squeezed her eyes shut and forced herself to remember. She exhaled long and slow, quieting the antagonizing din of her mind's chatter.

"I tapped this morning." She stood tall, opened the door, and left without giving in. That should be a gold star for Earl's homework assignment. She smiled the entire walk to the bus stop. But the moment she stepped onto the bus, her smile evaporated.

What if you only imagined tapping the door this morning?

The bus door closed before she could turn around.

Too late now.

The next stop was fifteen minutes away. Going back would make her almost an hour late, and she'd be written up this time for sure.

"I did, I did, I did," she told herself as she took a window seat at the back.

City buildings passed in a blur. Morning condensation fogged the window. Dava's skin prickled with invisible heat. She bounced her right foot. With her index finger, she drew on the window. As she traced three cat eyes over and over, her panic waned.

It's a message of awakening.

Dava inhaled so sharply that the man in front of her turned with a look of concern. She didn't make eye contact.

Why am I remembering this now?

Her foot bounced harder, causing a knee to rub against the back of the man's seat. This time he glared at her, but she had more pressing concerns.

Who's the message for? Who's the messenger?

Lost in thought about all the possibilities, Dava nearly missed her stop.

"Wait!" She jumped up as the doors were closing, and pushed up the narrow aisle.

"Pay attention," the bus driver snapped and reopened the doors.

Head bent low, hiding behind the collar of her jacket, she exited. The bus's brakes hissed as they released, and its engine revved as it drove away. She walked to her office building without looking back.

Dava's role as the assistant to Thenurgee's office manager was the same role she'd held for nearly ten years—a far different trajectory from her aspirations of being an astrophysicist. She'd spent her youth excelling at sciences and math, only to get cold feet after being awarded several university scholarships. She could never leave home, and the only schools that wanted her were several hours away.

Instead of studying the cosmos, her days were filled with delivering mail, ensuring the canteen was well stocked, attending meetings, and taking notes for her manager. Dava enjoyed the routine and stability of her role. And for the most part, she was genuinely happy with it. Except for lunchtime—the worst thirty minutes of her day.

Employees were encouraged to eat in the canteen rather than at their desks. The company believed this stimulated collaboration. Dava often sat alone and observed others congregating, having fun while on break. On one hand, Dava wanted to join in but felt she needed to be invited. On the other, most conversations were superficial—discussions of dating, shoes, and reality TV, things for which Dava couldn't spare the brain capacity. But today was different. Three employees from the engineering department sat at the table next to her, and Dava eavesdropped on every word.

Marge recounted her Sunday afternoon matinee date to Lauren and Toby. "The movie was okay. A bit too much gore, but I thought it was cool how they portrayed multiple universes running in parallel."

On the table's surface, Dava traced cat eyes with her finger next to a ham and cheese sandwich. She chewed the inside of her cheeks as words formed in her throat, swallowing hard to keep them at bay. She wasn't a part of this conversation.

"I love the thought of parallel universes—that there are infinite versions of me, all existing simultaneously." Lauren giggled.

"Of course, you'd love that," Toby grumbled.

Dava couldn't hold her tongue any longer. "There are not infinite 'yous' existing in parallel."

"Wha—?" Lauren's face contorted into a mix of confusion and annoyance.

Dava placed her fingertips on the table, tenting them as she looked at the group. "A new universe is created at a decision point, branching out until there's another decision point. Each point has an infinite number of choices. For example, at a decision point, you split in two where one 'you' creates a new universe by going left and the other 'you' creates one by going right." She lifted her hands, drawing in the air in a frantic attempt to illustrate her point. "While they may exist in parallel within the constraints of space-time, each decision you make alters 'you' by sending that version's future in a different trajectory," —Dava pointed at Lauren— "so there is no Lauren in any universes like you…"

She sucked in a deep breath, placed her palms down on the tabletop, and continued. "There was once one universe—think of it as a tree trunk. Each decision made in that universe caused others to branch off. The crazy part is that the infinite number of universe branches spanning space and time never touch. They may pass by one another, but they don't make contact. They exist within their own stream, taprooting through their past branches to the origin universe."

Dava's eyes widened as her mind drifted past galaxies, black holes, and supernovas. She spanned the vacuum of space as time folded in on itself. Dava wanted to say more to them but struggled to summon the proper descriptions. No human words existed for what she saw—things that rendered conversations about movies and dates infinitesimal in the face of the vastness of this universe. If only she could project her thoughts at everyone, so they could understand too.

"So, you're wrong, Lauren; parallel universes don't exist in the way you think. There's only one of you in all the universes combined. And it's in poor taste to think there's an exact replica of you in every universe because your existence is meaningless in this stream and non-existent in the grander scheme of all universes." Dava stared at them and tapped incessantly at the tabletop.

Lauren started to cry and ran from the canteen.

"What is wrong with you?" Marge glared at Dava, then went after Lauren.

Toby rolled his eyes and said, "You're weird," before following the others.

Dava sat back in her seat with her hands over her mouth. She clenched her eyes shut, and in the darkness behind her lids, three purple cat eyes pulsed in sync with her racing heart. Sweat poured from her body in a steady stream. Suddenly, it felt like she was being crushed inside a small box. She couldn't orient herself amidst the spiral of negative self-talk and chastising thoughts tumbling through her head.

Where are these thoughts coming from? Why can't you shut up? Why can't you be normal?

Dava bolted to her feet, her chair clattering to the floor. Everyone in the canteen looked, but she ignored them. Running from the room and out of the building, she saw her escape on the other side of the street—the bus stop. Dava stepped off the curb.

Stabs of electricity and pain lanced through her body as she connected with an oncoming cyclist. The warm, oily smell of the asphalt filled her nostrils just before her face smashed into it.

Rings rippled around Dava's feet as she shifted her weight, fracturing her reflection into countless versions. She stood on the glassy surface of an ocean as dark as the deepest reaches of space. Above her, stars punctured the inky sky, but none of them reflected off the water's surface.

A scrape, like a fingernail tracing down her neck and spine, sent shivers through Dava, causing her to turn and face a towering being. An intense heat blasted against her, and she shielded her eyes with her palms to keep from being blinded by the prismatic light radiating off its body. Just as she accepted that the heat would burn her alive, it dissipated. She mentally assessed her body, noting no traces of pain.

Dava slid her hands from her eyes. The light subsided, and she could clearly see it. A long, thin tail swayed lazily above the water's surface, humming with a shimmering energy. Its humanlike hands and feet were a dark gray, that morphed into a twinkling rainbow color as it ascended its limbs. Crowning its head was a tuft of gray fur between two pointed ears. No nose or mouth was etched on its face. And its eyes…

Dava dropped her gaze as fear flooded her body. No human being should ever look upon this creature.

But its eyes...

The eyes that haunted her dreams stared down at her—the ones she couldn't stop drawing or thinking about. An ache bobbed in her throat, and the skin of her thumbs burned as she scraped them with her fingernails.

Dava relaxed her fingers and raised her head. "Why am I here?"

{A message} It spoke in a two-toned voice, both male and female at once. The sound came from far away, yet boomed inside Dava's head.

For the first time in Dava's life, her mind didn't churn with thoughts. Usually, a thousand replicas of her voice wandered through her head all at once, giving her reminders, parroting useless facts, replaying past failures, or simply worrying about an endless stream of things.

"A message for me?"

Silence.

"For you?"

Silence.

"Tell me something!" Dava shouted. "What is the message? Does this have something to do with *awakening*?"

The creature shrieked and vanished. Dava gagged, and arched her back—her chest cramped as though her lungs were being pulled out from the inside. Stars rained down from the sky, shattering the glassy surface around Dava and rendering her vision an agonizing white.

Then everything stopped. Her body relaxed and settled. Her surroundings came into focus as the blinding white dimmed.

Dava wasn't standing in an endless ocean of falling stars anymore, but lying down in a completely unfamiliar room. She was on her back on an uncomfortable bed with arm rails. Stark white walls surrounded her, with a lone TV hanging in the corner, and a machine chirping behind her head.

Dava tried to look, but a white-hot flash of pain prompted dizzy lights to steal her vision. She returned to her original position.

A news channel droned away on the TV. She ignored it and groped for the watch on her wrist. Her fingers found only a hospital ID bracelet.

She didn't know when or how she ended up in a hospital. Part of her wondered if she was still in her dream and hadn't woken up yet. Pinching her arm, she flinched—not asleep.

The being. A message of awakening. She remembered the details of her dream—every last detail. But why this time? Why now?

A low rumble rattled the room, pulling her from her thoughts. Unsure of what was happening, she pressed the call button secured to one of the bed railings. After a few minutes of no response, Dava hit it again, clicking it repeatedly with her thumb.

The rumble came again, louder this time.

Maybe it's thunder.

She turned her attention to the TV to check the weather. The woman on the screen talked to her co-host about a natural disaster. But Dava couldn't focus on the woman's words or the images of mass destruction that flickered across the screen. What held her attention was the date and time in the bottom left corner of the news ticker.

It was nine-thirty in the morning.

Wednesday.

No, it's Tuesday. It has to be Tuesday! I was just at work. A corded telephone sat on the nightstand to her right, and she gritted her teeth against the pain that shot up her leg as she reached for it. Grasping it in her hands, she pulled it on her lap. Sure enough, the date and time on the phone's screen matched the TV.

She'd been hospitalized overnight and didn't wake up in her bedroom. Her door remained untapped. Dava hurled the phone across the room, where it clattered against the wall before falling to the floor.

Bad things were going to happen if she didn't get home. Tremors tore through her body as she ripped the leads off her skin, sending the machine behind her into a tizzy. Her empty stomach churned in disgust as she tore the IV from her arm, clamping a finger over the puncture until it clotted. Scooting to the edge of the bed, she slid off, screeching as her bare feet landed on the cold linoleum floor. She lifted her right foot and saw it wrapped in bandages. A faint line of red had seeped through the white dressing.

She would deal with her injury later.

As she limped toward the hospital room's door, another rumble came. This time, the entire room vibrated. Dava didn't look out the large window on her right to see if there was a storm in the sky. There was only one thing on her mind.

Have to get home. Tap, tap, tap.

She pushed the door. It wouldn't budge. She tried pulling to no avail.

Looking through the narrow window on the door, she saw a medicine cart lying on its side in front of the door, wedged into place by a toppled wheelchair braced against the nurse's station counter. Glancing up and down the hallway, the entire floor appeared void of life.

Dava tapped at the door to signal for help and to quell her flaring distress.

But this wasn't her bedroom door; tapping here would do nothing.

Another rumble shook the room so violently that Dava fell to the floor. She'd been right about her morning ritual and how it kept the world safe.

Pushing herself to all fours, she looked at the large window on the back wall. Maybe she could signal for someone outside to help. Using the wall as a crutch, Dava climbed to her feet. The pain continued to sear up her leg as she limped toward the window.

The sun shined bright in the sky, negating any idea that the rumbling was thunder. Pandemonium stretched for as far as she could see.

Chaos reigned in the parking lot as hospital staff scrambled to get patients lying on hospital beds or in wheelchairs away from the building. People scattered and screamed as the right wing of the building collapsed in a pile of rubble, trapping all who'd stood nearby. Past the hospital's boundaries, smoke dotted the horizon.

Dava started to cry and tapped her right index finger in three repetitions against the glass, hoping to suppress the bedlam outside.

The building lurched, throwing Dava forward. She cracked her head against the window, spider-webbing the glass. Wet warmth trickled around the corner of her right eye. She looked through the cracked glass as the reflection of something black loomed in each fractured piece. Leaning left to gaze past the shatter, Dava froze.

A black mass stood against the horizon—an obelisk towering toward the sky, shifting left and right as it grew larger.

"Not an obelisk," Dava whispered, placing her fingertips against the glass.

Long legs stretched at least two city blocks with each careless step as it approached. The black fur covering the lower parts of its arms and legs morphed into an iridescent white that caught the sunlight and cast kaleidoscope prisms. A long, thin, white tail waved behind it. And its head—triangular and mouthless—was topped with two pointed ears and a tuft of black fur. But Dava couldn't draw her attention away from its eyes—three of them, all vibrant and purple. This creature looked like the being from her dreams, albeit shorter, lankier…childlike.

Tap, tap, tap on the window, Dava willed the beast away with the action, thoughts drifting to her dream. A message of awakening—a message of *something waking.*

She kept tapping as the creature approached, stepping on cars, homes, and buildings. The tapping turned to pounding, her fist recoiling off the glass. Tears streamed down her face, and she avoided looking down, where screams of terror ended abruptly as people were crushed into the ground by its tremendous feet.

Dava battered the glass with both fists, further spreading the spiderweb until all she could see were thousands of splinters of her universe—each one containing this creature.

Live Free or Die

Danny Brzozowski

Blood roared in my ears, muting the sounds of hall passing time. Stampeding feet, chatter, the bell all underwater. I tried to remind myself everyone had their own drama, no one was paying attention to mine but gossips already whispered. After the rumor mill had a day to grind, I'd be the talk of the town. Again. Briarbrook was too small, too inbred. Good ol' boy nepotism clashed with transplanted wealth. Contrived scarcity combined with too much entitlement meant privileged folks were sure there wasn't enough to go around. Some days it seemed like bigotry was the only thing holding the two halves of our remote village together.

Bigots build community by sacrificing scapegoats and I was about to be fired for being trans and teaching science: anthropogenic climate change, no biological basis for race, sex determination more complicated than chromosomes. They said I was divisive and grooming children; I'd be lucky to keep my license. Truth would be choked to death so the fear-mongers could create their scandal.

"I'll do everything I can," Jodi, the history teacher and union rep, reassured me. Her jutting chin and snub nose marked her as belonging to one of the old families who settled here before the Revolution, but a warm smile always softened her features. "We'll file a grievance with the labor board. Just don't get mad and quit. If you're no longer part of the bargaining unit, I can't help you."

"How could I possibly not be mad?" My nostrils flared but I kept my voice down. "But don't worry. I'll never let a spineless jellyfish like Marsh erase me." Fighting the unrelenting urge to vomit, I steeled myself and knocked.

Our school principal, Mr. Marsh, admitted us to his sanctum, dissecting me with his gaze under harsh fluorescent lights. Heavy mud-season rain pounded against the windows, framing him in dark thunderclouds. His shaved head, barrel chest, and ridiculously narrow tie wedged between a thick chin and broad shoulders made him look like a vicious bulldog begging for an excuse to break its chain. He'd been a bully twenty years ago as my gym teacher and hadn't changed as my boss. He casually threw his weight around, expecting others to get out of the way, while I spent a lifetime fighting for the right to exist, earning respect by inches. He was a coward with power, the most dangerous kind, defensive and unpredictable.

"I've received hundreds of complaints. Serious complaints."

"I was doxxed." My voice cracked, despite my best efforts to keep calm. Knuckles white, I gripped my seat until I could pull myself together. "People who've never heard of Briarbrook are harassing me."

"You should be more responsible with social media. Per your contract: 'Teachers will uphold high moral standards. The district reserves the right to take employment action in response to any conduct interfering with the effective performance of professional duties or district operations.' I think we can agree your current situation qualifies."

I glanced over at Jodi for affirmation. She looked at me apologetically and nodded. I didn't know who shared my information on a forum devoted to attacking trans educators, but the response was rabid. Most settled for threatening messages, but last month the district was hit with a DNS attack that shut down its network for days. Negative press, especially from nationally syndicated conservative media, shocked residents of our isolated town. Op-eds in the local paper made it clear that I should be sacrificed to restore the peace.

"I am careful. I've never posted anything inappropriate. People search school websites for likely targets. I'm trans and a teacher. That's enough for them."

"You don't have to be so obvious about it. Your they/them thing is hard on staff, and confusing to students and families." Marsh sat back and steepled his fingers, cocooned in smug self-satisfaction. "Believe me, I don't like this any more than you do. I never want to replace a teacher mid-year, but parents have challenged your license under the Divisive Concepts Law."

I ground my teeth and took a deep breath while Jodi furiously scribbled notes. "There are bounties for people who get a teacher's license revoked under that law. At least they get their thirty pieces of silver. You're selling me out for free."

A vein bulged from his temple like a leech. "The district is investigating. Parents are concerned you haven't taught both sides of controversial issues. Education already has a reputation for being too liberal."

"Science is a process for testing information. Challenging misconceptions can be uncomfortable but it's about evidence, not belief."

"Public school has to be a place where everyone is welcome. You can't discriminate because of their sincerely held beliefs. All of our students have the right to a safe learning environment."

My shoulders tensed, my fingernails clawing into my palms. What did anything matter if they'd already fired me? Why play nice to protect his feelings? He looked so calm, he enjoyed toying with me. "What about our trans students? They don't feel safe, witnessing this attack."

"Everyone should feel safe. Identity has nothing to do with it. Plenty of straight white boys are afraid to walk down the halls."

"Bullying is a problem here, but not the same problem." I couldn't hold in my outrage and keep my self-respect. I began to yell, "No one is afraid to come to school because they are straight, cis, and white."

Marsh pounded the table. "You are out of line. I will not have that slur used in my presence."

I backed off, recovering my professional tone. "Cis is a technical term from chemistry, the opposite of trans, not a slur."

"It's used to make normal people feel bad about having so-called 'privilege.'" He was turning red now. "This is exactly the kind of divisiveness the law prohibits. You're on leave, pending termination, while we finish our investigation." Marsh shoved two copies of a reprimand across the table. "There's a place for you to add any remarks, but they won't change anything. Sign now and go before you make your situation worse."

Words swam on the page and lines blurred together. I rested my palms on the table to hide their shaking. Even if it meant nothing, tiny acts of resistance were still resistance. I wrote, "District responded to targeted anti-trans harassment by terminating the victim," and signed my name.

He nodded and collected his copy. "Wait outside while Jodi gets your things."

"I have a lot of personal items, books."

"Come back after school and someone will escort you, but not while students are here." He held the door for us, the picture of patriarchal gentility, then closed it firmly behind me.

Jodi's voice was calm and reassuring. "Be patient. You have a good case for wrongful termination, maybe even a Title IX complaint."

"Thank you." I choked back tears. I couldn't cry here, in front of everyone.

My savings would cover a couple months of rent and bills, but no job meant no insurance. No insurance meant no testosterone. Maybe I could stretch what I had by halving the dose or look into alternative options from online pharmacies. One problem at a time. First, get away.

Hood pulled up against the downpour, I threw my weight into the door, fighting to open it against the wind. I snaked my way through a sea of puddles, water leaking through a hole in my shoe, squelching with every step.

The car provided some shelter and concealed my breakdown. I began to drive as I wiped away messy tears, replaying interactions with students, parents, and colleagues, trying to puzzle out who decided to ruin my life. I screamed helplessly at a huge gray truck with full-sized flags mounted on the back. "Nobody is treading on you, asshole. We're quietly living our lives." The yellow Gadsden flag was tasteless, and somehow nutjobs committed to advertising their patriotism never respect the Stars and Stripes enough to put it away in a downpour.

Torrential rain reduced visibility and made the winding road home treacherous. Trees closed in on every side as the car rattled over frost heaves. I slowed to maintain traction, transitioning onto a dirt road. High beams in the rear view blinded me, coming on too fast. I struggled to keep the car in control through the crunch of a rear impact. Goddamn drunk was going to kill someone. Before I could pull over, I heard the roar of the engine bearing down for another strike. Not an accident. Steering wheel in a death grip, I hit the gas, hoping against hope I could accelerate faster, get some distance between us, looking around wide-eyed for a way out. No cell signal. How far to the nearest house? No one locked their doors here. I could get inside, find a weapon.

Weapons. I'd never win in a fair fight. What did I have? Fuck me for not carrying bear spray. Sunglasses, tiny-ass flashlight, phone. Nothing. Looks like it would have to be keys in a fist like Mama taught me. I unclipped the carabiner from the car key, freeing the rest of the ring. The truck splashed past on the narrow road, spraying my windows with mud. He cut in too close. I slammed the brakes, yellow flag with that fucking snake filling my windshield before I skidded into the ditch.

I jerked the gear shift into reverse, gunning for the road, tires whining, unable to get traction. My door wrenched open. A tote slammed over my face. Eyes watering with the smell of spoiled milk and rot, I shrieked and lashed out with my keys. No effect. Thick, leathery cords constricted around my arms and legs, hurling me to the sticky wet ground. Some kind of rubbery bit forced the plastic material into my mouth, sour on my tongue, muffling my screams. Dead trees cracked under me, tearing my jacket and skin. I flopped like a caught fish as I was dragged through the mud. Biting down hard on the gag, I winced in pain, landing on a bruised shoulder in the back of the pick-up. A door slammed and the engine revved. I panted, short, wheezing breaths.

If I escaped the truck, maybe I could get free. I clenched my abs and jackknifed my body, pushing with my feet until I hit the wheel well. With each effort, the ropes tightened around my chest until I saw stars. I held my breath, twisting my arms up, and felt along the rusty metal wall for the edge, ropes digging into the flesh under my armpits. I hauled myself over the side as the driver hit the brakes. I lost my grip, but I was clear. Drunk on the euphoria of relief, I barely felt the cut of every branch, every rock as I fell, bouncing down an embankment, where he would never find me. I hit the back of my head hard, dissociating, recalling an old New England adage: all the stones you want sink and the ones you don't rise to the surface. Colors swirled before me and I passed out.

Cold water choking me, I gasp in panic. Damp fabric fills my mouth, the rubbery gag saving me from drowning. This time. I kick out, trying to get face up, to stand. Partial success. I flop to one side and get my knees under me. My head breaks water. Breathing through wet cloth burns my lungs but I manage. I blow hard, trying to make space in front of my nose, to no avail. Frigid water laps against my chest. I can't be in more than two feet, a shallow pool with a rocky bottom and slow current. I have to move. I can saw my way free if I don't die of hypothermia first.

The ground vibrates, pitching me face-first into slimy mud. An earthquake on top of everything else. Today even nature is against me. Slime oozes through my fingers as I grasp for something solid, crying in helpless frustration, trying to stay upright in the heaving streambed. This isn't possible. We don't get earthquakes here.

Mossy rocks slide under me. I moan as I slip backward, landing against something warm and fleshy, reeking of body odor. Hysterical screams, muted by the gag, shriek with every breath. I squirm away by inches, pushing against a yielding, fleshy beer gut. We don't get carjacking and murder here either, but here I am. Denial won't help me. He's breathing.

I freeze, body tense against imminent attack, but hear only water trickling over stones and gurgling breaths. I pull myself back towards the body and grab a handful of wet denim. No response. I can do this. Willing cramped muscles to move, I inch up his leg. I bite back revulsion, bile burning the back of my throat, worming my fingers under belly fat, following his belt until I hit the jackpot: his knife. Viciously sharp, it carves a deep gash in my fingers as I blindly maneuver it free. I grasp the slick bone handle hard when the ground shakes again, separating me from the man and depositing me on a bed of sharp gravel. The small stones sting as they grind into my wounds but remind me I'm still alive and fighting.

Warm blood runs down my wrist, dripping into the stream with a *plop, plop, plop.* The moment the rumbling stops, I've got the knife pointed at my face. I squeeze my eyes shut and saw into the gag. The cord is tough but pliable, with a solid core. My hands, slick with blood, shake from cold and adrenaline. More blood trickles down my cheeks where I cut myself each time the knife slips, cords twisting under the blade. I manage to miss my eyes and prize enough space to breathe easily.

Something pops under the blade and the gag falls away, salty warm blood spattering into my mouth. I shake my head, freeing it from the shredded bag, and spit the foul liquid out. An ominous voice in my head. *These outsiders come here, taking our jobs.* That's not my thought. Where did that come from? I can see my bonds now, thick and black with a diamond pattern, bizarrely organic. Some kind of hose, maybe?

Gulping air, I catch my breath tracing the curve of a yellow flag. Its coiled snake writhes in the flooded stream, pinned under the half-submerged truck, upside down, roof crushed in. Pink froth bubbles from my captor's mouth, glass embedded in his face, unrecognizable under a mask of blood. One side of his chest sags with each gurgling breath. I avert my gaze, hiccupping against the rising gorge. He would have murdered me, so why am I sick at the thought of leaving him to die? My stomach churns as I empty it into the stream. Chunky brown scum washes around my legs, sour sick mingling with smells of sweat and dank earth.

Loud grinding pulls my attention upstream. My skin crawls as I take in the sight of the dying man, blue-gray now, irregularly snorting each breath. I tear my eyes away and look past him. I can't think about him now. I have to focus. Boulders pushed ahead of a flash flood jam against narrow rocky banks. Debris and the truck's slowly shifting chassis dam the rising stream, but can't hold long. Frantically, I turn the knife and stab the bonds around my legs. Blood spurts from the incision, but not mine. I recoil in surprise, nearly dropping the knife. I've opened a gash into bright red muscle under iridescent green-black scales. Not a rope. This thing is alive. I twist around, unable to understand, trying to find knots, or the ends of the snake constricting me. This can't be happening. We don't have giant snakes here. Shouting, "No" with every stroke, strengthened by the sound of my own voice restored, I grip the knife harder, stabbing deep to find the spine. Probing for a gap between the bones, I wedge the knife tip into a cartilaginous disk. I twist with all my strength, leaning my weight into the knife, straining to tear the vertebrae apart as my fingers go numb.

The ground under my knees writhes and falls away, a void filling with water, sucking me under. I pull furiously, desperate to hold onto the knife, but I can no longer touch the bottom and it's stuck too deep to extract. I let it go, kicking, every breath a battle to keep my head above water. I'm hyperventilating. I know I have to take slower, deeper breaths to stay afloat. I barely have the strength to breathe against my bonds. It's impossible. I'm not ready to die here. Not when I am so close.

An ophidian arch rises before me, tearing the streambed apart like a broken zipper. I open my mouth to scream, a mistake. I'm sinking, burbling as silty water enters my mouth and nose. Thrashing, fighting for the surface, until I'm lost in the cloudy water. Lungs burning, I can no longer tell which way is up. I hit bottom.

Bottom hits me back. Harder. Hurling me up the opposite bank. I land with enough force to knock the wind—and half a lungful of water—out of me. I cough, sucking in ragged breaths. Wrapped in the twisting body of the serpent rising from the stream bed, my captor's limp form dangles, broken. Bones crack under pressure. I scramble backward up the slope, wedging my body wherever I can, trying not to slide back between each push. I can't hear my screams over the thundering roar as the dam breaks, releasing the fury of the flood. Metal screeches as boulders tear the truck apart, flinging it in pieces downstream.

Battered, the arches and coils of the creature retreat into the sinkhole, dragging the corpse into unknown depths. With its retreat, constriction around my body loosens, coils slithering away, disappearing as soon as they are free of my body. Dizzy with exhaustion, I draw my first full breath in an eternity and collapse into the leaf litter. I never want to move again.

A surge of adrenaline saves me from sinking into desperate inaction. I have to move. I'm not safe here. Have I ever been safe? My fingers and toes ache with cold, my throat the only dry part of me, as I climb out of the gully on hands and knees. I have to find some way to cross back to my car. Even if the water wasn't dangerously high, there's no way I'm setting foot in that stream. If I survive this night, I'll never go swimming again.

The smell of woodsmoke leads me along the ridgeline, down the opposite slope, where, despite the recently passed storm, someone is holding a party with a large bonfire. I stick to the trees, trying to make out shapes in the gloom. Tiki torches outline an erratic path on the yellow early-spring lawn, casting long, flickering shadows up the walls of a converted barn home. Alongside expensive SUVs and a few electric vehicles, a convoy of trucks decorated with Gadsden flags line a serpentine driveway. I'm desperate to warm myself but I shiver from more than cold. Was my kidnapper bringing me here? For what purpose?

Yellow-robed figures dance around the fire, spiraling in and out, breaking in chaotic darts and weaves, hissing a sibilant chant. In the golden light, dress shoes, work boots, brand name sneakers, and off-brand rubber clogs snake by in an endless stream, the whole county represented. I squirm, trying to see faces obscured by deep hoods.

Familiar voices complain behind the row of vehicles. "Damn it! Cody was supposed to be here with the sacrifice two hours ago."

Icy fingers crawl up my spine when I realize he's talking about me. Did he mean Cody DuBois, the police chief's son? We'd gone to school together. It had been years but back then he seemed like a nice guy, always willing to help a neighbor. I never would have figured him for my attacker. What happened to him?

"Unbelievable, he's probably drunk at the wheel again. And we have an initiation tonight." I gasp, breaking sticks, covering my mouth in panic. It was the rough, gravelly voice of Mr. Marsh.

"Did you hear that?" Jack Wheelock, our state representative, comes around an SUV, head on a swivel. How high does this thing go? I flatten myself to the ground, willing myself to be small, invisible.

"You going soft on me? Backing out?" Arms crossed, Marsh posts up behind him. "The dance has begun. We'll make do. Besides, you felt the tremors. It's awake. If it strikes before we drain it, well, Chief DuBois will make sure no one asks questions. One more deadbeat ODs in the woods. Let the bleeding hearts cry. Nobody really cares."

"Are you challenging me?" Wheelock rounds on Marsh, spitting his words. "Without me, you'll never drink the Ichor of Union again. And don't think you can go to another enclave. Your eyes will be closed to the truth. You won't even think for yourself anymore. Next thing you know, you'll be brainwashed by the liberal media. Maybe you should be our next sacrifice. Go get your candidate. Time to set her mind right." He turns his back and strides across the lawn, arms outstretched. At his approach, the dancers fall to the ground, silhouettes writhing, tangling, sliding over one another, hissing and rattling.

Marsh deflates, slinking to the house. I'm about to creep towards the road when Jodi emerges blindfolded from the patio door. I'm shocked into stillness. How could Jodi be part of something like this? Why did she submit to the thick tendril snaking out of Marsh's hand, wrapping around her waist, her shoulders, her neck? Why does she allow it to pull her forward, following Marsh across the grass?

The hissing of the crowd intensifies as Jodi steps onto their backs, treading over the golden field of revelers. I'm held in place by pathological curiosity. Wheelock raises a wicked hooked blade above his head. Is that a fish scaler? He rakes it across Jodi's chest. She stumbles to her knees. As one, the crowd sits up. Eerie silence blankets the woods, broken only by the rasp of metal as a hundred knives are drawn, biting into arms or legs, smearing blood on the grass. Rattles echo off the hills, in every direction. It's too late to run. The ground in the center of the crowd bulges, clumps of sod and burning wood flying in every direction as a great horned serpent, as wide as a truck, erupts from the earth.

Wheelock grabs the back of Jodi's dress, hauling her to her feet. He rips the blindfold from her eyes and presses something into her hand. The serpent towering over her, poised to strike, pinning her in its gaze until Marsh shoves her roughly forward. Firelight glints off a sharpened metal cone as Jodi raises her arm high then drives a maple sap spile into meaty flesh. She lowers her mouth to it and sucks, bracing her hands against the coil, still spooling up into a towering wall. The rest of the crowd surges forward with their spiles. They fall on the beast with jubilant cries, its head collapsing, power drained as they drink.

With the cult absorbed in their ecstasy, I hobble to my feet, clothes shredded, mulch sticking to my mud-covered skin. I stumble down the driveway, desperate to get away, to drive as far as I can, and never look back. I climb into the first truck I see. Everyone leaves the keys in their truck here.

The Silent Letter

Chris Nelson

"I fear," Theresa Hayes's voice recording says, "that the real challenge in grappling with The Silent Letter will not be trying to understand it, but ensuring it does not exterminate us. Its *explanation*—to the extent such a term even applies—may very well be one that brains like ours simply cannot comprehend. Nature does not select abilities that do not confer a reproductive advantage, and human language is less than a million years old. Linguistic evolution, you see, has finally surpassed our own biological evolution—overtaken us, and produced a threat that we did not evolve to contend with."

The other voice on the recording asks: "Theresa, what *is* The Silent Letter?"

She replies: "A virus."

"A memetic virus," suggests the other voice. "One that infects the mind."

But Theresa Hayes says: "No—the analogy is that of a computer virus."

What we know is this: a search party discovered The Silent Letter while looking for a tour group that had six days previously gone missing in [REDACTED] Cave, an expansive limestone system some forty kilometers southwest of the nearest population center. We call it "The Silent Letter" because that's what is written, in English, at the top of the first page of the manuscript they found. The envelope, now lost to us, is reported by our first surviving agent to have had "Eshmak E" written on it in black ink.

We also know the letter itself consists of twelve typewritten pages because we have acquired, at great cost, three fragments of the manuscript, one of which bears the text "page 5 of 12."

Only after losing three investigators to the pernicious effects of the text did we finally recognize the cause. That it took us *so long* to notice only serves to highlight how incredible the pattern is: everyone who has read The Silent Letter is now *silenced*, either by catatonia or by death.

Experiments involving both illiterate children and adults literate in languages other than English—subject to legitimate ethical concerns though they are—corroborate the idea that it is a conceptual, as opposed to sensory, stimulus that causes these deleterious effects. We have now confirmed that even *photocopies* of the original letter produce the same results. Indeed, it was a photocopy of the manuscript that Theresa Hayes and her followers took with them when they returned to the cave. This is why the Sans Doctrine is one of containment, why Deborah Sans herself ordered the mouth of the cave destroyed.

Fragment One:

"The buzzing hovered just above the threshold of my ability to perceive it, irritating me with its intermittent absence. I said aloud that I did not remember what had happened, and a rasping voice replied: there had been an accident. The memory-loss, the voice assured me, was temporary.

My eyes adjusted slowly. I turned towards the tall windows on my left to see what was outside—or thought I did. Instead, I realized that my body, which was sitting in a chair, could not move as expected—nothing below the shoulder responded. This too, said the voice as it receded, was because of the accident.

The ward I found myself in was high-ceilinged and dimly-lit, with a single wide door opening onto a hallway passage, perhaps a dozen meters away.

That I could neither move nor remember anything seemed strange to me—as though I ought to be able to move, as though I should be able to remember what had happened more than a moment ago. Then again, without any memory I had no knowledge either: For all I knew, the strangeness was what constituted the place.

I could feel no emotion: neither sadness nor anxiety nor any pain. But as I strained again towards whatever lay beyond the windows, paralysis seized upon me as though it were some hungry fungus—blind but waiting to sense me move.

The old man had been sitting in the corner of my eye the whole time, muttering something in a language I did not understand. Finally, in heavy accents but in my own mother's tongue, the old man—who, if he could be believed, was an Uzbek—spoke: part of the punishment was that it did not fit the crime."

The following is the second transmission we received after the destruction of the cave mouth:

"We have identified a sequence of four stages in which individuals affected by The Silent Letter predictably progress.

Stage 1, Infection:

Speechless A, a 37-year-old female, was the first individual into whom The Silent Letter was intentionally introduced, and the first to extrapolate the *letter* from *epistolary* to *alphabetical*. She thought that 'The Silent Letter' referred to the first letter of the word *gnaw*. In contrast, Speechless B, a 27-year-old male, believed The Silent Letter was the final one in the word *solemn*.

Stage 2, Hush:

Once The Silent Letter has been introduced, the victim falls silent and typically remains so for between one and four hours (One outlier was hushed for almost two days before entering Stage 3). Speechless D, a 65-year-old male, was sure The Silent Letter was a *g*, but refused to say whether it was the one in *feign*, *gnarl*, *sign*, or *gnaw*.

Stage 3, Glossolalia:

Victims invariably speculate as to the identity of The Silent Letter during this stage, although to date no two have agreed. According to Speechless E, an 88-year-old female, The Silent Letter was the "E" in "Eshmak E": she pronounced the name *"Esh-mack,"* leaving the standalone letter silent. She holds the record for longest time spent in glossolalia: she spoke for almost forty-one minutes before entering Stage 4. Speechless F, an 88-year-old male, was certain The Silent Letter was one of the *t*'s in the word "letter" but entered Stage 4 before specifying which one.

Stage 4, Petrification:

At some point during glossolalia, a victim's eyes widen, their volume increases, and an intense *rigor* turns *mortis* unless artificial life-support intervenes. Nearly seventy percent of victims loudly utter 'Eshmak' before succumbing to this final stage, and another twenty percent say 'Eshmak E.' Speechless G, a 20-year-old male, believed that we would never discover the location of The Silent Letter, because The Silent Letter was also invisible."

Fragment Two:

"[…]page 5 of 12

philologist, 'specializing in the religious sects of those liminal regions in which civilization has been pushing against original mankind for a thousand years'; however, I found this unlikely in the context of this asylum.

'My work, from which I am retired,' the old Uzbek explained, 'lay east and a little north of this country. I feigned a heartfelt passion to deliver the Gospel to the heathens of what is today Siberia, though my real objective was almost the opposite. I had to know: what was The Silent Letter? I could feel that my ignorance was necessary, not due to any paucity of indications.'

Though the lights were now all off, the droning continued unabated.

'Contrary to my expectation, the people of those primitive lands were actually believers, and could profess the name of a single God with their lips,' the old Uzbek continued. 'They even knew our Christ, calling Him by the honorific "The Stillborn King." This concatenation, derived from their word for "born" and one of their many words for "dead," alluded to His human incarnation and to His subsequent crucifixion, respectively. Their word for the devil was "Eshmak E"; I irrationally hoped the Eshmak E was not borrowed from the Caucuses. It was the Turkmen man Aziz Garayev who discovered these redemptive correspondences between their cult and our own religion. He said that words were everything, that language was the greatest power attainable to Man; and I believed him, because those Siberian aborigines could perform miracles.

'This is why I have retired to this asylum; this place affords me the chance to lay down my sanity for a while and let it rest. It has had to absorb so much: I once saw the Eshmak E.

'Aziz Garayev was the first to commit The Silent Letter to writing, in the pages of a Bible he had brought to share with the isolated people of that valley, who had only ever taken him out into the forest where their shaman lived. That ancient person remembered the oldest traditions of the Stillborn King: that the Eshmak E dwelt sulking in Bactria for many years after the delivery of the Stillborn King; that the Eshmak E was disquieted when the Stillborn King resurrected ("was dead and stood

up" was their gloss); that the last time a living human being saw the Eshmak E, He was walking away northward from Samarkand. There were things up there in those remote boreal forests, the shaman told him, silent things, that "shake"."

[REDACTED] Cave represents a bright line demarcating the current boundaries of our understanding of The Silent Letter, beyond which lie darkness and ignorance; what form, if any, it had before it was discovered there, three kilometers underground, can only be conjectured.

On approaching the epicenter of The Silent Letter, our first surviving agent encountered a large capital "E" scrawled in dried human blood on the left-hand side of the passage, although its orientation suggested to him an "M." About twenty meters further down our agent found another message, also in dried blood, across a ridge on the ceiling of the passage, and a forward-pointing arrow. The capitalization (or perhaps *handwriting*) was unusual: approximately "behoLd thE STillborn king!"

Just beyond this advertisement the passage falls steeply downward before opening up into a significantly larger chamber, perhaps twenty meters by thirty meters, with several other passageways leading off it. Almost eight-hundred instances of the word "Eshmak" were found on nearly every surface of the chamber in many different sizes, handwritings, and materials the tour group had brought with them into the cave. Near the center of this chamber, our first surviving agent found all but one member of the tour group. Twenty-two were heaped in a roughly circular pattern on the floor around one standing erect. This center figure, the corpse of a 20-year-old male, had its head downturned, its arms hanging at its sides, and was vertical: it had been, for want of a less abrasive word, skewered onto a single large stalagmite in an approximately standing position. And there, at the feet of the vertical body, were The Silent Letter, the envelope from which it had been removed, and our first three agents. Critically, this agent was the first to report back before reading the letter himself.

Our agent realized that not all the bodies were dead; but certain measures are prohibited under the Sans Doctrine.

Other documents name all twenty-four members of the tour group, and speculate as to the whereabouts of the missing one. Other documents meticulously describe the crown of five human hands the central figure wore, and what was used to connect those hands and whom they came from. The writers of those other documents are strong people, brave ones whose work is important even as it is futile. This document can only be what it is, for if it were *different*, then *this* document would have gone unwritten.

There was a schism in the aftermath of this discovery, and an altercation at the mouth of [REDACTED] Cave between Deborah Sans and Theresa Hayes, her erstwhile mentor. There was information exchanged, and some kind of compromise arrived at. Perhaps the two Doctrines will ultimately prove reconcilable; we need more evidence. Nor is it clear how long Theresa Hayes and her group can survive down there, now that the mouth has been destroyed.

Fragment Three:

"*[…]was real and I was there.*

The Eshmak E, said the Uzbek, was even now mimicking a human walking down the hallway passage toward us, making no sound even as He vigorously stalked and lurched, using elaborate movement to cover such a brief distance—all soundlessly.

I wrenched, in vain, panicked, toward the windows, for even that immense glaring darkness would be better than any light rebounding off the body of the Eshmak E. But someone had placed those windows there, and at that angle, on purpose.

The Uzbek said: 'It was, perhaps… ten or eleven moments before I realized He was in front of me, staring at me from at least two degrees of remove, possibly more: a reflection of a reflection of the Eshmak E who crouched around the corner in the hallway.'

The old man's expression changed suddenly; I waited for him to tell me it was a nightmare he had had—a joke, unreal.

But: 'My eyes were closed, *I tell you,' he said. 'This is only how the thing appeared to me* through my eyelids.' *He shuddered violently, and had to force himself to suck air in through his nostrils before he could continue.*

'The Eshmak E,' he said, 'was like—a big, smiling, camel-faced man humped with two shaggy, drooling breasts, squatting atop another huge lobe of Himself, shivering with opossum tails and haloed in big, slow, droning bodies that buzzed as loudly as blaring horns. The leering camel face of the Eshmak E was split open into many labia, always smacking and extruding to reveal ever innermore lips, and above that endless, insatiable mouth the skin was being stretched and pulled tight into empty

sphincters where eyes should never be, all dilating in eyelike coordination, roving in ecstatic contemplation of human suffering on Earth—and from His forehead an imposing unknown untranslatable Silent Letter blazed and blazed with so much blood and meaninglessness and fire.

"THIS BEAUTY SEPARATES US FROM THE STILLBORN KING, *the Eshmak E signed absolutely silently, using too many padded hands instead of His awful mouth, which could only be used for screaming—until the screaming, too, resolved into intelligible blasphemy:* HE… ENVIES… US…

The Uzbek seized suddenly into a rigor from which he never relaxed.

It felt like a long time before I could sleep again. Perhaps it was never again.

I was still sitting there beside the old man, because my body could not move. But all the lights in the ward were out, and where he had been sitting there hunched an almost-meatless skeleton in a rusted wheelchair.

Time, I reflected after some had passed, was not an aspect of the world I now found myself in.

'Oh my God,' I heard myself say, and recognized in the sound of my voice that I had been trying to weep. Even as I uttered these words they were my last: I could feel the paralytic fungus finally crawl, slowly but ineluctably, to just above my upper lip.

As if in mockery of my last words, heavy metallic doors far away down the hallway squealed and slammed; but after that, for a long time, I could hear nothing, though I strained to listen. Only once I heard the intimation of many softly padding hands and feet.

I don't know how long I sat there trying to hold my breath; feverish half-waking nights, perhaps.

Suddenly I could feel that the Eshmak E was there, now a measurable distance away from my body, looming just around the corner in the hallway, squatting—inching, as slowly as cool magma, toward the rectangle of visibility that separated the extinct from the hideously extant.

I blinked desperately, unable to think, helpless against the inevitable arrival of the Eshmak E: His doorward progress was mathematically smooth. As my capacity to feel emotion suddenly began to heal painfully and stitch and thaw I knew that terror—fresh, world-foreshortening terror would soon overcome me. Mouthless now, I could but squeeze and thrash my eyelids—which, by sheer tragedy, froze open.

The chances were even, and my eyes happened to be open when the paralysis took them. This, after everything, was when I knew that there could be no king, liveborn or otherwise.

If I know anything at all, I know from my own memory that this world had a beginning. Yet there is no reason to think that it should ever end—and all that while my eyes will be open. I cannot now even close my eyes against the onslaught of the Eshmak E.

I see—just the merest sliver of His outline bulge from the doorframe's edge, changing Him from a possibility into a thing that I am looking at right now, the visible fraction of His body as yet so infinitesimally small that it can contain no attributes but which is so[...]"

This is where the Hallway Passage ends and uncertainty prevails. Our best theorists, as they so often must, resort to enumerating the possibilities: either the Sans Doctrine aligns with what is represented by the Stillborn King, and the Hayes Doctrine with the Eshmak E, or else the reverse is true. Either we have saved three individuals by deciding to maintain them on life-support even after petrification, or else Theresa Hayes is right and we have needlessly condemned them to suffering of unprecedented magnitude. We say *petrification*—but if anything, brain activity has increased.

The following is the third and final transmission we received from [REDACTED] Cave: *"It is not technology that will supplant us, my dear Deborah, but language."* To the best of our knowledge, adherents to the Hayes Doctrine are still down there, still exposing humans to fragments of The Silent Letter. It is beginning to creep into our awareness that The Silent Letter is achieving a result, otherwise unachievable, by indirection. Theresa Hayes herself, moments before petrification, implied that the accumulating sentences of The Silent Letter were projecting what could be called holograms of the real Silent Letter into readers' minds, a pattern that coalesces perhaps… only ten or eleven moments after you've read those final unforgettable words of The Silent Letter, which trigger the onset of Stage 1.

Effigies of Monstrous Things

Pedro Iniguez

His world shook and the earth opened like a maw to swallow him and Julia whole, their bodies tumbling down a muddy, chthonic pit where the shadows slithered like eels. The sensation of falling is what jostled him awake. Instinctively, he reached for Julia and grabbed a handful of the comforter where his wife should have been.

The back of his head was damp, as was the pillow cradling it. Marissa stood in front of the window, a beam of waning sunlight creating an orange halo around her as she rocked his shoulder with gentle hands.

"Papi, it's happening again," his five-year-old said in a soft voice. "And the air conditioner is broken, too."

The sun sank below the window and Mario grunted as his eyes adjusted to the growing darkness. The air conditioner sputtered as it blew warm, suffocating air through rusted vents. The smell of mildew wafted across the room, the source of which he couldn't identify. He sat up. In the heat and all that sweat his shirt had stuck to his body like a second skin. "I'll look into it, baby."

Satisfied with his answer, she skipped out of the room, her curly brown locks bouncing with every hop. His lungs burned and his throat felt raw again, as if he'd swallowed a handful of jagged rocks.

Mario shook off the discomfort and lifted the frame he kept on the nightstand. In the picture, Julia beamed, her amber eyes glistening with what joy remained at that point in their marriage. Marissa had inherited her mother's brown, curly hair. The hair of a goddess he used to say. Julia hadn't crossed his mind in ages. How long had it been since she'd left? He walked to the bathroom as he plumbed the depths of his mind, but it was all a haze—the answer wouldn't come. He shook his head. His memories lately had been filled with holes, like a cotton t-shirt decimated by moths.

The dreams, though, had become frequent. Nonsensical terrors. Visions wherein his family met strange, horrible fates he'd rather not dwell upon. He chalked it up to the pressures of being a single parent while working the lumber yard and attending night school for a nursing degree. Which reminded him...

A quick glance at the clock on the wall confirmed his fear: he was running late. He shuffled into the shower and turned on the water, waiting for it to run hot. The pipes groaned behind the walls. As the steam billowed, he pursed his lips. The showerhead was speckled with scum and black mold, as were the grooves between the tile walls. Not again. He could've sworn he'd scrubbed it clean. Mario soaked a cloth with bleach and wiped down the walls and the showerhead.

After a quick shower he opened his sock drawer and stared at the empty orange pill bottle. Fuck. It looked like he'd have to get by on will power tonight. He got dressed and padded into the kitchen. Marissa and Yvette were at the dining table hunched over their homework. Something was missing. He regarded the old booster chair tucked behind the table that had grown dusty. Why hadn't he ever thrown it away? Nostalgia, perhaps. Memories trying their damnedest to cling on to what little life they had left.

"Where's your sister?" Mario asked no one in particular.

Yvette sipped from a glass of water, eyed him quizzically, and returned her attention to her schoolwork.

"It's just us two, Papi," Marissa said, gripping a red crayon as she scribbled on a sheet of paper. She'd sketched some abstract monster with horns, a large tail, and a multitude of small, crab-like pincers running the length of its torso.

"What are you guys working on?"

"Finishing up my book report on *Charlotte's Web*," Yvette said, her eyes fixed on her paper. She was studious, certainly more so than he'd ever been at ten.

"We're supposed to draw something for Halloween," Marissa said, "a monster of our own making." She stood and pinned her drawing on the fridge with a magnet.

"Aren't they all?" Mario said.

"Sink's leaking again," Yvette said, coughing into her hand. She cleared her throat. "Mr. Hartwell cut corners. Like always."

Mario grabbed a small flashlight from the junk drawer and crouched by the cabinet under the sink. He opened the doors and tossed the light around until he spotted the spring in the PVC pipe. Gray water wept from the elbow joint in a steady trickle, pooling directly underneath.

"Shit," he muttered, quickly lifting his shirt over his nose. Black mold had taken hold along the drywall backing. Mario lowered the shirt from his face and backed away from the sink. He fetched a pot, slid it under the leaky pipe, and closed the doors. "I'll talk to Mr. Hartwell tomorrow. Just stay clear of the cabinet. And don't drink from the tap."

"He's not going to do anything." Yvette pushed her glass away with two fingers.

"I'll be extra persuasive. Anyway, I gotta get to class. You know the routine."

"Be in bed by nine at the latest," Marissa said.

"That's right, baby," Mario said, smiling. "Love you, girls. I'll be back later."

A wave of humidity enveloped him as soon as he stepped outside. Beads of moisture began to dot his brow. It was early autumn but in Los Angeles, summer still had its say. He locked the door and when he turned, he noticed Miss Lucinda in her wheelchair, the tank of oxygen at her side. She peered blankly out over the second-floor guard rail which overlooked the courtyard of the apartment complex.

Her son, Marvin, was a substance abuser who'd vanished some time ago, devoured by the city like so many others. The man never got the help he needed. Not from his friends, not from the city, no one. And Miss Lucinda was too old to do anything about it. She'd been hindered by her COPD and other financial hardships. Just like everyone here.

"Good evening, Miss Lucinda," Mario said. She said nothing as she turned her attention across the street. These days, she didn't say much of anything.

Mario followed Miss Lucinda's gaze towards a neglected billboard looming over the neighborhood liquor store. The corner flap of a faded movie poster had peeled away, revealing the graffiti painted on the backboard. It was a red, snaking pinwheel that terminated in what appeared to be a horned head on one end. The billboard's LED underlighting created an eerie, hellish effect on the enigmatic image.

Mario made his way downstairs, his hand catching rusty flakes as he clutched the rail. He wiped his palm on his scrubs. Everything in this complex was falling apart.

At the gate, he checked his mailbox and rifled through the day's correspondence. Nothing but a stack of bills. Most days he felt his debt was insurmountable. A malady he'd carry to the grave. Even subsidized housing couldn't unburden him.

When he got to the bottom of the stack, he saw another one of those Have You Seen Me? cards with the picture of a missing child. This one he thought he'd spotted playing in the neighborhood not too long ago. Jackie Hodges. A Black boy. Twelve. Last week it had been a little Latina girl, but her name eluded him. She'd had brown skin, an infectious smile, and wild, curly hair like Marissa's. Disappearances had become too frequent a thing around this part of town. He wondered if everyone just crumpled up the cards, moved on and forgot about them. The thought of his own children disappearing caused a flutter in his stomach. Like a monster lurking over his shoulder.

There was nothing more he wanted than to pack up and leave. Anywhere but the inner city. But he lacked the means—the money. Mario peered up at his apartment, thinking about his girls. They deserved so much more. He contemplated the barred windows, the metal screen doors, the great wrought iron fence barricading the perimeter of the complex. Never in his life had he felt so much like a prisoner.

Every day it felt like the world was conspiring against him and people that looked like him—subtle cruelties that kept him down. Thousands of small cuts that amounted to slow exsanguination.

Unquantifiable little crimes.

They could tell you exactly how many people had been murdered in L.A. County last year, but they could never tell you how many times a colored man got turned down at the bank for a loan, or lost out on a job offer for speaking a certain way. Phantom infractions that could ruin a life and keep someone locked up in a place like this.

Before he walked out the gate, Mario spotted Hartwell in the courtyard smoking a cigarette beneath a sky the color of bruised flesh. Hartwell's eyes followed a young boy riding his bike on the curb as the street lights flickered on.

"Evening, Jake," Mario said.

Hartwell turned his face away and blew out a cloud of smoke, hacking as he did. His mustache had bristled with yellow, nicotine-stained hairs. He wore his typical jeans, boots, and a white shirt spattered with red paint. He'd more than likely been tending to one of his better properties in the suburbs. "Hey, Mario. What's the word, amigo?"

"Hey, listen, my pipes are leaking again, the air conditioner's busted, and I've got mold growing all over the place. Can you help a brother out?"

"Yeah, I'll get to it," he said with disinterest in his voice. Hartwell took a hearty drag from his cigarette and turned away.

"I've got two girls in there, Jake. I don't want them breathing in that mold. Can you handle the leaks at least? Maybe replace those old pipes?"

Smoke flared out his nostrils. "Mhm."

"Listen, Jake, we both know I'm within my right to report you. You've left us hanging too many times. The whole fucking place is falling apart."

Hartwell dropped his cigarette and stomped it out. "You do that and I'll call Child Services on your ass. They won't like that my tenant is a meth addict who leaves his girls home alone at night."

Mario gritted his teeth and balled his fists. "You know I have night school, Jake. It's fucking hard enough as it is on a single father."

"Like I said, amigo, I'll get to it." Hartwell grinned and walked towards his van.

Subtle cruelties. Unquantifiable crimes.

Mario's fists unclenched. He was used to feeling powerless, but the thought of his girls getting sick didn't sit with him. He had to do something. And it wasn't just him. It was common knowledge that the other tenants had been dealing with the leaky faucets and sinks, dirty water, broken air conditioners, and that persistent mold no one could seem to expunge. The heat and moisture had no doubt spread the rot, circulating it through the vents. It seemed like it'd been going on forever.

The flashlight, he realized, had been in his pocket. Perhaps he could look for himself. He wasn't an expert, but maybe it had something to do with the aging plumbing system. Fuck, it was worth a shot.

Mario shoved the mail back in the box and made his way around the back of the building where the boiler room was located. Overgrown weeds were there to greet him in an empty lot where bedsheets fluttered from clotheslines like ghosts. He tried the door to the boiler room but it was locked. Of course.

Moonlight caught on heaps of dirt that had been piled along the lot as if there had been some recent excavation. What appeared to be wheelbarrow tracks cut across the lot and led to an old grate on the bottom of the wall. There was a chance he could find access to the boiler room from there.

After looking around to make sure no one had seen him, he pried the cover loose, crouched inside, and waved his light around. The crawlspace was tight, just big enough for him to duck walk through. As he squatted past the mouth of the crawlspace, his socks and shoes sopped up moisture from the muddy ground. Once inside, a wave of oppressive heat swarmed his body and it wasn't long before sweat began to trickle down his face and seep into his eyes.

Ducking below the joists, Mario followed a maze of corroded copper pipes which dribbled from their joints. Everywhere he looked, black-blue fuzz covered the rotten beams above. The building moaned as it settled, specks and spores fell from the planks and danced in the cone of his light. Mario sneezed into the crook of his arm. A subtle tingling sensation filled his nose and ran down his throat.

The crawlspace terminated abruptly where a plywood wall bisected the building. The pipes descended into a small cavity—a six-foot plunge into a concrete floor that stretched into darkness. The pitter-patter of droplets echoed in the distance. He considered turning back but he'd already be marked as absent from class tonight. May as well keep going. He sighed and wriggled down the hole which was just big enough for him to slide through.

At the bottom, he found himself inside a narrow tunnel, the walls carved from the earth itself as if the place had been hastily buried and bored through again. Stacks of large, dusty iceboxes had been stacked on the floor along the walls. Old Igloo coolers; the kind you took to the beach in the summer.

Mario wrinkled his nose. The air smelled of decay. Like spoiled meat and mildew. He followed the pipes on the ceiling until the tunnel opened to a dim, spacious room filled with old water heaters, broken pumps, rusted pipes, and assorted HVAC equipment. Above, a few overhead light fixtures swayed lazily to invisible currents of air. An antiquated boiler room. Subterranean remnants from an older Los Angeles.

The building groaned again, this time like a wounded animal, and earth sifted from the ancient walls. He heard the drip of water. His light skimmed past something glimmering, moving with inky fluidity. A fountain. A bird bath, really, overflowing with murky water. It had been placed directly beneath a leak springing from the ceiling.

Behind the fountain his light caught the outline of something peculiar. As he approached, his probing light touched the jagged thing and it cast a shadow against the wall, imbuing it with the illusion of life. The thing in question appeared to be a sculpture of a horrendous winged demon, its serpentine form a depiction of tanned flesh and exposed bone. Like an excavated fossil or mummified beast. It stood on a round, raised platform of marble. Mario ogled it, partly in fear, but also in bewilderment. Who had made this? The thing looked like it had been crafted from plaster and PVC pipe matted with papier mâché, but upon closer inspection it reeked of rot. The longer he gazed upon it the more he had the suspicion the abhorrent thing had been a patchwork of leathery skin grafted onto human bones.

Mario stepped towards the sculpture. His heart raced. If his nursing studies had done anything, they had confirmed that his suspicions were true. What stood before him was a jigsaw of disparate anatomy. A human pelvic bone formed the base of its head, where coccyges jutted from either side of the crest like makeshift horns. The obturator foramen appeared like gaping eyes, black holes staring back at him, judging him.

A mandible had been fused to the bottom of the pubic bone, its teeth removed and replaced with a row of severed pinkies. An abnormally long spine ran down its head forming a faux serpentine tail that stretched deep into the shadowed recesses of the boiler room, fused, he surmised from multiple human vertebrae. Several ribcages had been joined to cover the length of its spine. Outstretched humerus bones and fanned-out fingers extended from its back, webbed with taut skin like bat wings.

The demon sculpture bore femurs and tibias for arms with elongated fingers for hands, made from numerous proximal bones. Rows of small, crab-like claws sprouted from its ribs. They appeared to be small human hands, their digits removed, except for the thumb and forefinger to give the appearance of clawed appendages.

Mario stepped back, a rush of bile surging up his throat. What had he stumbled onto? He approached one of the iceboxes along the wall and flipped the lid. The rotting remains of children, all packed tightly in various states of decay, greeted him. Hips, hands, faces, scalps bearing curly, brown hair. Putrid flesh mingling with bone shards. One bore a face resembling that little boy, Jackie Hodges.

He opened another. It held only bones, like an ossuary. This couldn't be real. He moved on to another cooler and opened the lid. Julia stared back with lifeless eyes, her cheeks sunken in, her skin swathed in blue-gray mold. Her head sat atop a pile of discarded organs and fatty tissue. The rest of her was gone.

A wave of nausea overcame him and his breaths became shallow, burning gasps. He stumbled over his feet. The world began to spin and blur. Footfalls echoed down the tunnel, a muffled voice following close behind. He turned off the flashlight and threw himself behind a water pump just as Hartwell entered the boiler room.

Mario made himself small and peered from behind the pump. His landlord stepped towards the fountain, cupped his hands inside, and brought the water to his lips, drinking like a man deprived. Hartwell muttered to himself in hushed tones, stringing together crazed sentences Mario could just barely make out.

"It slumbers beneath…shall awaken once more…blessed be this effigy, born in tribute to its splendor."

Mario pressed his back to the pump and felt warm tears stream down his face. All those children. Julia. But she'd left him ages ago, hadn't she? The way she looked, she couldn't have been dead that long.

"The sculpture is nigh complete…just a few more bones…a few more *children*."

His mind reeled as he thought about his girls. He needed to get back to them. Call the police. Mario's lungs suddenly began to burn. A tingle ran up his nose. He cupped his hands over his face and fought the urge to cough, to sneeze, to yell and cry.

In the depths of the boiler room, he thought he saw movement, as if the shadows themselves were dancing, slithering, coiling into themselves.

The building creaked as its old bones settled. Spores fell from the ceiling, dusting his world like snowfall. The fire in his lungs spread to his throat. His eyes watered and stung and itched. He sneezed.

Hartwell emerged from behind the pump, his body appeared to be covered in a black aura, a seething energy of shadowy, writhing tendrils. Mario felt himself lifted off the ground and dragged to the fountain.

"Drink," said Hartwell.

Mario felt his limbs grow weak, his consciousness slipping. What was happening?

"Drink!"

Mario's face splashed into the cool water and he felt it slither up his nose, down his throat. A rancid taste filled his mouth and singed his tongue.

There came a voice from nowhere and everywhere at once.

"Make me whole again."

Mario tried to scream for help but no words came. His throat became coarse, a useless meat pipe. All around, the spores fell, clinging to his clothes, his skin, his lungs.

The voice came again.

"Make me whole. Finish the effigy."

And then, darkness.

Mario woke in his bed, damp, covered in sweat. The dreams had spiraled into haunting, turbulent affairs. How long had they been going on now?

The air conditioner sputtered as it exhaled hot air, spreading the smell of mildew. The sun sank beneath his window and the world grew dark. He cursed under his breath. Time to get ready.

As he sat up, Julia eyed him with loving eyes from the frame at his bedside. A familiar pang festered in the pit of his stomach. How long had it been since she'd left him? The answer wouldn't come. All he knew was that he still missed her.

In the bathroom, the walls of the shower were covered in mold. He thought he'd cleaned it. It had become a tedious, laborious cycle. He'd make sure to speak to Hartwell. Running late, he ignored it and showered.

It wasn't until he got dressed that he noticed the house had been strangely quiet.

He walked into the kitchen. Yvette sat at the dining table hunched over a book. She sipped from a glass of water, looked at him, and returned to her reading.

"Where's your sister?" he asked, looking around the kitchen. It felt spacious, empty.

Yvette looked up from her paper, mildly irritated. "It's just me, Dad."

"Right. Right."

He looked at the booster chair behind the table for a moment before his eyes settled on a sheet of paper pinned on the fridge. A juvenile crayon sketch of a terrible horned monster. He had no idea where it had come from. It seemed familiar and yet so alien. Like a memory stolen. Mario hung his head and wondered what other things he'd lose the next time he woke.

Six Underground

Vicky Velvet

One's preferred environment can tell you a lot about someone. This is obvious enough for animals—fish, birds, moles, all unique products of water, air, earth— but it was true for people, too, and that was something Anh Coleman took to heart. Anh was not egomaniacal enough to think infecting the rest of the galaxy with humanity was their destiny, nor were they a morbid loner fixated on the cold clamminess of a tentacle sliding down their back.

Anh was not a bird, or a fish. Anh was a mole.

"Help me with this, will you?" Air hissed from the emergency air tank as they attempted to remove a large stone from a nearby crevice. In the faint light of the lamp between Anh and her husband, it was clear that the stone wasn't budging a millimeter—despite the strenuous effort.

"It's not going anywhere." Phillip slouched against a nearby rock—as if there was nothing else for him to be doing. Anh was glad they couldn't quite make out his expression. Phillip knew their chances were slim and it weighed heavily on him. "It's too big, the space is too small, and I may not be the geologist, but I'm sure that rock is impervious to everything short of a nuclear bomb."

Anh shot him a look. They were usually the snarky one but, realizing the absurdity of being offended by the theft of their role in the relationship, they relaxed.

As much as they could, trapped six miles underground.

"You can see it though." Anh pointed at the thin stream of light descending from behind the stone. "The Sun."

"Not enough."

It was a miracle that the incident had allowed enough space that a single photon fit through the cracks. Removing the blockage would at least add more air to their dwindling reserves. If the stone remained unmoved, they would soon hit zero.

Anh slid down the wall and let out an exhausted sigh. They had been so excited to realize their dream, and now they were going to die underground with Phillip. The way things had been, not even that comforted them.

Anh recognized their own part in the problems. They'd dismissed Phillip, convinced he didn't see their vision. When Anh *did* talk to him about their work, they came off as condescending—oversimplifying the details or spouting so much jargon he had no chance of understanding a single word.

The two of them sat in silence, wondering how long they would have to await Death's scythe.

"It wasn't an earthquake." Anh would have sworn hours had passed, if not for the tank's needle only just sliding into the red.

"It couldn't have been anything else. Not with how violently the whole place shook. I thought my bones were going to shatter, and I'm not entirely sure they didn't."

"You know exactly what it was."

Phillip said nothing.

It wasn't in his nature to argue. He was always supportive, quietly writing for a local magazine while Anh set their sights on bigger prizes. He submitted literary essays when they needed a second income, and took care of the house when Anh was busy or away.

Since being approached by the people at Morian Development Anh had been hard at work, planning endless networks of tunnels and chambers adding up to an underground metropolis all of their own design. A pocket of caverns extending out into the sea had been found with multiple underground lakes that would keep temperatures cool enough for humans, exactly the necessary conditions described in Anh's thesis, which had proclaimed the possibility of "revolutionizing the way civilization evolved." They knew Phillip thought it sounded ridiculous, but at least he kept the thought to himself.

The CEO of Morian Development, who was doubtlessly dead given his position when the ground swallowed everything in sight, had spoken of his business to Anh's aunt at some event, and the offer was made later that day. While fortunate, it did leave a bad taste in Anh's mouth. Their lineage was the only thing that allowed them to pursue such an impractical career, but they swore that even if the opportunity had been handed to them on a silver platter, the results would be earned.

Naturally Phillip came with them, cheering as Anh attempted to create a functioning pocket of civilization six miles underground. It was a change of pace, obviously, but he trusted Anh. Even if they could be irritable, flighty, and unreliable, their passion was the burning flame that fueled their every action.

But Anh never suspected there might be natives.

Phillip groaned. "I don't care what the yokels say, these caves aren't infested with man-eating lizard people."

"They're more like canines actually, based on the claw and teeth marks we've found..."

"It's nonsense!"

"You believe in them too." Anh didn't have the energy to say anything, but still the words came out, each one ragged, labored, and sad.

"I don't."

"You're not an idiot, Phillip. You just don't want to believe. It's how you stayed sane when I started losing it after the kids—"

"I don't want to talk about this."

"Phillip, please—"

"You're *wasting* our air."

Anh froze in mute shock. Phillip's face melted into regret. It was the angriest he'd been in the years since he became Phillip Coleman.

"I'm sorry." He sounded like he meant it.

Anh didn't respond. They simply sat there in the dim blue light, as if they were already dead.

The dreadful silence broke as Anh switched to a fresh air tank, only to once more blanket them for a small eternity.

"They're real." Anh spoke so suddenly that their heart skipped a beat.

"No." Philip muttered the only thing he could muster the willpower to say.

"But, the disappearances." Anh forged on, undeterred.

"Just that—disappearances."

"We found them."

"I'm sure those were animal bones; a bear or something, maybe—"

"Not the monsters, you stupid bastard!"

Phillip's eyes widened.

"The missing diggers," Anh continued, "and the sketch artist, and the two little girls who snuck past the fence and never came back."

Phillip stared at them. "You found..." He blinked. "You found them?"

Anh's hand slid into one of their pockets and tossed something. Unprepared, Phillip didn't catch it, and had to root around in the pale blue light to find it again.

"This is just junk." He held it up to his eye, his tired lungs using more and more of their oxygen. "This isn't anything, it's just a lump of metal..."

"It's a tooth." Anh told him flatly. "The artist lost a tooth in a car accident and—"

"It's just metal!" Phillip hurled the object into the darkness. "You heard that story and the second you found a shiny bauble convinced yourself that it was a clue. It's a delusion Anh, at least wait until we're out of air before inviting the cave goblins to our tea party."

Anh stared at him for several long, silent moments, the lamp's warmth doing barely anything to stave off the freezing cold.

"Rachel," Anh whispered. "That was one of the girls. While we were searching for her and her friend..."

"What, Anh, you knew she wore braces and then you found a tangle of metal wires, or a strand of fabric that must have come from a scrunchie?" He fumbled for his next words before asking, "What are you going to show me to make me believe stories about cave monsters told by a bunch of drunk hillbillies trying to scare each other?"

Anh raised their hand. "Be quiet, and I'll show you."

They took a thick bag out from behind the rock the lamp sat on, and dropped it in front of them. Phillip frowned. Anh had been carrying the bag while inspecting the latest passage. It was a heavy equipment bag, but Anh had no trouble lifting it.

Phillip swallowed hard. "What's in the bag, Anh?"

Anh pushed the bag dead center between them, and drew the zipper down. "Look."

Phillip's vomit nearly joined the bag's contents, but he'd averted his eyes so quickly that it missed completely and splattered against the cold stone wall of their subterranean cell instead.

"Close it!" His scream was hoarse. "Fucking, close it!"

Phillip continued to scream long after Anh zipped the bag. Eventually something close to sense came back to him and he lapsed into silence. The silence lingered as Phillip continued his efforts to compose himself with the occasional quiet sob or heavy breath.

"Tell me why you had that," he demanded, breaking the tense silence. The lamp illuminated a ghost of his tortured expression

"I had to find them." Anh snapped, but managed to keep their expression blank—neutral. "And once I did, I stopped going anywhere without them— daring those monsters to come get me. As we moved deeper, I could feel their eyes on me. So many eyes tracking me, and what I'd stolen from them."

Phillip's jaw hung open.

"They were ruining my dream." Anh's heart was on the verge of ripping in two. "If I could prove they existed, maybe the project could continue, or I'd be famous enough some other company would hire me to do it again…somewhere without monsters."

"You did this." Phillip's voice cracked through fresh, choking sobs. "You murdered all those people and are blaming it on…mole people!"

"Do you want to spend our last moments thinking of me as a deranged killer, Phillip?"

"Something was going wrong, wasn't it?" His expression showed that he was certain he'd worked out the truth. "They were going to shut everything down, so you did this…"

"Yeah," Anh's spirit shot past heartbreak straight to rage, responding venomously with, "I'm not only a murderer, I'm a failure, too."

"I've always had your back…"

Anh almost laughed, their voice becoming a low hiss. "And you hated every second of it. You're so quick to believe I'm a murderer because you already thought I had screws loose. A fucking city underground? Did you read my thesis and decide I'd be an easy lay who wouldn't have enough brain cells to realize you were cheating on me with your fucking editor?"

Phillip's righteous anger faltered for a moment, and his face grew paler in the dim light.

"It doesn't matter." Anh seethed, tilting their head with narrowed eyes. "He can find another dick to ride, because the creepy crawlies won. I'm sure they'll hide the new trophies better."

"Insane…" Phillip heaved, wasting more oxygen. "I married you…and you murdered people."

Anh was so tired of him. Tired of everything. They never really cared that he fucked around, because they didn't care about much of anything as long as he continued to support what little they did care about. That had clearly come to an end. Worse than not supporting them anymore, Phillip had become a millstone around their neck—holding them back and wasting their time and energy.

"You're not helping." Anh told him. They lifted something that had been laying next to the rock they sat on. "In fact, you're fucking useless. You think I'm a killer? Fine."

Anh crept closer to Phillip, their hand passing through the light to reveal the diamond-bladed power saw. "All you're doing is using up my air." They growled like an animal. "And you know what? We've been down here so long…I'm starting to get *hungry*."

The tool clicked on, its scream drowning out Phillip's as Anh bore down on him.

Anh lay alone in the luminous haze of the lamp's blue light. Their belly was full, and their mind at peace—a first for their family. Anh's grandmother had committed suicide after losing her position at the university for an affair with a student. When Anh was young, her mother went missing after years of struggling with mental illness and was found with her head almost entirely gone. Seeing the closed casket lowered into the ground is what first awoke Anh's interest in what lay beneath their feet.

And now Anh was buried too, though not yet dead. They decided to not bother using the last air tanks. Better to strip out of their clothes, pile everything as out of the way as possible, and lay on the cold stone floor with their eyes closed, letting their breathing slow as the air around them became thinner and the lamp's battery trickled out its last drops of energy.

Deeper in the cave, Anh heard heavy footsteps and raspy, guttural breathing. The lamp gave out, and all was dark.

You Have Joined the Livestream

Jessica McHugh

@theRealGhostBros is live!

Kayden dances into frame, his pointed chin and massive grin giving him a natural-born Ghostface mask. As he shows off the "No Guts, No Gory" shirt BigBadBoo.com sent the Ghost Bros earlier that week, a neon purchase link appears at the top of the screen. He dances to royalty-free techno as Matty bounds in front, swinging a black velvet pouch that erases the floating text with a dramatic whoosh. Animated hearts pepper the screen when Matty does his trademark bicep flex, and laughing emojis follow when Kayden pokes his tongue against the inside of his cheek and mimes a blowjob.

Matty chuckles. "You know I can see you, right?"

"You can?! I honestly thought you only saw yourself."

"Usually you're right, but I've got eyes everywhere today. On me, on you, and…" He dangles the pouch in front of the lens. "…on all the haters tuning in to see if we're going to puss out."

Kayden releases a singular cackle. "Fools! We are the unspookable Ghost Bros! When it comes to us, it's 'down with *puss* and up with *pus*!'"

Matty winces. "I hope that motto doesn't stick." Leaning into the camera, he adds, "Don't listen to him. I'm very up for *puss*." He claps his hands. "But that's another video for another day. Becaaaaause…" He tosses the bag to his partner. "It's time, Kay. We're finally putting the beef to bed."

"That's the hope anyway. Most of you know we've got some so-called ghost hunters putting us on blast for no reason. We aren't naming names…" Kayden coughs, "*Chrissy and Cat,*" followed by "*Marta, Trish, and Betz,*" and pounds his chest. "Pardon me, I had a little hag in my throat."

"No worries, buddy. It's going around. Our loyal fans know we've tried to squash this shit without a show, but some people just can't cope with being second best, so we're shining a light on their accusations and shutting them up once and for all."

"We've got a handful of haunted locations in our bag of tricks." Kayden swings the pouch between his knees. "Each submitted by a paranormal investigator that's accused us of being shady."

"That's right. We put the power in our haters' hands to prove we're the real deal." He shakes the shiny blond hair out of his eyes, but it slides back in when he smolders at the camera. "Whatcha think about that, GeeBees?"

Comments whizz up the screen:

> *We're here for you*
> *Hot as hell*
> *Hiii Matty It's Carrie remember me?*
> *Click here for new offer --->*
> *don't got the stones*

Matty waves at the screen. "Of course, we remember you, Carrie. Those cookies you sent were fire!"

"Literally!" Kayden flaps his collar. "Did you put habanero in those suckers or what? No complaints though. I'd love some more."

Matty snatches the velvet bag. "Work first, bro. Then cookies."

"Ugh, that's what you always say. You sound like my mom."

"No, if I wanted to sound like your mom, I'd say…" Pitching his voice into a grating falsetto, he waves his finger in Kay's face. "Come over for dinner, Kaykay! Help me reset my router, Kaykay! Why don't you ever answer your phone, Kaykay?"

Kayden teeter-totters his hand. "Ehhh…the words were right, but that nasally woodchipper voice sounds more like Chrissy." He laughs as he taps his chin. "Or Cat. I can never remember which is which."

> *Fuck you*
> *Hahahah*

YOU GUYS
y u fear nature
ur tears are delicious

"Speaking of witches, I wouldn't be surprised if there are some witchy suggestions in our bag. We've got some of Salem's sloppy seconds in our local lore. And considering the mental state of our submitters…"

"Shit, you're right." Kayden winces. "I'm kinda scared now."

Matty thrusts the bag at his friend. "Be brave and open her up, bro. But be gentle. She's been hurt before."

With a sinister giggle, he opens the drawstring, and Matty's falsetto returns when he plunges his hand inside.

Hi @twdsavior2000!
@CandCBooSickFactory posted a new video

"This might surprise you…"

In a dark blue room lined with purple twinkle lights, a sleek woman with a shaved head and vibrant Ankara earrings leans back in her chair, more exhausted than relaxed.

"…but Chrissy and I don't hold any grudges against the Ghost Bros. Honestly, we don't think about them *at all* unless they tag us. Which they do…" She leans forward, eyebrow raised. "…*A lot*. They asked *us* for a submission the same as everyone else they obsess over. If you don't believe me, click here for the receipts on their own damn feed."

She points to a video link so carelessly colored it's barely visible against the black background before it blinks red and transforms into a GoFundMe link for Chrissy's medical bills.

"The Ghost Bros spearheaded this stunt. They compiled a list of so-called 'haters'; Chrissy and I didn't know who else they included. We didn't hold some clandestine meeting to embarrass them—they do that easily enough themselves each time they steal our research and fake their findings. So, I speak for my partner and myself when I say we don't give a rusty fuck what they do with our submission, their show, or their sad little lives."

Hi @twdsavior2000!

@therealGhostBros posted a new video

As the boys' laughter rises, the clip from *@CandCBooSickFactory* turns monochromatic, and their video squashes Cat into oblivion. While Matty flexes for the camera, Kayden throws his hands in the air.

"Here we go again, forced to defend ourselves against the Witches of Yeastwick. I wish it was the last time, but I seriously doubt it."

"It's true we reached out for submissions, but we asked for legit shit, you know? Different suggestions from different haters."

"Despite what they say, it's obvious they banded together to assault the integrity of the paranormal investigating community."

"It's too big of a coincidence to be anything else. Especially since they all submitted…" He overturns the bag, and paper slips flutter out. "…Milk-Tooth Mountain."

A booing crowd effect rises and falls as Kayden waves his hands. "It's not the location that bugs us! I've been wanting to do Milk-Tooth Mountain for years. It's one of those haunts everyone discusses but is too scared to investigate."

"Not us, though. And we're not watching any videos from other ghost hunters on the subject. They're all gossip anyway. Big talk about demons and elder gods and teenage witches. Too much conflicting info to trust anything but our own research."

"Especially with our haters stacking the odds." Matty wags his finger at the screen as Kayden shows slip after slip marked with the same location. "Not cool, ladies. And lying about us doesn't help your cause." He winces, then adds, "Sorry…*lady*."

The boys snicker. "By the way, Cat, we were *devastated* to hear about Chrissy's head-on collision with 'fuck around and find out,' but that's what happens when you choose rioting over patriotism. Good luck with the fundraiser though. Too bad you'll probably have to run another when the clot shot catches up to you."

"You'd think these sheep would have tons of extra money lying around after the government paid them to lock themselves up for months on end."

Kayden pouts. "Their loss. They're gonna miss out on our brand-new merch! In conjunction with BigBadBoo.com, we're releasing limited edition tees ahead of our soon-to-be legendary exploration." Kayden holds up a shirt with the Ghost Bros neon green logo, then flips it around. In an oozing font, it reads, "Milk-Tooth Mountain Can Bite Me."

He chomps at the camera and Matty squeals in falsetto.

"Whew! Watch the teeth, sweetheart!"

"Careful, bro, you might trigger the hags."

"Pssh…they're all bark, no bite." Matty crinkles his nose. "All Negan, no Lucille."

Kayden laughs. "All Twinkie, no cream."

"All hoe, no garden."

"All milk, no tits."

Matty points at Kayden, snickering. "All mountin', no comin'."

They howl, desperately pleased with themselves. "Saturday, 1 PM Eastern," Kayden says, wrapping his arm around Matty's neck. "Tune in to our exclusive livestream for all the lore and gore, cuz The Ghost Bros are coming all over Milk-Tooth Mountain!"

☺

Hahahahahhaha

Flesh peddlers

Moss curtains --> last offer

Cant wait 4 this!!!!!

Ur the worst

another stream?

You have new notifications!

@allbetzerov
@twdsavior2000 viewed your profile

@whatagirlhaunts
@twdsavior2000 viewed your profile

@CandCBooSickFactory
@twdsavior2000 viewed your profile

@therealGhostBros
@twdsavior2000 reposted your video

@twdsavior2000
@therealGhostBros viewed your profile

@therealGhostBros is live

To a geyser of animated hearts, the duo leaps into frame, their headlamps grossly ineffective at lighting the cramped interior of Milk-Tooth Mountain. Only their faces are clear, making them look like stark white skulls floating in the grainy ether.

"Greetings, GeeBees!

"It's your favorite paranormal investigators, the Ghost Bros, broadcasting live from Milk-Tooth Mountain!"

"I can't believe we're finally here. This place has been a source of gossip for over two hundred years when people started disappearing without a trace. The mountain has allegedly gobbled up hikers, photographers, influencers, and more than a couple criminals trying to outrun the police."

"All the lore we found blew our minds, and we can't wait to share it, but we want to start by thanking our loyal followers for the support this past week. There have been a lot of low-blow videos since we announced this event, but you all stuck by us."

> *Go Bros!*
> *ur the stuck one*
> *Light& your teeth offer --->*
> *Hey guys it's Carrie remember me?*
> *Take a juicey bite*

"Hi Carrie! Good to see you. I'm still waiting for more cookies." Kayden sucks air. "Ooh, that would've been a good idea: loading up on Carrie's spicy cookies just in case the mountain tries to eat us like the skags from *@WhatAGirlHaunts* predicted." He winks. "That's right, we heard what you said about us in your last video."

"Not that we watched it. We *do* have lives. Well, except for all those Saturday nights Kay spends with his mom."

Kayden's face tightens into a bullet of embarrassment. "What? No, I don't."

"Dude, you hang out with her all the time!"

"I haven't even seen my mom in—" He stops, brow furrowed. "I—I don't know when, but it's been a long time." Rubbing his pointed chin, he frowns.

"Seriously, I can't remember—"

"I'm sure you'll have the opportunity to make new memories next Saturday…and the Saturday after that…and the Saturday after that." When Kayden punches his arm, his laughter turns to a moan. "Hey, cut it out! I'm not judging. Your mom's way cooler than all the man-hating pronoun pushers who love attacking us. But maybe they'll change their tune after this historical event. You think, Kay?"

He aims his camera at his partner, who's staring at the rocky floor, his forehead crinkled and jaw hanging loose.

"When was it…?"

> *He doesn't look good*
> *U ok, K?*
> *#blessed*
> *More offerss here -->*
> *See any teeth yet?*
> *You're losing it*

Matty snaps his fingers, and Kayden clears his throat.

"Sorry about that." He holds out his phone as he spins in place and shows off the glistening ivory stones jutting from the walls. "We're in the first of many caves branching off from the entrance of Milk-Tooth Mountain, but no one's gotten footage from beyond this point."

"Some say the mountain's full of bums who chase away anyone who enters. Others say the mountain itself eats intruders. But I don't see evidence of either. No trash, no clothes. And…" He runs his hand over the wall. "…no warmth. This is probably a run-of-the-mill haunting that got blown out of proportion after the most famous incident in the 70s, which we'll cover shortly."

Kayden slips on the harness for his camera mount and adjusts the flexible arm. "And once we're good and deep, I'll use the Estes Method and our trusty spirit box to communicate with whatever's spookin' up the joint."

With straps tightened and cameras secured, the boys hoot as they test the grip with bounces and twists. Satisfied, they high-five, the echo of which sounds like bones breaking as they plunge phone-first into the mountain. As they walk side by side, their screens show the area from their shoddy headlamps to their popped collars. The deeper they go, the darker the white walls become, distorting and consuming the path behind them—but only on their phones. To them the rocks remain glinting ivory. But on screen, the boys resemble bleached jack-o'-lanterns hovering in the soft palate of an abyssal throat.

"That's weird. Check EMF, will you?"

Kay frowns at the detector. "Nothing."

"*Yet*," he says. "There's gotta be a hot spot somewhere."

When Matty sees a flash of white on the right side of his screen, he assumes it's Kayden falling behind. But then it happens on the left, and twice again on the right. He skids to a stop and swings around, but there's nothing behind him. No strange shadows, no sounds of life or flashes of white.

The selfie cam tells a different story.

As they continue walking, the screen shows black walls increasingly dimpled with large white holes.

"What the hell? Kay, do you see this?"

His partner doesn't reply. He's staring at the wall, his hand on the stone.

No… not *on* it.

In it.

To Matty, Kayden's arm looks like it's been lopped off at the wrist, but on the livestream, it's penetrating a grainy white orifice, into which he extends the EMF detector. The tunnel pulses with red light when the trembling needle shoots to the precipice of the "high-activity" quadrant.

Kayden reels back the machine to show the viewers, but the needle flips back to green. He sticks it in the tunnel, and the needle goes wild again.

The Ghost Bros grin at each other, not a word spoken before rushing into the dark. After a sharp left, the path opens to a large cavern in which the phone screen reveals even more holes.

"Grab the box, will you? And the blindfold." He leans his phone against a rock while Matty fishes the spirit box out of his bag.

Spirit Box from Spirit Halloween
FAKE AF
this feels endless
not even an SB7
Any bites?

"This is better than the bullshit you see from our competitors," Matty says. "This method is the only surefire way to link up to a real spirit. And the key is sensory deprivation. For most people, that's easier said than done. Luckily, my good pal Kay doesn't have much sense to start with, so it's easy for him to block out the noise."

Kayden flips him off, and he tosses over the blindfold.

"But he's not the only important part of this puzzle, loyal viewers. We need you to give us your trust, your faith, your open hearts, and open minds. That's the only way this will work because—"

@CandCBooSickFactory posted a new video
@twdsavior2000 bookmarked your video

"—shared belief thins the veil, my friends. Just like the living, who so often cry out with their first and last breath…" Chrissy bows her head, and Cat squeezes her hand. "…most spirits want to be heard, to be acknowledged and reassured that someone out there still cares."

@therealGhostBros is live

"We all want to be heard," Matty says, "and shared belief parts the veil between worlds."

As he sets the spirit box on a stone ledge and fiddles with the dials, Kayden tightens the blindfold and waves his hand in front. The radio crackles and squeals until Matty finds a steady river of static, and Kayden's face jerks upward.

"Do you hear something?"

"No, I…smell…something. Something sweet."

Matty sniffs the air. "You sure we didn't bring any of those cookies?"

"I finished those ages ago." He shrugs. "Hook me up, bro."

Matty gleefully twists the plug into the radio jack, turns up the volume, and Kayden slides on his headphones.

@whatagirlhaunts Your video has uploaded!
@twdsavior2000 bookmarked your video

It begins with a closeup of Marta's black lips purring, "Milk-Tooth Mountain…" and the camera zooms out as she continues. "It was originally called Marbery Mountain Pass and served as a refuge for weary travelers, but the truth is…it's never served anyone."

She wiggles her nose; her silver and amber bracelets jingle as she slides a folded piece of paper to her investigation partner. Trish opens it slowly, revealing an illustrated map of the woods leading to the mountain during the 1800s. The forest is so overgrown, it's hard to tell where the treetops end and the mountain's mossy stones begin.

"This is the earliest depiction we have, and there's not much to see, except..." she points to a dot between the trees. "The entrance was a lot smaller back then."

"Here's what it looks like today." When Marta holds up her palm, a photo of the mountain appears, the entrance of which takes up more than half of the rockface. "Maybe it was erosion. Weather and time."

"Or maybe, after so many years of eating travelers, it wanted to open itself up to other opportunities."

@therealGhostBros is live

"Once better roads were constructed, the passage stopped being used by travelers and became a haven for vagrants and junkies," Matty says in disgust. "There have also been rumors of witchcraft and satanic rituals dating back centuries. But the most notable incidents don't date back far at all."

@allbetzerov Your video has uploaded!
@twdsavior2000 bookmarked your video

"Milk-Tooth Mountain really got into its feelings in the 1970s." With a filter that turns their high ponytail pink, Betz growls at the camera, and the background ripples into a photograph of the mountain's gaping entrance. When they snap their fingers and duck out of frame, cartoonish fangs appear on its stony maw, and the voiceover begins. "Though similar stories occur every few decades, the most famous involves a group of girls in 1973 skipping school to have a picnic in Marbery woods." When Betz reappears, they're holding a picnic basket and wearing a crown. "These boss bitches were having the time of their lives when a harrowing storm drove them deeper into the forest—"

@therealGhostBros is live

"—where the rebellious teens took shelter in this very mountain." Matty curls his lip. "That's the fairytale version anyway. They were actually wannabe witches who believed the mountain had special powers and came to cast a spell on a boy from their school. But it didn't turn out so well. Only one girl turned up after the incident, and they locked her in the looney bin when the boy from their school went missing too. For years, she maintained her friends 'ascended' while she was chosen to 'tend the mountain'…and the boy's soul, which remained inside."

Kayden shushes him. "I hear something." He tilts his head. "I think it's the girls. Their spirits are still here."

"They didn't ascend? Shocker." He cackled. "What are they saying?"

"It sounds like they're negotiating. Or…making an offer?"

Matty blows a crumb off his phone screen. "An offer to who?"

"Something else. Something bigger. I can't hear it yet."

Matty keeps his eye on the WIFI, which stays strong as comments fly up the screen.

it's so dark where you are
what do you see
what do you hear
Wanna know a secret/
Final offer--> prism keep sakes
you're both gonna die

"We'll find it. No ghost trapped in no haunted house has ever given us the cold shoulder."

Kayden's back hunches and a gravelly groan rolls up his throat. "It's not trapped in a haunted house."

"Sorry?"

"What lives here: it's not trapped in a haunted house." He lifts his head with a hiss. "It *is* the haunted house."

The EMF detector flashes and the stressed needle bends against the boundary of the red sector until it snaps.

Matty gasps. "It's happening, GeeBees! Reminder that we are *live* from Milk-Tooth Mountain, where the Ghost Bros are the first paranormal investigators to speak to the spirit haunting this mountain."

"Not even a mountain. It is a mouth, with stones strong enough to gnash us all to paste, even riddled with cavities." Kayden's voice is a tree branch on a tin roof. "Not the rotten kind though. Not yet. All these empty spaces that made the first of us call it Milk-Tooth Mountain: they're holding cells. For old bones and new earth, but mostly for lost souls. That's the real rot, we've found. We who tend its hunger."

"*We?* So there's more than one spirit here?"

Kayden growls. "You're not listening."

You never listen.

"You never listen."

You never learn.

"You never learn."

You never change.

Matty's ears perk. "Wait, I can hear them." He turns up the volume on the spirit box, and Kay screams as he rips off his headphones.

"What the hell, dude?"

All these years, all these rituals...

Kayden and Matty stare at each other.

All these rituals...

"It's not coming from the box."

Keeping you here...

As they spin in the cave with phones in hand, more holes open around them. While Matty investigates a tunnel to the left, Kayden's chin tilts to the ceiling.

The voice grows louder. More complex.

@CandCBooSickFactory has joined the livestream

It widens.

@allbetzerov has joined the livestream

It deepens.

@WhatAGirlHaunts has joined the livestream

It triples, then quadruples.

"That smell again."

@CookiesByCarrie has joined the livestream

Dazed, Kayden drops his phone and stands on tiptoes. "It's coming from above me."

"Wait, Kay, don't—" By the time Matty reemerges, his friend's white sneakers are vanishing into a hole in the ceiling.

"How'd you do that?" With the opening too far away to reach, he clips his phone into his chest mount and searches for something to stand on. "Kay? Can you hear me?"

"Where'd you go, Matty? There are too many tunnels."

"Stay where you are. I think the ghosts are messing with us."

Impossible.

"Who is that?!"

We speak for the mountain.
And the wannabe witches.

Kayden whimpers. "We should go. I'm gonna be late for dinner with my mom."

"Yeah, you had your fun," Matty bellows. "Let us out."

You can't make demands of the mountain.
It's too ancient.
Too busy.
It doesn't hunt anymore.
It prefers a long meal. Lots of little nibbles.
That's where people like you come in.
crunch
Trish, can you please stop breaking the circle to eat chips?
I'm hungry.
We're all hungry.
She's done this every year since 2020.
Can we please refocus? My grandkids will be home from daycare soon.
Sorry, Carrie.

Kayden groans. "Carrie? Like, with the cookies?"

> *Told you they wouldn't remember.*
> *They never do.*
> *That's the part Milk-Tooth likes eating most. The reality.*
> *When I ascend, whoever takes over is going to realize how annoying all this*
> *dawdling is.*
> *Sorry again, Carrie.*
> *Join hands. Concentrate. Restart the spell.*

"Matty, don't move. I'm gonna head your way."

> *To the moss-curtained stones*
> *We offer these bones*

"I'm not moving." He whimpers. "Jesus Christ, I *can't.*"

> *To the deep mountain blessed*
> *We offer this flesh*

"I…" Kayden's voice clots. "I can't either. Can you see anything?"

> *To the nature we fear*
> *We offer these tears*

"It's too dark." He coughs. "Wait, I see something…"

> *To the secrets we keep*
> *We offer these teeth*

As Matty's selfie cam glows from his chest mount, and comments fly up the screen, the boys realize they're side by side on the cave floor, their pale faces turning blue as cookie-speckled bile pours down their chins.

> *In word and blood*
> *and time and light*
> *To lock this evil*
> *in prisons tight*

Jessica McHugh

We offer up
a juicy bite
For another stream
of endless nights

They're a pair of broken baby teeth on the mountain's tongue, something to giggle over in the group chat as the ancient creature enjoys a midnight snack. And as the permanent fixtures gaze down in amusement—a hater in every hole, a cackling in every cave—the Ghost Bros share a moment of clarity.

This isn't a livestream. This is a repost.

Cracks

Mary SanGiovanni

Through the usual chaotic blur of shouts and running, hiding and seeking, flying balls and gleaming slides and pendulum swings awash in color and squeaking noise, Angela Melfi noticed the small group of third graders in the corner of the playground. It had been their tentative postures—both furtive and curious—that had arrested her attention. They stood gathered around something on the ground, all nudging elbows and secretive, cupped hands. And Angela, who had been a third grade teacher long enough to hazard a guess as to why, assumed they'd accidentally done something they shouldn't have and hadn't quite worked out a course of action. She heard no crying or shouting, no finger pointing or accusations of telling. Probably, no one was hurt. That was a good sign. There was something strange, though, about how very quiet they were, almost as if they were in awe. Or fear. And that was probably not so good a sign.

Though there had never been real problems with the students at Thomas Edison Elementary before, Angela had heard horror stories from friends teaching in other districts—kids experimenting with pot or pills or oral sex acts, kids cyberbullying and catfishing, even at the tender ages of nine and ten. She shuddered. She thought she knew her students pretty well; she'd had them almost nine months by then, long enough to carry their minds to term, in a way, and she couldn't realistically imagine any of the little huddled heads engaged in those behaviors. She certainly hoped it wasn't anything like that. Angela missed the days when the worst she might find at the center of their circle of fascination was a weird bug or some remnant debris of the teens that sometimes used the park after dark—a cigarette butt or a condom wrapper for them to giggle over and speculate about.

What she found as she reached them and crested their little heads to peer into their midst was a rock, faintly luminescent, resting on a blue-plaid handkerchief on the ground where the wood-chipped turf of the playground met the grass of the field. For a moment—just a moment—she thought that luminescence, a kind of faint aquamarine, was reflected in their eyes, blinding them, absorbing both iris and pupil and filling them with that light.

"What's going on?" she asked just over their heads. It occurred only in the back of her thoughts that she'd seen no illumination from the ground or between their little bodies, from even a few feet away. "What's got you all so interested?"

No one answered. None of their eyes rose to meet her, although the whispering had died off completely. She was reminded again by their postures and downcast expressions of children caught looking at something they found interesting for reasons they couldn't quite understand and shouldn't be messing with—a dirty magazine, a dead squirrel, an untouched cigarette.

"Did you find a rock?" she asked, keeping her voice light. Some part of her wanted to yank the children away from the thing, to pull them free of its turquoise glow, but the common-sense part of her, the teacher part, knew that was irrational. For God's sake, it was just a rock. Plus, it would cause undue alarm in the small gathered group at best, and draw further interest from their classmates at worst. It was best to name this discovery, disarm its mystery and fascination, and make the children think they were done with it and moving on.

When none of them answered this inquiry, either, she tried a different tact.

"Cindy, where did this rock come from?"

Cindy was a quiet little girl with perpetual flyaway strands of blonde escaping her messy braids. She wore lavender stretch pants with hearts on them and a lavender and white t-shirt with a name Angela recognized as a pop singer, but didn't really know. Cindy's skinny arms folded over her little chest defensively. She looked at Billy, then at Karleigh, and shrugged. "We found it."

Angela looked from Cindy to Billy. "Oh? Where did you find it?"

Billy kicked at the dirt, but not near the rock. "I found it in the woods yesterday. I brought it to show the others," he mumbled. He looked...put out, was the best way Angela could think to describe it. Angela had inconvenienced him and his little crew by interrupting the revelation of this discovery.

"Well, it's a very pretty rock," Angela said, forcing a smile. "It even looks like it glows a bit, the way it's catching the light."

"My dad says that's from the minerals," Billy replied in a marginally uplifted tone. "He says it's from a meteor." Billy finally looked up at Angela, meeting her eyes, and for a moment, his own flashed the turquoise light. "It's not radi-active, though. He said it's okay. He's got a thing that checks radiation."

"Well, that's good," Angela said, and meant it. That the rock might be radioactive had fluttered just beyond the fringe of conscious thought—an attempt, however feeble, at labeling the unease she felt in the rock's proximity. "But recess is just about done, kids. The bell's going to ring. Maybe you should put it away now."

Again, that look passed over Billy's face, a soured expression of annoyance. He bent and scooped it up, rewrapping it and tucking it into his jacket pocket. It made a big lump there at his side, but the jacket fabric muted the glow.

"Thank you," she said, and gave them a smile again. They didn't return it. They simply trudged off toward the area by the bleachers where they lined up to return to the school building. Billy and Karleigh, the twins, were first, as if leading Cindy, Scott, Brayden, and Flora. Angela watched after them, frowning. It wasn't just Billy's expression mirrored in the others' faces; their movements were the same, too—furtive, cautious, almost stalking. And the protective way Billy cradled the lump in his pocket with both hands....

Other kids passed between them and Angela, so she didn't see who tripped Kenny Madison. She saw him fall, saw him hold back tears as he dusted off the gravel embedded in the heel of his hand, saw him glare at Billy and the others as he stood and then moved to take his place in line.

Billy and the others watched Kenny without expression...or, at least without an expression Angela could identify. There was a feral wariness in their advancement along the line, though, that Angela didn't like. They moved like a pack. Angela wondered if she should mention the incident to someone—the guidance counselor, Mr. Morris, maybe, or the vice principal, Reggie Barstow.

Then the bell rang and the children filed inside.

The rest of the afternoon went by in blissfully uneventful fashion. The group— Angela had taken to thinking of them as Billy's rock group—seemed to have forgotten about the strange rock in Billy's jacket pocket. They were animated, warm, engaged as children their age ever were in English class. All trace of the feral wiliness was gone. Despite the occasional glance back over their heads to the coat closet in the back of the room, Angela relaxed. She'd been worried for nothing. End-of-the-year stress, maybe, was taking its toll, seeing problems where there were none.

By the time the final bell rang and the kids were lined up to go out to the buses, Angela had just about forgotten about the rock...until she saw Billy showing Oscar the contents of his jacket pocket as they waited for the bus.

Immediately, a sinking feeling gripped Angela in the pit of her stomach. She couldn't help but feel Billy was spreading something dangerous, something worse than the rumors and common colds that kids spread to each other all the time. The rock *meant* something—she could see that much in the reverent expressions and body language of Billy and his rock group—but what?

That was silly. It was just a rock—a cool rock with pretty colors, but just a rock all the same. Billy had said it was a meteor, right? Of course something from outer space was bound to capture their interest and imaginations. A space rock, then. But still just a rock, and not some omen of evil. She repeated the logic as the children burst forth into the early May afternoon sun, joking and laughing and jostling each other on the way to the bus. She repeated it as the buses pulled away from the curb. It was just a rock. Just a rock.

She never quite believed it, though.

That was on a Tuesday. By Friday, the weather had warmed up and the children were restless, but there had been no sightings of the space rock the rest of that week. Angela had been listening more carefully than usual, though—in the bus lines and lunch lines, in the pockets of gathered children not playing ball or running around the playground. She'd listened in the girls' room and in the halls when it was her turn to monitor. Most of their chatter was the innocent third-grade type—talk about the Marvel movies and toys they wanted and the latest song by some pop star only a decade or so older than they were.

But there was the occasional odd, cryptic thing she'd hear Billy's little rock group imparting to others in that same wily but reverent tone, as if they were protecting some great secret.

Scott can break backs when he steps on cracks.

Karleigh saw one of them in her closet, and it told her [muffled giggles].

Oscar knows Red-Light/Green-Light is more dangerous than Red Rover, especially along the walls....

No—not just them. Anyone. And that's not all. He can change his face.

When Angela drew close enough to garner their notice, close enough to ask them what they were talking about, they clammed up, regarding her with those stony expressions of mild irritation at being interrupted. Their eyes were listless and dull, as if the removal of the rock's glow had somehow sucked out the life and vibrance naturally to be found there. She thought the hue beneath their skin looked wrong, too—unnatural and unhealthy, though it seemed to change and recede in certain light, or if she looked at it directly. She could swear, though, that sometimes there was the faintest turquoise tint, leaching the warmth away from their limbs and faces.

And then, that following Friday, Mrs. Appleton had her accident.

They said Eleanor Appleton had had the right of way, that the truck which had t-boned her car had blown through a red light. The truck driver had tried to stop, had slammed emphatically on his brakes, but the line had snapped. It was, investigators said, as if something had dissolved the line clear through, although the truck driver, a Grady Harrison, had claimed a tune-up the day before had caught no such issues with the brakes. It was an accident, they said around the teachers' break room—a horrible, horrible accident. The substitute, Susan Myers, would talk to Mrs. Appleton's fifth grade students about what it meant to be in a coma, and would have them each make a card for her. The teachers planned to send Harry Appleton a fruit basket and several covered dishes.

Just an accident…but Angela had bad dreams all that weekend. In them, she saw through Grady Harrison's eyes, saw the child with the glass spheres for eyes standing in the middle of Owens Road. She swerved and then corrected, not an easy thing to do with such a big rig, and then hit the brakes, in order that she might go back and check on the child.

There was no child in the rear view, and the truck wouldn't slow. She pumped the brakes, then practically stood on them to get the truck to stop. She saw the car at the intersection, saw it fill with a turquoise glow within, just seconds before she plowed into it and woke up screaming.

In the light of day, there was no reason—absolutely no reason whatsoever—for Angela to think the rock that Billy and his little group had found in the woods had anything to do with Mrs. Appleton's accident. Angela knew that. Even with the children's weird talk, with whatever strange little game they were playing since the meteor's discovery, there was no train of logic that even remotely suggested a connection.

And yet…

That Monday, she heard things. She caught Cindy filling Annabelle's ear with whispers behind a cupped hand, something about "the light that blinds then makes you see" and how "coma doesn't mean what they say." She heard Karleigh telling Oscar to "watch the stars for the sign." She heard Billy mumbling to Devon about "the bleeding between her teeth" and "the opening of the way." She never caught all of what they were saying, nor could they be induced to repeat or elaborate on anything she heard. She didn't push; if she made a big deal of it, she made it exciting to them, and they'd just keep perpetuating the game. She did mention it to the guidance counselor, Mr. Morris. He said he'd keep an ear on their little game and pull children in to talk to if he thought there was an issue.

That Tuesday, Scott's grandmother was taken to the hospital with a broken back. Her daughter, Scott's mother, suspected a fall down the stairs, but the old woman, who EMTs assumed was delirious from the injuries to her head, had muttered something about sidewalk cracks and something stepping on her, and of the snapping of bones before she had even taken the first stair.

On Wednesday, Mr. Morris was absent from school. Angela was handed a note from Mr. Barstow's secretary that informed her that Mr. Morris had been mugged on his way to his car in a grocery store parking lot. It had been a violent attack; the police believed some type of gardening tool had been used, something with prongs. His tongue and three of his fingers had been removed. He had been adamant, gesturing wildly to his wife and the nurses, that he did not want the students to visit or even send cards.

Angela had been a teacher for fifteen years; she knew that accidents happened. In a community of families as large as a grammar school, there were bound to be heart attacks and car accidents, illnesses and hospitalizations, and even sudden or violent deaths over the course of a school year. In all the time that she'd been a teacher, though, she'd never seen *so many* such tragedies befall the families of one single class in two weeks.

Kyle's older brother Ben went missing on Thursday afternoon. When he didn't show up to baseball practice, his coach called his parents, and his parents called his friends. No one had seen him since the high school let out at 2:50 p.m., nor would anyone see him again.

Thursday evening, an ambulance rushed Carrie's father to the hospital after a heart attack and a stroke, despite him being a regular runner in good shape.

Flora's grandfather drowned in a bowl of Campbell's chicken noodle soup on Friday.

Ellie's aunt and uncle died in a house fire Friday night.

Jennie's cousin Sasha jumped from the Overlook Bridge off Kerrigan Road late Sunday night, going into Monday morning. She'd missed the water and landed on an outcropped rock.

Oscar's Uncle Tio slipped in the shower Monday morning and broke his neck.

Mollie's baby brother nearly drowned in the bathtub Tuesday evening.

On Thursday morning, Billy's older sister was electrocuted by one of the outlets in the living room and sent to the hospital.

And with each violent event, the children whispered more feverishly. They grew paler and leaner, but moved with the kind of power and grace normally attributed to predatory animals. They would watch the teachers now with that same look they'd given little Kenny, that look of cunning beyond their years, and if Angela happened to catch their eye, even for a moment before they sharply turned away, she was sure she saw twin points of turquoise light.

On Friday afternoon, when the bell rang signaling the end of the school day, Angela calmly dismissed the class.

"Billy," she said, doing her best to keep her voice even, "may I see you a moment before you go?"

Billy's little rock group exchanged glances of knowing and irritation. There was something in the look which seemed too mature, too jaded for children that age. Billy nodded to them and they filed out the door, not running and shouting with the other children, but silent and serious. Did Angela actually hear Kayleigh whisper to Flora about "another obstacle to be removed," or did she imagine it?

Her heart pounded as Billy approached her desk. He looked very pale, his blue eyes nearly hidden beneath the fringe of blond hair grown long in the last week or so. His clothes were rumpled. As he got closer, she thought he smelled of the deep dirt of old places—ancient woods and crumbling cemeteries.

"Yes, Ms. Melfi?"

"Billy," she began, forcing her voice to stay even, "I just wanted to make sure everything was okay. At home, I mean, or here in school."

Billy put on a smile that was almost convincingly warm. "Of course, Ms. Melfi," he said. "Why?"

"If there's something going on, say, with you or any of your friends, you can tell me. I can help you," she said.

"Like what?" The smile still clung to his face, but it looked distorted. Certainly not warm at all.

"I don't want to make assumptions," she replied. "You seem tired, though, and you look pale. Are you not feeling well? There might be a bug going around the school. A number of students—"

"We're fine," Billy cut her off. "All of us. We're better than ever, actually."

Angela stared into his eyes a moment, hoping he'd flinch and maybe admit to a game or a joke which had run its course. He didn't.

Finally, she leaned across the desk and said, "What is that rock you found? What is it doing?"

She'd half-expected a look of surprise or confusion or even amusement. What she found in Billy's eyes, though, was a glint of smugness, as if he felt superior in being the keeper of a great secret.

He said, "Are you really going to ask questions? Like Mr. Morris or Mrs. Appleton?"

Angela felt cold in her chest. "What do you mean?"

Billy's smile slipped off his face. "Or Scott's grandma? Or Flora's? Or Oscar's uncle or Kyle's brother or my sister or Jennie's cousin?"

The cold slipped into her stomach. Was he threatening her? Implicating himself or the other kids in their families' accidents? It couldn't be. He was nine, for chrissakes. "Billy, what are you talking about? What do those accidents have to do—"

"It doesn't like when people ask questions," Billy said, that irritation returning in turquoise glints across his expression.

"What doesn't?"

"The One Who Blinds So You Can See. The Sepsis from Ithsrath." Billy paused, and part of the smile returned. "It knows a lot of fun games. It's teaching them to us."

"Billy, I think maybe we need to talk to your parents about all this. It sounds…" Her voice trailed off. *Crazy*, was what she'd wanted to say, but was it? If she was honest with herself, wouldn't she have to admit that some part of her believed that there might be at least *something* to what Billy was saying?"

Billy put a hand on her blotter. It was so small, so pale, and yet she flinched at the soft thump it made hitting her desk. "Ms. Melfi, I don't think you want to do that. It doesn't want you to. You're a good teacher. We like you. You could help us teach others the games—the special ones that bring about the changes."

Angela started to rise, but sank back to her seat under the withering gaze of the child on the other side of her desk.

"Billy," she whispered, "what is that stone doing to you?"

"It's not the stone," Billy said, his hand sliding off the blotter. It had left a wet print there, faintly turquoise. "The stone is just a key to a door, a horn blasting a calling note through and beyond the void. It's the Other that is giving us the way to evolve, to make this world right for passage."

"Do you hear yourself?" Angela's voice was small. "Do you even understand what you're saying, the words you're using? Who is teaching you this nonsense?"

Billy took a few steps back and in the next second, the hand that had touched the blotter seemed to ripple before becoming solid again. "Listen, Ms. Melfi. This is a final warning. It has already seen you and is watching. Right now, it's watching. And like I said, we like you. But don't go asking questions. Don't make it harder to play the games."

"Billy, I—"

"It will make you bleed between your teeth, if you're lucky," he said, but the voice wasn't that of a little boy's. Neither were the eyes. What filled the sockets in the boy's head were pits of bright turquoise light.

Then, in the next second, he was a regular nine-year-old boy again, strolling out of her classroom.

Angela rose and ran to the door, looking frantically up and down the empty hallway. Billy was gone.

She had just enough time to make it to the ladies' room in the teacher's lounge before she threw up in the toilet.

At home that evening, she'd foregone a glass in favor of the whole bottle of Riesling as she searched Google on her laptop. She'd typed in *glowing stones* and gotten a number of Pinterest results not related at all to what she was looking for. A search for *One who blinds so you can see* brought up advertisements for window blinds. The search on *Ithsrath* returned *No results found* until she'd typed *The Sepsis from Ithsrath* in quotes. Three results came up that time, two of them dead links.

The third was a Wordpress site for some type of organization called the Hand of the Black Stars. Its home page spouted what looked to Angela like doomsday cult rhetoric, with wildly skewed pseudo-religious language honoring deities with terrifying honorifics. The page had a *Deities* link, as well as a *Messengers* link, and one called *Travelers*. The first two yielded catalogs of monstrous entities from other dimensions and universes. It was on the last page, Travelers, where she found a reference to Xonarith, the Sepsis of Ithsrath, also known as the One Who Blinds You So You Can See.

Xonarith is the Sepsis, dweller of Ithsrath, moon of Xionathymia. Xonarith is the One Who Blinds So You Can See. He is the Light inside the Darkness inside the Light, the Breaker of bones, He who Travels the walls, He whose minions rival the stars in number. It is from Him that the children are bestowed the gifts that bring the Change…

Angela couldn't read any more after that. That much alone led to two nights of the most terrible, most realistic dreams….

That Monday she called in sick. She gave Mrs. Fergus, the school secretary, a story about coming down with the flu over the weekend, delivered in what both women found to be a convincing sick-voice. Angela pulled the blinds on all the windows and locked both the front and back doors, checking every few hours or so to make sure the locks still held.

And she waited. She waited.

Monday night came, settling darkness all around the house, while inside, the rooms blazed with light. Angela had turned on all the overheads and lamps around 4:00, when the late afternoon shadows slanted the scant light coming through the blinds.

There was nothing in these actions which struck Angela as practical, really. She didn't know if the thing or things taking over the children of Thomas Edison Elementary could bypass locks, nor did she know if light afforded any protection whatsoever. Still, she had nothing else by way of weapon—no gun, no crosses or holy water, no ancient book of banishing spells. She had locks and lights, and she'd have to make do.

None of these measures kept out the whispering. It seemed to be coming from corners where walls met ceilings or floors, where cabinets formed sharp Ls against the wall, where door jambs met in mitered Vs. The whispering sounded a lot like children telling secrets.

She called in sick Tuesday and Wednesday. Mrs. Fergus suggested a COVID test, fluids, and plenty of rest, and Angela weakly agreed that all three might be in order. She was distracted, though, by the way the light seemed to have made its way through the blinds in the living room, and appeared to be playing Red-Light Green-Light on the wall.

She really was feeling poorly, though. A low-grade ache gripped her head above her eyes, and if she turned her head too fast, she caught turquoise glints in her periphery. Her stomach burned. Twice, she had run her tongue over her teeth and tasted blood. She couldn't sleep. She had lost her appetite. She tried showering, but it was too much of an effort to do more than stand beneath the jets of water.

By Wednesday night, she knew she had to kill Billy and his rock group, before their infection spread further. But was Billy a snake head or a hydra head? How many would she have to kill to truly cripple Xonarith?

On Thursday morning, she drove out to Home Depot and bought an ax and a kitchen lighter. Then she drove over to the BP gas station and filled her spare gas can. Mrs. Fergus called on her cell phone but Angela didn't answer.

She sat in her car, waiting for the final bell to ring. The children would be lined up like chattel, to be herded out to the bus in a neat and orderly fashion. She could get them there, at least two or three, she thought, before anyone recovered enough from shock to tackle her. She liked to believe the other teachers knew what the children were, and would maybe even applaud her efforts, but she thought she knew better.

Angela was alone.

The ax, the can of gasoline, and the kitchen lighter sat next to her on the passenger seat.

She felt surprisingly numb. Not calm—she would never feel peace again—but numb. Maybe that was just as good.

The bell rang, and Angela gathered her things and got out of the car just as the front doors of Thomas Edison Elementary opened.

She moved quickly, spotting Billy at the head of the line all the way to the right. She gripped the ax in one hand, the gasoline and lighter in the other, and waited until Billy met her gaze.

His eyes were turquoise blue. She smiled.

Angela had a game of her own to show him.

The Things We Did in the Dark

Julia Darcey

I spilled the wine on my very first day in the sepulcher.

My uncles sold me in the morning, and by the afternoon I stood in the grave of the Long-Sleeping God, fouling the second of the twelve sacred rites. Wine the color of blood, to dull His senses, to keep Him dumb to the world, running all down the onyx stone thighs instead of into the black pit of His mouth.

The other nun, my teacher and sole companion, was only a few years older. Still, she slapped me, shouting, "You are an idiotic little girl!" I would kill us both, she said, when my errors awakened the One Who Must Not Stir.

So I tried to keep silent and follow her lead. Hovered a half-step behind, as she left our niche every morning, and followed the winding stairs into the depths. My hands trailed the weeping walls to steady my too-large feet. She never stumbled.

I stood quiet in the corner of the tomb, trying to ignore how the cold curled up from the dirt through the soles of my shoes, and watched. Watched her bathe the dozen stone arms in milk and oil. Watched her burn the goat carcass and braids of human hair, to remind Him of the scent of those who resisted Him turning to ash. Watched her feed fat purple livers to the Mouth with No Eyes in the center of the pinwheel of limbs. A deep black hole between those lips, leading down.

Some hero had tricked this God amid His rampages. Traded the villages at His feet for a promise the God would sleep in luxury for eternity. Twelve rites performed by maidens every day, to feed Him, bathe Him, soothe His pride with ancient songs of His strength. And if we had to live in darkness til our demise, at least we would protect everyone else from His rage. That's what she told me, instead of her name.

We had rituals of our own when the day's rites were done. She gathered the offerings dropped into our pit by surrounding towns; always enough to sate the God, never enough to sate us. I lit the stove but she cooked, knowing we wouldn't have enough food to last if I burned even a morsel of it. I washed the robes, though it took weeks before she was satisfied with how I scrubbed out the smell of burnt bones. We dried them over the fire, the only hot, dry space here, beneath the surface of the earth. I only singed one once. It was my robe that blackened and not hers; I was proud of that.

We never spoke about our lives outside of this pit. I tried to ask, the first week. She didn't hit me. Only ran me through with the despair of her dark eyes, catching the orange candlelight. And that was worse than any beating.

Every once in a while, if we finished all our tasks early, she let us go to the hole where they dropped the offerings—where they'd lowered me in once, like a bucket down a well. We pressed our heads together and stared up through the shaft to the sky above. Sometimes we felt rain. Sometimes we saw stars. I hoped that one night we'd see the moon. But I wasn't foolish enough to speak it out loud.

We never saw the sun. When the sun was up, there were rituals to be done.

I had always been a clumsy girl. I suppose that's why they sold me. Sometimes I nicked the skin of the livers, marring His feast. Once, I dribbled mother's milk down the chin of the Mouth with No Eyes as I shivered in the tomb's frozen air. Each time, she saved us: catching my wrist in her hand, mopping up the milk, snatching the broken liver before it went into that black pit. Each time, she beat me. Said it was a greater curse to be locked with me in the dark than left alone in it.

And yet. When I sliced my hand on the dull knife and nearly awakened the Deep One with the perfume of virgin blood, she crept back to my corner of our room, after the beating was through. With a sliver of soap and strips of cloth, she cleaned and bound my wound. In the blackness left by our dead candle, I could feel but not see her lift my bandaged hand and lay her lips upon my knuckle.

Wondering if I dreamed this strange kindness, I watched her, too often, during the ablutions. Watched as her steady hands poured the soapy water over the smooth stone limbs, and, later, the oil, which she rubbed in with long slides of her small hands, her back arching and contracting like a cat's as she worked.

I tried, desperate to please her. Not to stop the beatings, because they'd always been meant to scare rather than scar me—nothing compared to what my uncles had done with a switch. I tried to see her smile. If I poured the milk well, if I sang the hymns of the terrible God's power without drifting off-key, she would smile all night in our niche. Sometimes, she would take the fat we cut from the livers, melt it on the stove, and rub it into my hands, red and cracked from the cold.

One night, when I had long lost count of my days in the dark, we sat beneath the shaft, gazing up at the narrow slice of sky. Feeling bold, I whispered, "Who was she?" Because there must have been a girl before me. There must always be two maidens.

She tilted her head up, a halo of light across her sharp nose and her small lips, chapped from the chill. The starlight seemed to unravel the knots always there between her eyes.

I didn't think she'd answer, only gnaw at the flakes of skin on her lower lip. But she said, "She was even younger than you. She was good. She…tried. But when I wasn't looking—"

She turned down to the stones, banishing the pale blue light from her cheeks. "It took two months for them to bring you. All that time, alone, to think about how I…I couldn't…"

I touched her shoulder, to spare her from finishing. She glared at me, stars catching on her tears, and told me it was time for sleep. But in our niche, she reached out and crushed my fingers in hers.

So our nightly rituals shifted, even as we remained slaves to the angry God by day. I still made mistakes, but those brought only sharp words in place of slaps. In the evenings, we spoke in low tones in our lightless niche. We braided each other's hair, twining it in crowns above our heads where it would not get in the way of our work. I waited for her to put her lips again on my knuckles. It didn't come. But still, her fingers in my hair sent shivers up my spine. This was something, some flickering light in the dim.

We had our rituals, by day and by night. The things that gave structure to our time in the darkness. The things that kept us breathing. The things we did not say. It was not enough, but it was not nothing. And, because I was a fool, I thought we could go on like this.

But I was always a clumsy girl. And how could it be any other way, living above a God whose maw was always open for error?

I saw, one day, in the milk as I poured, a skein of red swirling from my hand, skin cracked by the cold. Her brown eyes huge with fear. Her steady hands trembled like I had never seen them.

I stood, as the grinding of the shifting beast made the stones shudder beneath our feet. I would not run from what I had done. "I'm sorry," I told her. "I am not afraid."

Out from the Mouth with No Eyes, from that pit that held the eternal blackness of the underground, came its shriek. A voice crying out in every octave the human ear could hear.

I stared at it, the horror seeping through my rib cage like the cold. But she did not look at it. She only looked at me. She did not scream or tremble now, as she neared me and grasped the edges of my hood.

"No. Forgive me," she whispered. "You were only a foolish little girl. You did not deserve this darkness, or mine."

She kissed my lips, dry skin rough on mine. Kissed me while that thing that was no god reached the first of its dripping gray arms out from the pit. Kissed me while it groped blindly across the onyx, claws scraping on stone.

Then with all the weight of her—which was scarcely enough—she shoved me out into the hall. My back hit the ground as the stone door clapped down.

Screaming, I pounded on the stone. Shouted nonsense instead of her name because I had never known it. Tried to lift it until my fingers went bloody, and I did not know how I would pour the milk tomorrow.

For I would, I knew, wake up tomorrow to the open door and the monster masquerading as a god waiting in his hole. I would do the rituals again. I would add my own, lying down each night with her spare robe tangled in my arms, and curse it for no longer smelling of her. I would sit beneath the sky and keep watch for the moon. When I finally saw its silver swell, I would tell myself it was her spirit, floating above this place, finally free from the dark.

Until they sent me a new girl, perhaps even worse than me. Because I had been no error. I understood that then. This hole had been built to please a monster playing god, demanding obedience, punishing those who failed to give it. A series of rituals so complex, girls so hungry and frostbitten, an error would always come. That was the bargain the hero struck. This is how they kept him happy, how they kept him fed. Because there is nothing an angry god loves more than rising in righteous rage and slaking rage with blood.

I pressed my ear to the door until my cheek froze. Until the blood on my fingers dried brown and my tears turned to frost on the stone.

But I heard none of her voice inside. And never would again.

She died to save the people who put us down here. And so would I. Unless I woke up tomorrow and did not pour the milk, or burn the goat, or sing his songs. Unless I let him starve. Starve, until he climbed from this pit and raked his hundred claws over the villages that had broken their blood bargain.

The villages that dropped the girls they did not want down this pit, thinking we would follow their rituals without a word. Never believing, not for a moment, that we would fight.

In the House, There Were Teeth and There Were Eyes

Ichabod Cassius Kilroy

FIRST STORY

Outside of the house, he could take up space. His eyes had a skull to sink into, and his teeth had long, thin lips with which to frown and sneer. These were just some of the things he had taken for granted before moving into the house.

At work, there were long, thin hands on long, thin arms, and he used them to neatly pack boxes in an assembly line. He never went anywhere besides work and then back to the house.

Work. House. Work. House. Work—it went on like that.

To be in the house was to become the absence of a man. A negative space where a man could be, but wasn't. In the house, he didn't have the same soft footfalls, the same little huffs of breath that he did outside.

One of the house's biggest problems was that it was simply too large to be the home of nothing more than the space where a man could have been. He had no living family and very few of what might be called friends. The few friends he had weren't the kind you could reasonably be expected to live with. And so he was alone.

Only him, and the three stories in the house (not including the basement).

Because the house was so large, the teeth and the eyes slept in the walk-in pantry. None of the other rooms felt hospitable.

The walk-in pantry was next to the laundry room and the laundry room had a side door leading to a side yard.

The pantry's doors were French and wooden, and the shelves were built of another, darker wood. He'd laid out a sleeping bag and put his alarm clock and

92

the charging base for his phone on the second lowest shelf the night he'd moved in. Now a neat little pile of dust lay at their bases.

He kept his food in the wooden linen closet that was in the backmost hallway since the pantry had become his bedroom. The closet was beside another side door. Occasionally, he would get confused and open the wrong door, and find himself faced with the narrow stretch of wooden fencing that enclosed the side yard, instead of the smiling faces on his boxes of cereal.

Everything in the house went back to wood. Wooden floors. Wooden decks. Wooden stairs. Wooden built-in cupboards and bookshelves. Wooden accent walls in the bedrooms. Somewhere else, this might have been nice.

The problem with this was that none of the woods belonged together. All mixed up in every room; an unreal cemetery for an unreal forest, where pine and mahogany and ironwood and cypress all merged into an unpleasant range of browns that echoed and thumped when they came into contact with each other.

The absence had never had strong opinions on the architectural importance of wood until he'd moved into the house. Now he hated wood because it was easier than hating the house.

Then there were the first story baseboards. The man's wanting presence was pretty sure they were oak, and while unattractive this wasn't the main problem he had with them. The issue was that the baseboards in the first story had wept. Hot, salty tears that ran in silence all through his long and lonely nights in the house.

"It's a structural problem, though," said the contractor he'd called to re-caulk the baseboards. The contractor was leaning against the wooden entryway to the living room, beside another side door, when he said this. "Bad bones. You'll be up to your eyes in all the mess again in another few years."

The place where a man wasn't shrugged. He couldn't afford to move in this economy. Not when the house had been inherited outright. Besides, what were a few tears to a pair of disembodied eyes and a set of unsubstantiated teeth?

The contractor sighed, in understanding. The contractor was having his own financial difficulties. "You see this thing all the time in these custom new builds. There's no architects. No integrity. You'll have to stay vigilant for any other problems and get on top of them fast. Do you have the blueprints?"

The teeth and eyes didn't have the blueprints. Or, if he had them, he had yet to find them. The emptiness in the house had attempted to be filled by his dead relatives with lifetimes of paperwork.

There were birth certificates for people he was reasonably certain had never existed, and death certificates for people who were still alive. He'd found a whole laundry basket of receipts that had been made into terrible blackout poetry, and piles of letters written in codes for which he couldn't find ciphers. Worse still, the weeping baseboards had washed out much of what was left to be sorted through.

He said as much to the contractor. The contractor tutted and shook his head. The contractor ran a scarred, wide hand through his hair. "Well, you have my number now."

And the empty place that was a man nodded, and said he did, and he tipped the contractor in cash. The contractor left.

The contractor went home to his wife, who was as beautiful as she was terminal, and they spent most of dinner talking about how sad it would be to be only teeth and eyes and ignoring the ever-growing pile of medical bills and the looming presence of her hospice nurse between them.

SECOND STORY

The house was very newly the teeth and the eyes' house. Before that, it had been his grandmother's and before that his great aunt's, and she had built the house on the leveled space where another family's house had once been. Before that, it was impossible for the teeth and eyes to say.

It had been some time now since the baseboards had been repaired, and the house was finding new ways to pain his life.

It started in one of the second story bathrooms. When he moved in, the walls were white, which had been a nice break from all the wood, but then they started changing. A horrible jaundice had encroached upon the space, first yellow and then a slow build to brown. The room stank of bile and the walls seemed to shudder and sweat. A low moan was coming out of all the plumbing.

Then, something happened in the bedrooms. He missed the beginning of this because he was so rarely upstairs, to begin with, and when he was, he was trying to get control of the bathroom's jaundice, but both bedrooms on the second story had started growing side doors.

The master bedroom had two now, and it looked like a third could spring up at any moment from behind the headboard. All of the side doors led to the same spot in his side yard.

He knew this for certain because he'd taken up smoking, to deal with the stress of his job and the house, and so he left a ceramic ashtray outside the door nearest the pantry. It looked like a cabbage leaf. That same ashtray was outside of every side door the house produced.

Just as he was trying to decide if a jaundiced, moaning bathroom and spatial rift side doors were enough to justify calling the contractor again, all of the lightbulbs on the second story began to fill with blood.

The teeth threw up from a stomach that he didn't have. It splattered against the wooden floors and walls. The whole story smelled of iron and bile now, and then the blood got hotter and hotter and stank more and more and so he threw up again, prolifically, and fell to the ground near tears, only to find that the baseboards on the second story were now also crying.

He laid there, exhausted, in a pile of his own sick and the house's tears for several hours, just watching the baseboards cry.

When he could, he gathered himself and went downstairs to call the contractor.

The void of a person got the contractor's voicemail, and so he left a rambling message about the side doors, and the bloody lightbulbs, but neglected to mention the jaundice and the weeping baseboards.

He immediately remembered that he'd forgotten to mention them, and called back. He hung up before it finished ringing through, and then called back again to leave a voicemail, begging the contractor to return as quickly as possible but again neglecting to mention the specific problems he was facing.

It didn't matter, as the contractor was having problems of his own. The contractor was taking time off to plan his wife's funeral and would be gone for the next long while, attending to her personal affairs.

THIRD STORY

The teeth and the eyes hadn't been to the third story since the day he moved in.

He'd done a check of all the rooms with his grandmother's lawyer. He'd been given a big string of jingling keys and a pat on the place where he'd had a shoulder, and then he'd been left alone in the house.

The third story, which was an open floor plan, had more windows than anywhere else in the house. Every window was as round as one of his eyes, and full of thick, bubbly glass. Light reflected and refracted in terrible ways. The place where he'd had skin felt hot. He'd stood there, in the center of a brightness, until the sun set, letting the light dance and change across the floor.

Long after the sun was gone, the windows' lights remained.

Was this what ants felt like? When he'd gone to work the next day, his skin was pink and blistered. His manager had complained.

That was the last time he'd gone to the third story.

Regardless of his careful avoidance, its windows had started sinking through the floor. A few windows were trapped between the third and second stories, but most were on the first story now. One was even falling into the basement, still luminous.

He had the contractor on speed dial, but the contractor was busy with probate court and blocked him.

He couldn't get any sleep. Alone, in that big wooden house, the teeth and the eyes were spiraling. If he had lungs, surely he'd be hyperventilating.

He stopped showing up to work. The house was too big to be left empty. His manager had him on speed dial and the phone's voice echoed everywhere, but the omission of a man was busy dealing with the house and blocked him.

The new windows on the first story blinked and turned inward, and the man's dearth quivered in terror. He was up to his ankles in the baseboard's tears.

After one last attempt at calling the contractor, who was mourning his wife in every bar in the country, the teeth and the eyes dropped his phone in the rising water, and headed, after much confusion with the side doors, down into the basement.

BASEMENT

In the basement, there weren't any floors.

Everything expanded into the endless maw of the universe. There were no light fixtures, and so the only light that came in came from the doorway at the top of the stairs or the falling third story windows, which spiraled out into space and became pinpricks in a formless sky.

However, the longer he stood there and the more lights that came in, the worse things felt, because then he could see where the light was going. Then he could see the teeth in the maw of the universe.

The teeth and the eyes laid down at the base of the stairs.

Quiet engulfed him. It was silent in the basement save for the occasional drip of a tear from upstairs, and again with great clarity, he felt the loss of the little human sounds he could make outside of the house.

His eyes rolled back in the head he was missing, and the arms he'd once had tried to pull his missing knees up to his lacking chest.

The uncaring universe subsumed the man's wanting presence.

Then came the gnawing.

A Dampened Embrace

Christopher Hann

It was the first week of summer and the events that transpired were thus:

Mother passed away on Sunday

She was buried on Wednesday

Her grave was reported to have been robbed on Friday

And on Saturday, at the first light of a dreadfully humid morning, my mentally unstable father called me over landline, informing me that he had come into possession of a mermaid.

I sat for an hour thinking about the worst implications possible, and the ghastly predicament I was now forced to resolve—should these implications be true. I questioned the plausibility of the scenario at hand. A frail old man could not possibly unearth an entire grave overnight. Perhaps the events weren't related at all—a mountain hog was to blame for Mother's missing corpse, and Father's call was a mere display of his condition—fragmented delusions of a deteriorating mind, made acute by the onset of grief.

But then I remembered how Father jumped into the grave and wept atop Mother's casket. How he screamed indecipherable chants of lament and heartbreak. How the topsoil wasn't filled at the time due to this commotion. I doubt the workers ever returned to finish the job.

Perhaps the authorities had to get involved, should the situation be as ugly as I imagined. I left for my father's house promptly at noon.

The holiday traffic gave me ample time to wallow in my dread.

Hot. Humid. Summer. Mom. Body.

Mermaid.

I tried my utmost not to dwell on these words, for the image they formed made me ill. Strangely enough, however, in the roiling cauldron of emotions that assailed my stomach, one that could not be found was sorrow. No sorrow, no pain—just like when I had heard of Mother's passing.

Something to do with her thyroid. She was brought down with hormonal shock, developed a fever, and just as easy as that she was gone.

Admittedly I was coldhearted, for Mother and Father were never the ones to ill-treat their son and—in hindsight—I believe they tried their best to love me. Alas things weren't so simple, for as far as I am aware, estrangement and antipathy are common symptoms when reluctantly raised in a family of shamans.

Shamanism isn't some mystic art, nor a rarity where I come from. Even in 21st century metropolitan South Korea, where cities shine bright and billboards even brighter, shamanism still lurks, walking a tentative line between monks and tarot readers. At the risk of criticism, I will call them what they are—or at least what I believed them to be—charlatans whose perceived abilities of mindreading and fortunetelling only delve as far as the faith in their façade. I would even go on to say that some of them were predators—snouts keen to sniff out the naïve; jaws vicious in their assault upon the desperate. If there was money to be squeezed, shamans knew how to squeeze it.

Say these prayers or you'll fail your exam (it'll cost you).

Carry this emblem or you'll have an accident (it'll cost you).

Perform this ritual or your child won't be rid of cancer (it'll cost you—a lot).

Fear and doubt were the crutch of their rhetoric—never hope. If it isn't apparent by now, the disdain I hold for certain members of this "profession" remains profoundly intact to this day.

Mother may have been a charlatan, but she was no predator. Either that, or she was very bad at her job. Our family never escaped material scarcity, let alone saw wealth of any kind. As for Father, he was not a shaman *per se*, but a shaman's assistant, if one could call it such. The "deity" that had descended upon our bloodline was apparently female, so evidently it required a female "cup." Myself, being a son, was not subject to the deity's shenanigans—which was great, for even as a youngster I didn't buy into the nonsense. It wasn't ideal growing up—I could never invite friends over in fear of being ridiculed, and every so often a classmate might jeer, asking if the cloud-gods might tip them in on the upcoming lottery. For the most part I wasn't bothered. Mother's job was just that, a job, and how she made a living was none of my business, and my opinions on the profession were none of hers. The years went on without incident, and despite the obvious wall which loomed within the household, we were moving through life with relative serenity.

And then my sister was born.

I was fifteen at the time, and was old enough to be concerned about the implications of having a girl in the house, and the uncanny path of life that Mother might try to lead her through.

"This cup is drying," I overheard her one night, confessing her worries to my father. "It's been drying out for some time. The princess requires a new goblet."

I knew what this meant: they were going through with the "descension." A rite in which the deity flows down into the body of a juvenile vessel, the senior practitioner passing the torch to her protégé. Superstitious jargon aside, they were going to raise my sister as a shaman.

That night, I crept up to the baby's crib. Pudgy little thing, just six months old. She awoke, and instead of breaking into a squeal like her usual self, she waved her baby feet in the air and said "Rah!" as she recognized my presence. She goo-ed and she gah-ed, and she flapped her arms around like a penguin trying to fly, and then she looked straight at my face and repeated "Rah!"

And then she smiled.

What infinite potential, I thought. *What boundless joys, and sorrows, to be had in life; what adventures to be undertaken and challenges to be overcome. What fortune it is to be blessed with normalcy.*

"Rah!" she said again, and I smiled back.

All tossed away. In the pursuit of fraudulent devotion. A delusional life saddled with stigma and poverty. And, when the time came, the miserable cycle would repeat itself.

There was a dull pain in my chest. It traveled up my neck, swelled through my face, and swelled into my eyes. I realized, for the first time in working memory, that I was capable of loving a family member. Perhaps I had forgotten, but now I was reminded, and I wanted the best for this child.

I reached out to my extended relatives, who—as luck would have it—were rational human beings. They spoke to Mother and Father. Mother, much to everyone's concern, was upfront and adamant in her views—her daughter was to be raised a shaman and none could say otherwise. Fortunately, such outdated sentiments did not fly in modern Korea.

Child services got involved. Legal battles of which I will spare the details followed.

One of our aunts ended up taking custody, until my sister reached three. She was then adopted into a wealthy family, and sometime thereafter moved overseas.

Needless to say, the rift between myself and Mother became irreparable. *They snatched her right out of my heart,* she used to say. *And you helped them!* It didn't bother me too much—or at least, I didn't allow it to. I left home at the age of nineteen and never looked back.

The cicadas greeted me as I exited the vehicle, belting out their last screech at the final hours of sunlight. To my right flowed a stream and beyond that lay a valley, and I was reminded—despite the harrowing circumstances—how hauntingly beautiful the surrounding vista was. As a tranquil retirement home for an eccentric old couple, I could imagine no better place.

It was ironic then, that Father's symptoms developed after moving here. He was, after all, a shaman's assistant, so a skeptical layman may have questioned his sanity to begin with. But he was never the one to blur his fantasies into the solid reality of the material world. Dreams may be messages sent by his deity, but he never *saw* such in his lucid, waking life. That changed after moving into the valley.

Something to do with the starlight, he used to ramble. Something to do with the shining granules of dust that poured nightly upon the still black water. Conjured from within was the visage of his newfound deity, whispering words so soothing, issuing commands so profound—yet utterly indecipherable. Its visits had become frequent as of late.

Mermaid.

The word hit me again as I knocked on the door. I was afraid that the first thing to greet me would be the stench of death—that foul stink of a rotting corpse, recalled only through my memory of roadkill. I was afraid that I would smell Mother before I saw her, proving true my worst assumptions.

Father opened the door. There was no smell.

He greeted me in a dull fashion, then he led me to the living room and served some tea. I scanned quickly for signs: bruises on his limbs, dirt under his fingernails, an oddly misplaced shovel lying someplace in the corner but found none.

I took a seat and drank the tea. "How are you holding up?"

He managed to mutter some kind of response—devastated, certainly. But consolation was not the purpose of my visit.

"You wanted to show me something," I said. "What is it?"

No response.

The longer the silence dragged on, the greater my trepidation—a sickly regret that maybe I should have stayed home, locked myself in my room, and let *whatever this was* sort itself out. Mustering what assertiveness I had, I asked. "Is it a mermaid?"

Father closed his eyes, shook his head, then spoke up grimly, "Not *a mermaid.*" There was vexation in his voice—defiance, even—as if I had somehow made light of a sanctified subject. "*Mermaid,*" he scoffed. "I only used that word as a reference."

"So, not a mermaid." I sighed. "What is it then?"

"It is a…" he started. "It is *a m…*" He was trying to articulate, but couldn't string together the right words—the revelation of some great secret, some marvelous phenomenon, some remarkable discovery that just had to be shared with his long estranged son.

"Dad," I snapped before he could finish. "Where is Mom?"

I couldn't take it—the neurotic, delusional drivel that was about to come pouring out of his mouth—I just couldn't take it. Either I needed to be here, or I didn't. If I didn't, then I wanted to leave.

"She's in the other room."

The grandfather clock hit seven. The cicadas still screeched outside.

There was a droning voice in the air, repeating: *Son, it is a miracle. I know it's hard to fathom, but truly it is a miracle.* I wished it would shut up.

Optimism—a tricky thing—probed at my psyche. He could be delusional. He *is* delusional. Mother might not be here at all. It could all just be in his head.

"I want to see her," I said.

"Not yet. We'll first wait for moonrise—"

"*Just be quiet*—all I want to do is check if she's here. *Okay?*"

"Son, I know you have doubts. I know you have concerns. But we can't ruin this, not now. Your mother gave her all to create this miracle. She gave her body; she gave her life—"

He stopped, and noticed. The bewilderment in my eyes, gradually transforming into disbelief. Then to wrath. "What did you just say?"

"It doesn't matter now. I managed to retrieve her body in time, so that was lucky. We—"

"You knew she was going to die."

"Son. I had nothing to do with her illness. That was coincidental. Her early passing was never part of the plan—"

"Plan?"

Fury. I knew what it was, but I didn't know I was capable of feeling it for Mother. Especially now that she was dead.

I grabbed Father by the collar, hurling him against the wall. *You poor, sick, sick man,* I thought. *What poor, sick, sick end to this poor, sick, sick family.*

"She took part willingly—willingly!" He croaked from within my grip.

Oh, of course she did. And of course, mermaids are real. There was no further point in humoring his delirium. Whether he had any part in Mother's passing, I did not wish to know. But grave-robbing was a crime, and—as miserable as it was—the safest place for this man now was inside an asylum.

"I'm calling the police."

GURGLE.

It came from the bedroom.

GURGLE.

We both stood frozen. Myself in terror; my father in exhilaration.

"It's happening," he whispered, freeing himself from my grasp.

He made his way to the bedroom, and I followed. In that room, I witnessed ugliness incarnate.

Mother lay on the bed, covered in scales. They sprouted like large toenails from under her eyelids, her nostrils, and her lips. They grew on the ridges of her hairline, and down her neck, sheathing her limbs. "I know it's hard to behold…"

I didn't catch the rest of the sentence. I crumpled into the corner, distancing myself as far as I could from the bed. My vision dimmed. All I could hear was: *tishk.* Father was removing the scales, by hand, one by one. They peeled off like scabs on a wound. I remembered I hadn't eaten the entire day.

Tishk.

Like an idiot at a fair, I watched. Trying to comprehend the horror unfolding before me.

Tishk.

I must have passed in and out of my stupor, for when I regained vision, the sun had already set. Alas, I could still hear that vile sound from the other end of the room. What might be a sane reaction, I wondered. Fright? Disgust? I asked in earnest to any deity out there—Jesus, Zeus, Ba'al, anyone—that I may be granted the mercy of waking from this nightmare.

Then I saw her face.

Younger, pristine as marble, her skin glowing with a soothing luminescence—subtle, yet captivating beyond measure—and the only thing I could compare it to was...

"Starlight," said Father. "It stirs within her."

I can't say why, but I walked up to the bed and began to help

There was an urge to free this woman of the seal that smothered her, to remove this layer of ugliness, so that she might shine true. And with each scale removed, it became bizarrely plain to me that this woman had loved her son in life—and perhaps thereafter—despite receiving no such sentiment in return.

I questioned my sanity, but the resounding answer to my doubts was *no, you are sound of mind, perhaps sounder than ever.* This was my send-off. A rite of farewell to the woman who brought me into this world, this time delivered in sincerity, and dare I add, a trace of affection.

Tishk. The final piece was removed.

There was a *gurgle,* a soft rumbling of sorts, which echoed from within her chest. She grew brighter—almost to the point of dazzling—but I could not look away; nor did I wish to. The room filled with starlight sparkling through the air in glimmers I had never seen, and pouring across the floor in shades I had never known. She gleamed with tranquil majesty. And then she blazed, like a comet hurtling through the atmosphere, its trail never-ending. Her visage infused in my heart a hallowed reverence, and filled my eyes with wonders. In her, all the secrets and terrors of the universe were revealed to me...

With a gasp, she melted into a puddle of liquid. From the puddle, it arose. A creature of the water, newborn and vigorous. It looked at Father, then at me, and said, "Rah."

I knew that everything had led to this: My birth into this strange family, the coming of my sister, which shattered it, every hardship, every trial, every decision we made had led to this one conclusion. The creation of life both as we knew it, and beyond. My days of cynicism were gone, for the creature before me was no work of a charlatan.

But the creature's vigor faded. The light in its eyes grew dim; its dampened body falling limp upon the sheets. First to grip me was panic, and then sorrow—all the sorrow I had unknowingly stowed away, all the bereavement I had foolishly denied myself—as I discovered for the first time what it felt like to watch a loved one perish.

"Quickly!" Father screamed.

We raced out into the cold, silent night and fell to our knees by the stream, Father coddling our dear-one in his arms. It was dying. The culmination of our family's journey—so little in its figure yet so grand in its purpose—was dying. Or, more accurately, it was *starving*.

Without the need for words, we both understood what had to be done.

The creature entered Father through his throat, whereby it nourished itself from the inside out. There was no grotesquery involved: just an infant in need of feeding, and a body willing to provide sustenance. Thereafter the creature emerged, swimming graciously onto the moonlit water. Glitter poured from the heavens once again, revealing not one, but many such creatures roaming the banks, mature in their figure and infinitely more glorious. The newborn gazed upon me for one final time. It blinked, bowed its head as if in acknowledgement, then whispered:

Rah. Rakshmana.

And all of them were gone.

Thus is the tale of my summer. As for Father, I'm sure no one will seek him so long as the bills are paid, but such things are no longer of importance. A terrifying yet magnificent discovery has been made and I of all people—an unyielding skeptic of over forty years—lay humbled in its wake. Hereby I record my true and honest accounts—my unadulterated testimony of entities beyond comprehension—and the miraculous transcendence they bestowed upon our parents.

Yes, *our* parents.

Song Ah, or Christine as you go by now, it was difficult for me to recognize you and it would have been impossible for you to recognize me. What a wonderful person you have grown to be, and what a beautiful family you have raised.

I remember back to that night, when you smiled up at me from your crib and taught me what it is to care about family. We've grown so far apart that we barely register each other's existences, but know that you have always resided in the deepest parts of my heart. I remember the illustrious life I wanted for you, what infinite potential I imagined for your future.

It wasn't easy finding you. Harder still was adding the star-laden water from the valley into your morning coffees at work. Even now you may feel its effects:

the inkling of a twitch behind your eyes, the viscous pumping of your heart, the irritable tingling on the soles of your feet and, moreover, that murky voice that calls you in your dreams: *come to the water.*

We won't be alone on this journey. Your beloved daughters—and my cherished nieces—have been drinking the water as well. So has your husband—a good man, might I add. When the time comes, he will offer himself as nourishment for the newborns—as will I.

You might feel frightened at this point. Repulsed. Violated, even. Please know that these feelings are natural, but transient. I too have felt them in droves, as apparent in my accounts to you above. Dear sister, these are no cheap tricks conjured by charlatans. Neither are they delusions of a self-proclaimed shaman. There are larger things at work which come to us not in the name of oppression or despair, but comfort and solace. When the time arrives—when the starlight beckons us with its ever gracious luminance—we will travel together to our watery home, where Rakshmana will hold us in its dampened embrace.

In the meantime, take care of yourself. I look forward to hearing from you.

24 Points

S.A. Cosby

The leaves fell like tears across the hood of the truck. Jarius watched them twirl and spin in the morning sun, rays of light filtering through them and splashing against the windshield. His father put the truck in PARK as his uncle took a sip from his thermos. The truck engine ticked like a clock as it cooled. His father coughed into his fist before he spoke.

"Alright," he said softly.

Uncle Ricky got out and Jarius followed him. They grabbed their rifles from the gun rack in the back of the truck window. Jarius pulled his bright orange knit cap down over his head as his dad pulled on his own blaze orange vest and Uncle Ricky slipped into his blaze orange baseball cap. Birds sang as they checked their rifles and filled their vests with ammo and clipped buck knives to their belts.

"Let's meet back here for lunch at 10. Jarius, make sure you keep your cell phone charged. Don't be playing games on it," his father said.

"I—" Jarius started to say then decided it wasn't worth it and stopped himself.

"It's cold as a witch's tit out here goddamn," Uncle Ricky said. He checked the scope on his rifle. "We should have brought the dogs, Cal."

"The stand's in a good place. There's an old salt lick over there. Deer be running through that old wash out where that old creek used to be. We get 'em set up in a big ass triangle. We don't need the dogs," Cal said.

"Go faster with the dogs. We gonna be sitting up in them stands colder than my sister-in-law's bed til we see a buck come by," Uncle Ricky said.

"I got a 12 pointer here last year. Timmy Dillet got two 12 pointers last month about a mile away. This a good spot. Come on, let's get it," Cal said. The three of them slung their rifles over their shoulders and made their way into the forest. They slipped between the elm trees that bordered the outer edge of the forest that then gave away to oak and maple trees that were losing their leaves like an old man losing his hair. The detritus under their feet crunched with each step. Jarius thought it sounded like bones cracking, like when his father would break the leg bones of deer after he cooked them to get to the marrow.

He heard a crow call out in the distance that echoed through the air like a baby's cry. It made him shiver. His grandfather used to have a crow he kept as a pet named Ahab who would impersonate the voices of characters from television. He remembered jumping out of his skin one day when he heard Scooby-Doo behind him in his grandfather's kitchen.

They had been walking for about twenty minutes when they entered a clearing encircled by a clutch of dead fallen trees. Overhead a flock of starlings blotted out the sun for a brief moment casting perforated shadows down over the three of them. Uncle Ricky paused and pulled out a flask.

"It's seven-thirty," Cal said.

"It's five o'clock somewhere," Uncle Ricky said.

Jarius laughed.

His father shot him a look that cut off his laughter in mid-titter.

A sound like thunder boomed through the early morning air.

All three of them turned their heads in the direction of the sound. The thunder came again. And again. And again.

"What the fuck is that?" Uncle Ricky asked in a whisper.

"Something big," Cal unshouldered his rifle and peered through the scope in the direction of the sound.

"Holy shit. Ricky, look over there. About three o'clock," Cal said. Uncle Ricky peered through his own scope. Jarius pulled his rifle off his shoulder and did the same.

"What the fuck," Uncle Ricky whispered.

Jarius felt his mouth go dry. About three hundred yards away through a field of pine trees was the biggest buck deer he'd ever seen in his life. It was a little hard to judge from this distance but he thought it might be five or six feet tall. It had a rack that, if his math was correct, was at least 24 points. Its fur was brown and gray with what appeared to be algae or mold growing on it. It was eating leaves from a tree that Jarius couldn't identify. Its hooves appeared to be the size of coconuts, Jarius thought it was bigger than some horses he had seen.

"Is that a fucking moose?" Uncle Ricky said.

"There ain't no moose in Virginia," Cal said.

"I'm gonna get it," Uncle Ricky adjusted the sight on his scope and placed the stock against his shoulder.

"Don't." The word came out before Jarius even realized he was going to say it.

"Boy, that's the biggest buck I've ever seen. That's the biggest buck anybody has ever seen. I'm taking that son of a bitch," Uncle Ricky said with a smile.

"Ricky," Cal said, but Ricky had already aimed and set his feet.

The crack of the rifle filled their ears. The sounds of the forest were so muffled Jarius felt like someone had shoved his head under water. That sensation passed as Uncle Ricky hollered out.

"Got him! Got that fucker," he yelled.

Uncle Ricky took off in a quick march towards the deer. Cal and Jarius followed him as they made their way down off the rise and over an old spillway framed on each side by the roots of the trees that lined it like sentries. They crossed over another clearing then worked their way through a field sparsely populated with saplings that stretched towards the sky like needles.

They hiked up to the top of a ridgeline and came upon the carcass of the buck. Jarius thought it was even bigger in person. It was laying on its side with a bullet hole through its front flank. The blood that stained the hole was almost black like molasses. The rack was massive. The antlers were dark brown and speckled with spots of gray like some of the buck's fur.

"It's old. It's gotta be old as hell," Jarius said.

"Watch your mouth," Cal said.

"How much meat you think we can get off it? This gotta be a world record, right?" Ricky asked.

Cal didn't speak.

"We can field dress and hump the meat back to the truck. Shit Cal we gonna have enough venison we can fucking sell it for the rest of the winter." Ricky pulled his knife and knelt by the buck.

"Ricky, wait," Cal said.

"For what?" Ricky asked.

"I don't know. Just…what if it's sick. Look at that shit on its fur. Looks like mold or something."

"We ain't gonna eat the fur Cal." Ricky braced one hand on one of the enormous antlers and placed his knife against the throat of the buck.

Jarius could see the dead black eye of the buck over Uncle Ricky's shoulder. It was as big as an eight ball.

It blinked.

"Uncle Ricky!" Jarius shouted.

Ricky started to respond when the buck wrenched its gigantic head to the right then the left. One of the antlers caught Ricky under his armpit and got entangled in his blaze orange vest. The buck struggled to its feet with Ricky dangling from its rack. Jarius backpedaled until he hit a tree. Uncle Ricky was screaming but his screams were high pitched like a tea kettle. The buck shook its head and then Ricky was flying through the air like a paper plane. Jarius watched as he slammed into the root ball of a fallen tree and then rolled down to the bottom of the ridge line. Cal aimed his rifle at the monstrous buck but when he pulled the trigger nothing happened.

Misfire, Jarius thought.

The buck turned around and bounded off through the forest. It crashed through the woods snapping branches and crushing the deadfall under its hooves. Jarius thought he could pretend it had never been there at all. He thought that might be what was best for him in the long run if he just told himself he'd never seen a white tail deer the size of a Clydesdale.

Then he heard his uncle moaning.

He rushed to the bottom of the ridgeline and found Uncle Ricky laying on his side cradling his left arm. It was twisted like a bread tie. There was a shard of bloody bone sticking through the sleeve of Uncle Ricky's sweatshirt. Jarius stood over his uncle and stared at the compound fracture. He didn't know what to do and his uncle was groaning in agony.

Then his father was there and pushing him aside.

"It's okay Ricky. It's okay. It's gonna be alright." Cal took off his vest.

"Give me your belt," Cal said.

Jarius didn't move.

"Give me your fucking belt Jarius!" Cal yelled.

Jarius pulled his belt off and handed it to his father.

"Alright Ricky, this gonna hurt but you bleeding bad and I gotta stop it," Cal said.

"What you gonna do? Ah, Jesus, Cal what the fuck was that thing? I shot it through the fucking heart. What was it?" Ricky asked.

"I gotta make a tourniquet."

"A what?"

Cal grabbed Ricky's arm and pulled it straight. Ricky's screams this time were nearly beyond the range of human hearing. Working quickly Cal wrapped his vest around the wound then took Jarius' belt and looped it around his brother's arm and pulled it as tight as he could above the wound. Ricky kicked his feet then gasped as Cal helped him to his feet.

"Can you walk?" Cal asked.

"Fuck Cal. I can walk but my arm man. My arm is on fire," Ricky groaned.

"We just gotta get back to the truck then get you to the hospital. Come on, I got you."

"Where's my rifle?" Ricky asked.

"Forget the rifle. Let's get the hell out of here. Come on Jarius, we leaving," Cal said.

"What was that thing Cal?" Ricky asked.

"I don't know and I don't care. Let's get back to the truck."

Jarius followed his father and his uncle as they walked back through the sparse saplings and over the clearing. They walked through the spillway and through the thick spate of maples. They walked and walked and walked until Uncle Ricky begged Cal to stop.

"Get me my flask," Uncle Ricky said.

"We gotta get back to the truck Ricky. Come on," Cal said.

"I need a drink," Ricky said.

Cal didn't say anything but he reached into Ricky's vest and retrieved his flask. He took off the cap and handed it to his brother. Ricky took it with his good hand and took a long swig.

"Cal, how long we been walking?" Ricky asked.

"I don't know. Twenty minutes?"

Ricky peered up at the sky. "According to the sun it's twelve."

Cal checked his watch. He stared at it. Jarius saw his father lick his lips.

"What's wrong Daddy?" Jarius asked.

"Nothing. Let's keep moving."

"What time is it Cal?" Ricky asked.

"Don't matter, let's get back to the truck," Cal said.

"Nah. What time is it, little brother?" Ricky asked.

Jarius watched as his father closed his eyes and took a deep breath.

"My watch stopped. Let's just keep going alright." Cal said.

Ricky laughed. "I shouldn't've shot at it."

"Just...don't worry about it. Let's just get back to the truck man."

They started walking again. They came up to a hill that Jarius was sure they hadn't seen when they went hiking after the fallen buck. His father helped Uncle Ricky climb up the hill as Jarius followed them.

When they got to the top of the hill, they found themselves facing three men standing shoulder to shoulder. The men were wearing loose fitting clothing that he realized were deer skins. They all had long reddish black hair that fell to their waist. They were barefoot and their feet were darker than their hands which were a dusky brown. Their faces were covered in red and black paint. Red paint over their mouths, black paint over their eyes and red paint on their noses.

Jarius noticed the forest had gone silent.

"White men came from across the water. They came here and were told this was the realm of Nyarlathotep. They were told her young bedded down here. They suckled from her great teats here. They were told to not harm them. They were told by the Werecomico and the Mattaponi but they did not listen. You are not white men. You were not warned. And so, you will be shown mercy. If...you give us the one who befouled the youngling. Give him to us and you may pass," the man in the middle of the three said.

Cal pulled his rifle. He ejected the misfired bullet and aimed at the man in the middle. "You're not taking my brother. I'll kill you where you stand."

Jarius thought his father was trying to sound tough but he heard how his voice trembled.

"She was old when the hills here were young. She was old when the mountains to the west were young. She was old when the ocean was still vapor. Old and bitter and without mercy. You will meet her. You will die." The man in the middle turned and walked down the other side of the hill. His two companions followed him. Jarius watched as they melted into the terrain like the mists.

"What the fuck is going on?" Ricky said.

"I don't know but we ain't staying here. The truck can't be far." Cal said.

They kept walking even as the sun began to sink below the horizon and darkness snapped at their heels.

Uncle Ricky stopped and leaned against a tree. "Cal. You and Jarius go on. I'm gonna stay here."

"Ricky, what you talking about?" Cal asked.

Ricky smiled but it never got to his eyes. "Whatever is happening, it wants me. You heard the fucking dude. You and Jarius go on. I'll be okay."

Jarius looked up at the sky. He could barely see it through the canopy. The night was inexplicably coming on like a blanket made of sackcloth. He felt his stomach clench.

"Let's go, Daddy," Jarius said.

Cal stared at him. Hard.

"We not leaving your uncle." Cal said.

"Daddy I'm scared," Saying it out loud made Jarius feel a little bit better, but not by much.

"You better man up then. We ain't leaving you, Ricky."

A fog suddenly materialized around them like a cloud. It didn't roll in from the hills or rise up from beneath their feet. One moment they were standing together in the dying light of the sun the next moment they were enveloped in a fog as thick as pea soup.

Voices, deep and guttural, erupted around them. They were chanting words Jarius didn't recognize in a language he didn't understand. The sun winked out and they were plunged into stygian darkness as black as midnight in a mineshaft. Jarius went to his father and grabbed his arm.

"Daddy let's go!" Jarius said.

His father shrugged him off.

"We ain't leaving my brother!" Cal roared. He started firing into the fog, random shots that ricocheted off the trees. Jarius covered his ears and dropped to his knees.

"Cal, stop," Ricky said.

Cal kept firing.

"Cal," Ricky yelled. "Stop!"

Cal stopped shooting.

The voices stopped chanting.

"She's here." Ricky pointed over his brother's shoulder. Jarius saw red streaks running down his cheeks and realized his uncle was crying tears of blood.

Jarius turned his head.

Her eyes were black holes, yawning expanses that swallowed stars.

Her mouth was the center of a galaxy, a widening gyre that glowed with celestial light that seemed to reach out with bioluminescent tendrils as long as the Milky Way was wide.

Her belly was an endless undulating mass of suckling young as numerous as grains of sands upon the beach. Mewling and blind maggots as large as cars, bleating sheep with umbilical cords that hung down for miles. Creatures that could not be effectively understood by what was left of Jarius's mind.

His father dropped his rifle.

Ricky picked it up with one hand and put the barrel under his chin. He braced the stock against the ground and reached for the trigger.

"Her young suckle at the teat of eternity," Cal murmured.

All they ever found of his father was his hat.

All they ever found of Uncle Ricky was his rifle up on the ridge line.

They found Jarius a week later. He was sitting on a tree stump. He'd eaten all the flesh from his fingers. When they came upon him, he was clicking the bones together like castanets.

On the Shores of Midnight

Marnie Desdemona

The first time Cordelia would see the Church of Midnight was while standing upon the cliffs. Near the cliff edge, the shore of white sand bright against the moonlight a hundred meters below, something peculiar took her sight. The shore started to retreat in on itself, like the whole sea was breathing in. Deeper and deeper, the ruins of the church revealed themselves from beneath the waters. The locals had talked about it before, but it was the first time she had seen it in the months since she moved there.

When her journey back down the cliffs ended, she would stand barefoot upon the shore, the water had already returned to where it had been as if it had never left. The church was gone from sight, the lapping water of the ocean biting her feet, stinging at the many lacerations upon them. A sealed envelope crushed in her hand, she let it drop to the shore to be swallowed by the sea.

Despite the late hour, there was no desire to sleep, no motivation to crawl back into the isolated little villa she was renting. She was not in the middle of nowhere, she could make it to town in half an hour or so, but it still felt at times like being the only person in the world. Waves of salt caused her to ache as she collected the gifts the ocean would give her, picking up various seashells and sea glass as if they were the most precious jewels.

She only stopped in her gathering at the sight of something washed up upon the shore. At first glance, it appeared to be a starfish of some sort, but when she leaned in closer, she could see something was off. Unlike the appendages of a starfish, its limbs were like the tentacles of an octopus, suction cups flaring as its arms thrashed. The thrashing quickly stopped after she arrived, the starfish creature starting to move in a clockwise motion like a gear. Its skin tone shifted from a deep purple into a color like the sand, burrowing deeper in, fading into the shore like it were part of it. Cordelia placed a piece of red sea glass over where it had been before walking away.

The next night, when Cordelia would climb the cliffs barefoot in her nightgown to stand too close to their edge once more, she would find that her usual place was already taken by another. In the months she had stayed in the town of Midnight, she had never encountered another soul upon the cliffs at such a deep hour. It was a woman in her early forties with Grecian features, her cheekbones strong, her curly chestnut hair blowing in the breeze. A trio of three unleashed Cretan Hounds lying on the ground beside her, snuggled against her torn jeans, their fur black, white, and a fiery orange. The white hound's eyes a pure red, the black hound's eyes a gray mist, while the orange hound appeared to have no eyes at all. The hounds' attention all turned to Cordelia while the stranger kept her gaze on the sea.

"I'm sorry for disturbing you," Cordelia muttered.

At the sound of her voice, all the hounds started growling, but with a wave of the stranger's hand, they silenced. The stranger's gaze turned to Cordelia, dimples forming on the stranger's face as she smiled.

"I am but the tourist here," the stranger said, "whose feet tread upon your land."

"This is not my land, I'm afraid."

"Then it is of your ancestors."

The stranger stepped forward, the hounds moving in sync with her, stopping before Cordelia. The woman was a good half a foot taller than her, and Cordelia felt like a young sapling beside her, despite there probably being only a decade between them. Cordelia froze at the stranger picking up a tress of her hair and letting it fall between her fingers.

"Eyes as emerald as the isle we dwell upon," the stranger cooed. "Hair like wisps of fire, and freckles that dot your face like its embers. Yet this fire is not real, so why dress so light against the chill of the night? You're shivering, my little flame."

The stranger took off the leather jacket they were wearing in a single motion, draping it over Cordelia. Cordelia wanted to step back, but she froze at feeling the fur of a hound against the back of her legs. The next sensation was even more alarming, the stranger's hand on her back guiding her to the edge of the cliff.

Cordelia's eyes grew wide watching the waters retreat once again, beneath them the church coming back into sight. A whimpering sound took the air, Cordelia watching the three hounds press their heads close to the earth.

"Dub, Dother, and Dain are frightened of the church," the stranger spoke. "But you're not. You came up here to try and see it again, didn't you?"

"How did you know I saw it already?"

"Shhh…listen. Can you hear it?"

Cordelia could hear nothing but the wind and the whimpering of the hounds, until after a minute or so, it reached her. It was the sound of church bells. Looking back to the church, she felt her heart tighten in her chest—it appeared as if there was light coming from its windows. Flames were burning inside.

"Maybe if you run fast enough," the stranger whispered in her ear, "you can make it this time."

Despite everything inside Cordelia screaming to remain where she stood, she burst away from the grasp of the stranger, making her way back down the cliffs. The pain of it all mattered little, her bare feet getting torn up even more, countless scratches on her legs and face from where she tumbled along the way. Only her arms were unscathed, kept safe by the leather of the jacket she was given.

By the time Cordelia made it to the shore, her nightgown was a tattered wisp, blood dripped down her body in the night, and the waters had risen back to normal. No church, no flames, and no sound of bells. Shivering in place, she pulled the leather jacket in tighter before remembering it wasn't hers. Looking back at the cliffs where she had been, she saw that the stranger was no longer standing at their edge.

Sitting upon the shore, she threw rocks and seashells into the water until dawn, and with the sun's arrival, she collapsed asleep in the sand. The waves pushed up and up, lapping at her waist.

Cordelia would wake near twilight, sitting up to see that she wasn't alone. Droves of the tentacled starfish were around her, but none were touching her— all of them moving in a gear-like motion centimeters from her flesh in perfect synchronicity. The color of their skin was blood-red at first, but upon her waking, their skin shifted into a pale gray stone. All of them started to burrow under the sand, Cordelia reaching out and grabbing at the center of one of their bodies.

When her hand would close around to grasp one of the creatures—as lightly as picking up a butterfly—she felt its body collapse under her touch. It burst like a balloon, the consistency of its insides like jam as its severed limbs started writhing around, burrowing into the sand by themselves. Cordelia rapidly wiped her hand again and again into the sand until its remnants were gone. The parts of its body that had shattered solidified on the shore, sparkling in the dying light, Cordelia picking it up. It looked like molten glass and had the rainbow sheen of bismuth.

That evening, in the heart of Midnight, she would ask many questions of the locals. She would ask if they had seen a woman with three hounds. She would show them the crystalline body of the starfish and ask what species it was. She would inquire about the church and its history. Each would tell her the same— no woman with three hounds had set foot in the town; there was no species of starfish that made home upon their shores; and that the church was an old wives' tale. The water levels were no different than they had been for thousands of years, and the tides had never been low enough for a church to be built.

That night, leather jacket warm about her, Cordelia decided to sit upon the shores instead of the cliffs. To wait for the ocean to breathe in, so that she might make it to the church in time. Yet, sitting hour after hour in place upon the cold sand, the ocean held its breath. The church bell never rang.

The following night, Cordelia would ascend the cliffs again, dressed more warmly, and wearing shoes. That night, Cordelia would once more find the stranger and her hounds upon the cliff's edge. The stranger was not looking towards the sea, but at the path leading up the cliff as if she had been waiting for Cordelia's arrival. Cordelia stopped a few feet from her, seeing that the eyeless hound was eating something, shivering at the sight of a torn apart rabbit in its maw.

"Dain," the stranger said. "You're disturbing our guest. Please do that elsewhere."

The eyeless hound growled, dragging the husk of the rabbit along as it moved down the cliff path. Cordelia moved a bit closer in its absence, removing the jacket, looking past the stranger to the ocean to see if the water had fallen or not.

"I'm sorry I ran off without giving this back," Cordelia said, jacket outstretched. "I'm happy I got to see you again, though."

"And I'm happy to see you again, Cordelia."

"I...I don't remember telling you my name."

"Of course you did. Just like I told you my name. Don't tell me you forgot already?" The stranger made a tsking sound as she took the jacket offered to her. "You're going to break my heart."

"Carman," Cordelia felt the name fall from her lips, blinking a few times while looking at the stranger, wondering how she could have forgotten it. "You're Carman."

"Indeed I am," Carman replied with a smile, draping the jacket back over Cordelia. "And this is a gift for you against the cold."

Carman's arm made its way around her shoulder, Cordelia not resisting as it guided her along to the edge of the cliff, as it gently pulled her down to sit upon it with Carman. Both their legs drifted over the cliff edge, feet hitting into stone, little bits falling to the ground so far below. Cordelia's eyes tracked the movement of the falling stone particles until they could no longer focus. Cordelia wondered if something heavier were to fall, would it fall silent as well?

"What brought you to these lands?" Carman asked.

"My grandparents were born here. They brought me here as a little girl, and I just remember...I just remember how happy I used to feel back then. How peaceful it was to run along the shore, to pick up shells, and see all the new animals."

"There's nothing much new anymore, is there? The colors aren't as bright as they used to be, and all the roads and the houses have driven the animals away. You're shivering still. You don't like the human animals much, do you?"

"I just don't know how to be one. I liked the world better when I was a kid."

"You know some species of animals come back to their homes when seeking new life. To find themselves something like a mate." Cordelia turned her gaze down, feeling a finger move along the back of her neck. "Of course, some species go back to their homes to find a comfortable place to die as well. When you think of dying, what do you feel?"

Cordelia's gaze returned to the ocean, watching as it was breathing in once again, the shore retreating even as the moon was full and the sea should be making it rise. Soon enough, the church came back into sight. The fires were burning inside it already, and the tone of its bell was crystal clear. Something else was in the wind along with the bell, sweet and soft organ music instead of the oft solemnity of church music.

"Everything feels still," Cordelia answered. "Everything feels quiet. It's like I'm floating in the ocean."

"Why did Dain's meal make you so unsettled?"

"Because a rabbit is innocent…it doesn't deserve to die."

"But you do?"

Carman's arm left its place around Cordelia's shoulder as she stood up, the hounds moving with her. Cordelia rose as well, looking between Carman and the church, shifting in place between the two.

"Listen to the music that's playing," Carman said, not looking back. "When you go back down the cliffs, keep listening to it, but never look to the shore. Just get in your bed and sleep."

Carman gave a wave, Dain running up to her from where he had been, the skeleton of the rabbit picked clean and clenched between its jaws. The bones were so much darker than what Cordelia would expect, looking charred almost. Hesitant steps moved her towards where Carman was heading, but she was unable to keep forward, instead looking back to the church…speckles of its fires reflected in her teary eyes.

Returning down the cliff, Cordelia would listen to the organ music, and she would keep her gaze away from the shore. She entered her villa, laid down in bed, and stared at the ceiling until every thought faded from her head like stars at dawn's arrival. From there, a semblance of sleep eventually found its way into her being. A deep, heavy sleep, with nothing but the taste of the void.

Then a weight upon her chest, and a barking stabbed into her ears, her eyes bursting open to see the face of one of the hounds staring down at her. The hound was white as snow, with eyes red as blood. Those eyes stared straight into hers, their consistency starting to waver, to look softer. The eyes reminded her of the starfish's body as it burst, the eyes pouring from the hound's skull like an open wound, falling upon Cordelia in a splattering of blood before it ran off.

Sitting up in bed, Cordelia's pure white nightgown remained untarnished, with no bloodstains upon it. The organ music had become thunderous in the air, accompanied by a new noise. A loud thumping, like something hitting into wood. Cordelia threw on the leather jacket, leaving the room, the thumping continuing throughout the villa.

Stepping out the front door, the thumping became much louder, and its source apparent. The strange starfish were all around the villa, hundreds and hundreds of them littering every piece of land around it except for the path leading to the shore. The starfish twisted in their clockwork motion, limbs striking against the walls of the villa. A loud growling in the air, Cordelia watching the two eyeless hounds tearing at starfish in their maws, shaking them about. Blood poured out until the starfish turned to crystal which shattered in their mouths, fragments falling like rainbow-hued stars to the earth. The black hound, its eyes focused on her, sat quietly in the path ahead.

Cordelia took tentative steps, her heart oddly calm, the black hound rose as she approached it and walked by her side. When her feet first touched the sand on the shore, it felt different than normal, looking down to see a dark oil that bled out on the sand from the weight of her steps.

A hushed chorus of sound grew behind her as she moved further down the shore, glancing back to see swarms of starfish rising from beneath the sand, the oil-like ooze bubbling up with them. Their skin color changed to the same pure black, all of them rotating counterclockwise, starting to drape over the shore like a creeping shadow.

The water was still pulled back—the ocean had held its breath for her. The firelight in the church burned bright against the night, the organ melody sweet and soft, the canvas of shadows trailing behind her.

Cordelia's first step into the sand that had been buried beneath the ocean was freezing like her blood had been flooded with ice. The softness of that sand was strange like flesh, not breaking to her weight. The black hound, ever by her side, walked faithfully until they arrived before the double-wide doors of the church. There, the hound dug into the sand, black ooze rising, and buried its head inside.

The stone of the church was smooth and worn like the sea glass Cordelia would collect with seaweed, barnacles, and plant life growing about it. Droves of the spinning starfish clung to it, and Cordelia looked back again to see that the shore had become pitch black. The shimmer of endless movement dwelt in the living shadow, the bright white and orange of the hounds still tearing at and eating the creatures.

A creak. The door opened itself a sliver. Cordelia slipped her hand inside to enter.

It was warm inside, all her body sighing in comfort, like a lost child being embraced by her mother. The smell in the air sweet like fresh fruit, put a lightness to her step. She followed the sound of the music, and let it guide her into the main hall of the church.

There were no pews for worshippers to sit, and there was no pulpit for a minister to preach. Round, stained glass windows were about the walls that depicted imagery of the starfish. The windows let in the moonlight, shining it upon what rested where the pulpit should be: a coffin, ebon black, with wood that looked as old as the church itself.

Barnacles encrusted the entire floor, Cordelia walked across them without flinching, the skin of her feet cutting open. The red of her blood painted the cold stone, which shimmered in the rainbow light. Moving to stand before the coffin, her fingers dug under the old wood, all of it rank with the smell of salt. Pulling and pulling, rusted nails came out of place until its lid tore off.

A torrent of seawater poured out from within the coffin, soaking her from head to toe, hanging heavy her clothes. The coffin was empty inside, save for one thing resting at its bottom. Cordelia knelt next to it, pulling out a sealed envelope with her handwriting on it, the paper dry and crisp…her fingers trailing upon its surface.

"Why did you even bother to write it?" she heard from behind her, tilting back to see pews were now lining the church hall.

Carman sat in the front row, the white and orange hounds curled up before her feet, while the starfish filled the rest of the pews. The pews the starfish covered were crumbling and melting away as if they were snow before a fire.

"It felt wrong not to say anything," Cordelia muttered, eyes frozen on the envelope.

"And what did you say, dear? If you don't mind telling me."

Carman rose from her seat, moving to where Cordelia was, leaning in, and pulling the envelope from her grasp. She tore open its seal, unfurling the folded letter within. The paper unveiled a mostly blank surface, except for a single sentence written in messy black ink: I'm tired. Carman then let go of the letter, it drifting back inside the coffin, her fingers trailing beneath Cordelia's chin and tilting her gaze up. Cordelia watched the pupils of Carman's eyes start to bleed out like tentacles into the iris, the pupils then started to slowly spin in a counterclockwise motion.

"What are you tired of?" Carman whispered into her ear. "Are you tired of being afraid? Of being lonely? Of the shame of denying what you desire for fear of what others think?" Cordelia gasped in a breath, feeling Carman's lips kissing at her neck. "You feel worthless. Everything feels pointless. It hurts. You're tired of not being able to pick up seashells anymore without feeling guilty about it.

You're no longer a child, you should be earning money. When are you going to grow up and live in the real world?"

Cordelia's breath sucked in more at feeling the trail of kisses fall to her collarbone before departing, watching Carman step ahead of her and stand near the coffin. Cordelia scrambled to her feet, Carman reached into the leather jacket Cordelia was wearing and pulled out a handful of thick, long nails.

"Do you want to sleep here, or back in your bed?" Carman asked, her pupils expanding and eclipsing her irises, eating out the whites of her eyes.

Cordelia glanced back, the pews completely gone, the starfish that had been dissolving them covering the floor, crystalized in their deaths. A rainbow sheen shining out so bright. The black hound entered the church and took a seat beside the other two, its eyes missing as well, all of them in quiet attendance.

Cordelia stepped into the coffin, the height of it a perfect fit for her, leaning back—it felt as comfortable as when she'd play all day as a child and collapse into bed. Carman picked up the discarded lid, placing it over the coffin, the inky black darkness consuming Cordelia. Only fractures of light came in through the ancient wood, slivered glimpses of Carman through the cracks, distorted and broken.

A knocking sound, a reverberation, as Cordelia could feel the nails being driven in. The hammering was like a lullaby, making her eyelids fall heavier and heavier, a stillness growing in her being. One nail, four nails, listening as they began to circle the coffin, sealing it tight. Just one more nail needed to tuck her in forever and let the tiredness end.

Before the final nail could pierce the wood, though, Cordelia felt something strange. She felt her arm move on its own, her fingers push through the last gap in the coffin lid and grip tightly. Her breathing grew heavier, flesh shivering at feeling Carman's fingers trailing over her hand, the tip of a rusted nail poking at her gripped fingers.

"I thought you were tired," she heard Carman whisper through the crack.

"I don't want to be alone," Cordelia muttered, pushing against the lid, it aching, but the nails held strong. "Please, please, please, let me out."

"You won't be alone." Cordelia felt as Carman gripped one of her fingers, pulling it loose. "Do you think I'd be so cruel as to leave you alone? You are my guest now. We are both far from our homes, so let us make a new one here together."

Finger after finger was pulled free until only a curled pinky was left hanging outside the coffin.

"I won't force you to," Carman's voice soothed in, Cordelia catching sight of Carman's eyes through the cracks, watching the inky black of them dissolve into crystalline, rainbow hues. "But I promise you, if you walk with me, you will find joy again in the shells upon the shore. You will see the world anew every day."

The last finger that held onto the coffin slowly but surely unfurled itself, Cordelia sighing as she listened to the final nail being driven in. She could feel the tingling warmth of Carman's body hugging against the coffin as if the coffin were her flesh, smiling with joy at the melody of the organ music and church bells. Smiling, as the roaring ocean let out its breath to blow her old life away.

The Eye of God

Rachel Searcey

Molly plucks a candied fruit from the cake and rolls it between thumb and forefinger, forming a minuscule sphere. She places it in the path of a black sugar ant, its body glittering in the sunlight. Thin antennas wiggle as it takes the offering in its jaws and scurries down a hole in the sand.

"If you don't want the cake, let me have it, Molly," I say as I adjust the parasol to block out the sun, now at its zenith. Father cleared the area for the house years ago and the handful of palm trees left on the island beach offer pitiful shade.

Molly lays on her side, hand propped against her chin. Her bare feet dig into the sand, to the cool layer still moist from this morning when the tide went out. Today, the ocean is smooth as a freshly made bed and appears almost black beneath the brilliant cerulean sky. Fluffy clouds, mounded high as whipped cream, crowd to the south of the island and darken towards the horizon over the Gulf of Mexico, promising rain.

A large flock of seagulls flies overhead and descends towards the mainland, several miles to the north.

"The cake is stale," she says.

"You're wasting food."

Molly closes her eyes. "Sylvia, what does it matter? I'm tired of fruitcakes and preserves. Have you checked the trap today?"

"Only shrimp. No fish."

"I won't eat the shellfish. Not after last time." Molly's thin face still carries signs of sickness. She clutches at her stomach, almost concave beneath her white dress.

124

I'm not doing much better. Despite shielding ourselves from the sun, the delicate skin on my décolletage is peeling and red. Lotions Father imported from France do little to soothe the sunburn or diminish the scratches on my forearms from wrestling with the fish trap. The scars are turning white against my tan skin.

The hairs on the back of my neck prickle as if I'm being watched.

A mile out, ripples break the water's surface. I narrow my eyes against the glare. The sun glints on a pod of sleek gray dolphins rising for air. They slip out of sight and the ocean is once again calm.

"I'm so hungry." Molly rests her head against crossed forearms.

I get to my feet, shaking sand from my dress and picking up the parasol. "I'll see what's left inside. Are you coming?"

The sun hits Molly and she rolls over into what little shade remains on the picnic blanket. "No. Leave the parasol."

Molly is wasting away, lolling on the blanket like a mermaid tossed ashore. It is difficult to refuse her. I arrange the parasol so it shades her and step onto the hot sand. My bare soles sting as I hurry towards the house. The noon sun blinds me and I hold up my hand to block it, but the reflection off the white sand is equally as strong.

It is a short walk from our picnic to the low fence surrounding the house, but my head rings and black spots dot my vision. A crunch underfoot—one of Mother's foreign flowers, long dead. They lay in desiccated mounds, ravaged by the salty ocean air and unable to grow in the sand. I mount the stone steps to the porch, shaking sand from my ruffled skirt.

The house is a sorry sight. During the last storm, a hole opened in the roof over the locked servants' quarters. Father refused to pay the servants when he caught them stealing food; they absconded with the only boat and returned to the mainland, stranding us on the island. Ocean breezes push into the house whistling through broken windows. Sand drifts into the foyer and across the wood floors, collecting in corners. Humidity hangs in the air.

Mother and Father are in the dining room. Rather than check on them, I go straight to the pantry in the back of the house.

A sudden, sharp pain in my left ear sends me staggering against the pantry door frame. I bite my lip; a flake of dry skin comes loose and I taste blood.

A change in air pressure. A storm? The incoming breeze carries the sweet aroma of rain. When we lived on the mainland, I always waited breathlessly for the heavy clouds to break. Molly and I shared tea and biscuits under the safety of the porch as we watched the many oak trees on our property sway, heavy with moisture.

We no longer celebrate the rain. Here on the island, we are at God's mercy. He has protected Molly and me thus far and we paid our penance for innumerable, unknowable sins. Will He grant us another mercy tonight?

The clouds darken to a slate blue. Lights flicker amongst the cloud cover. Gentle breezes give way to a more forceful gale and whip against the palm fronds. The waves churn against the shoreline. Jagged streaks of lightning strike the ocean.

Scratching and muted squeaks sound through the thin pantry door drawing my attention. I suppress a shudder and grab the broom. I fling the door open to find a swarm of rats fighting over a preserve jar they managed to knock from a shelf. Broken glass and bright red jam coat the floor in a sticky swath.

A year ago, I would have screamed and run from the room, begging Father to kill the vermin and spare my delicate senses. Anger courses through me now and steadies my hands as I beat at the rats with the broom bristles. If I kill one, Molly and I could eat meat for the first time in weeks.

The rats, unharmed, scurry into a hole in the wall. I gag at my debased thoughts; unhinged from starvation and dehydration.

The rodents were stowaways from the builders' boats; the men who constructed the house for Father. The workers left, but the rats remained, breeding to untold numbers. At night, I hear them beneath the floorboards, eating our scraps and each other.

I am glad Molly didn't see the broken jar, the twisting pile of rodents. Frustration seethes, but it will do no good to become upset. I sweep the glass into a pile and leave it in the corner. What does it matter? The pantry is empty now, devoid of purpose.

I gather the two remaining jars from the top shelf: green beans and orange marmalade. I scoop a small portion of each onto a plate and put the jars in our bedroom chest. The heavy cedar lid will prevent further interference from the rats.

Molly licks her plate clean and I eat the rest of her fruitcake. It will have to sustain us until the next day, as the fish trap fails to catch us a suitable dinner.

Molly's shallow breathing is drowned out by gusts pushing through the broken window. A fence board came loose during the last storm, puncturing the shutters, shattering the glass.

Molly's eyes flutter and she moans. I wrap my body around hers and hold her close. Her heartbeat is tiny, fluttering. She is so cold, despite the muggy weather. I fear she will die before me and I will be left alone. Can God be so cruel?

I pray, whispering into her thinning hair.

God, have mercy. If you take Molly, do not leave me behind.

I push the thought away and sit up in bed to watch the clouds shiver across the full moon. A thin spider web shifts and billows in the window corner. Tiny flies, mummified into black knots, hang heavy in the silky strands.

Unable to find solace in sleep, I wander the island. The cool sand crunches beneath my feet like freshly fallen snow, until the oppressive heat of the day becomes a faded memory. A breeze tugs on my unwashed hair, tucked into a low bun that lays heavy on my neck. Distant lights twinkle on the cusp of the bay, on the mainland shore to the north. Our old home.

How many nights had I sat here with a fire blazing, hoping someone would notice and send a ship for rescue? Maybe one of Mother's friends, wondering what happened, where we'd gone. They would hear of the servants' betrayal and ready a ship. But no one knows where we are.

Father spirited us away in the night, to escape the British invasion of the mainland. We witnessed the battle on the far shore. Cannons firing, musket blasts. Then all was quiet. We have no way of knowing who won; if it is safe to return. Father will be deemed a traitor and a coward, so we remain on the island.

Waves lap at my feet, warm as bath water. Tiny, jewel-backed crabs run back and forth in the rhythmic tide. A glimmer catches my eye, a twinkling cloud of blue-green lights like stars lies beneath the surface. I step into the water to investigate but a rumble of thunder takes my attention. Lightning bolts etch themselves on my eyelids when I blink.

When I turn back to the water, the stars are gone. A play of the moonlight, nothing more.

I return to the bedroom window, watching the storm draw nearer and nearer. Thick clouds eclipse the moon and the room is plunged into darkness.

Dawn never comes. The sun hides behind a veil of dense clouds. Molly sleeps and sleeps. I fear she will never wake and I will suffer the storm alone.

Rain hammers against the shutters, which I repaired with floorboards from our parents' bedroom. Molly clings to me in bed, shaking, insubstantial as a ghost. I will myself to be strong for both of us. Her bony hands and overgrown nails dig into my back, yet I hold her gently despite the pain she causes me, and bite my tongue when I want to scold her.

A nightmare woke her at almost midday, punctuated by lightning striking a palm tree near the house. The horrible sound filled the air. When I peek through the shutters, the burning trunk is the only light in the murky darkness, distorted by the rain-coated glass.

Beneath the constant rainfall is the sound of gushing water. *The hole in the roof.* I imagine the edges washing away, gaping wider as the storm persists. I hope the water will run out through the back door and not flood the house.

I lose track of time. Molly refuses to pray with me. I recite Scripture from memory; sing hymns until my voice becomes hoarse. My stomach aches and I bring forth the jars from the chest. We nibble on one green bean each.

"One more, Sylvia. What difference does it make?"

"No. After the storm passes, who knows what will happen? We must remain optimistic."

Molly's salty tears sting the scratches on my arms. She succumbs to exhaustion and her back rises and falls with gentle sighs. I leave her on the bed.

I feel my way through the dark house to find Mother and Father at the dining room table. I adjust Mother's dress, which had slid from her shoulders, and straighten Father's collar. Lightning flashes through the window slats and their skulls glow white against the black void of the room.

They starved to death after denying themselves food so Molly and I could eat. Mother gave me her tearful confession when she could no longer walk. I was furious with them. Yet, I tended to their every need in their last moments, while Molly wandered the island or sequestered herself in our room, unable to bear the sorry sight of our beloved parents wasting away in their beds.

Father was stalwart as ever until the end, reading to Mother and me from the Bible in a hushed voice. He never asked where Molly was or why she stayed away; he understood her anguish and fragile disposition.

I buried Mother and Father on the beach, in pitifully shallow graves. Molly was inconsolable and unable to help. After the first storm, almost a year ago now, our beloved parents came back to us. The crabs and sea birds picked their bones clean. Their clothes were in tatters and it felt wrong to leave them as they were, with nowhere to rest. I brought Mother and Father inside, put them in their Sunday best, and set them where we had the fondest memories.

Cheerful meals. The servants bustling in and out with platters of fresh meat and fruit from the mainland. Sweet desserts.

Nothing remains of our old life.

My stomach growls and I bend over, laying my head on the dusty table. The house shakes and trembles. A horrible thought seizes me- the roof will tear away, leaving us exposed to the open sky.

I stumble to the bedroom and wake Molly from her stupor. With my face buried against her neck, I weep. She comforts me as best she can and sings a lullaby from our childhood. Her voice croaks and she coughs. Blood spatters her nightgown. I help her sip boiled rainwater from the flask until her throat no longer seizes.

Shudders run through the house with each blast of forceful wind. Timbers creak and pop like old bones. A window shatters in the next room and the wind howls, invading our home. The storm is gaining strength. My body aches with tension.

Molly curls against me, her spine pressed into my bony chest. We lie with our limbs interlocked. Our heartbeats flutter as one and we fall into restless slumber while the storm continues to rage.

I dream of Molly's laughter and Mother's embrace. Father's baritone voice like thunder, reading us Scripture after dinner. Dolphins leaping from the water and eyes as bright as the moon, watching from the depths.

Dim light streams through the shutters and I hear the gentle lap of waves hitting the house. A lone seagull's cry breaks the quiet, shadowed by a dull, constant rumble.

At the front door, water covers the porch and kisses the doorstep. Shredded seaweed clouds the water. Tiny gray-blue fish dart in large schools across the submerged floorboards.

A towering, uniform wall of clouds surrounds the island. My vision swims and I feel disoriented for a moment, although I know our front porch faces the mainland to the north, miles across the water. The ocean heaves, breathing in time with an ever-present roar.

My eyes cross when I realize the clouds, still dark and heavy with rain, spin counter-clockwise around the island. A seagull flies with the air current, crying for its flock.

Sunlight pierces my vision as the clouds break. I squint against the sudden brightness.

The white-hot sun peers through an almond-shaped opening in the clouds, framed by the clear blue sky.

The eye of God.

I wade into what remains of our front yard and kneel in the sand, waist-deep in water. Clasping my hands to my chest, I recite the Lord's Prayer to thank him for our salvation. He opened an enclave in the storm. We are spared death for another day.

Splashing from inside the house announces Molly's presence and she joins me in the yard.

"Molly, pray with me!" I take her hand in mine and draw her into the water, opening my arms to the sky and reveling in the sun's warmth.

"Sylvia, I had the strangest dream." She shades her eyes. "The clouds look wrong," Molly says, her voice a whisper.

"Yes!" I embrace her as I begin to cry.

Molly's body heaves in my arms, like a cat with a hairball. She wretches and doubles over.

"Molly! What's wrong?" I pull the hair out of her face.

She vomits into the water. Chunks of green and red float on the surface before sinking. The small fish swim in darting groups and devour the droppings.

"I'm sorry," she says, using seawater to wash yellow bile from her mouth. "There's no more food, Sylvia." She covers her face with her hands and weeps with shame. "I found the jars in the chest and couldn't help myself. I'm so hungry."

Rage threatens to overtake my ebullience, but the wonders of God's miracle soothe my soul.

"God has bestowed His Grace upon us. He will send a boat, or open a path to the mainland, like Moses parting the Red Sea. His love has protected us. Do you see?"

Molly sits in the water, hands in her lap, shaking her head. Her nightgown billows like a jellyfish bell. "Sylvia, you have gone mad. There is no salvation. We are meant to die here. The ocean will have us."

Thunder rumbles overhead as if to mark Molly's prophecy.

Pendulous clouds sweep across the sun and darkness descends. A few scattered raindrops give way to a pelting downpour. Palm trees bend horizontally as the wind sweeps across the island.

A whipping gale tears shingles free, before the entire roof peels away in one stroke. It flaps like a sea bird before twisting up and away, carried into the darkening cloud bank. Shutters bang open and closed before being clipped by the wind, and ripped from their hinges. Mother and Father's bodies are carried upwards and away, spirited into the Heavens.

Molly runs towards the gutted house, to seek shelter, to follow our parents, but my hand claws at her nightgown, ripping the thin fabric down the back. It falls from her like petals from Mother's dying flowers. She shivers against the downpour, clutching her hands across her chest.

Molly screams at me but her voice is lost amongst the raging storm. She strikes me with her fists with what little strength she has left; bony knuckles bruising my chest and head. Her blows are caresses compared to the punishing rain. I can scarcely breathe for the water flooding my mouth and nostrils.

I struggle to my feet but the water rises to my chest in a mere moment. My dress tangles around my legs, threatening to pull me under. I tear the flimsy garment away. Let the tempest take it.

We stand naked before God.

Stinging hail pelts my scalp and would have drawn blood if not for the waves washing us clean. Currents tug at my legs and I fight to remain standing. Molly is swept under and I panic. I won't let her leave before I do. I search blindly under the black water until my hand finds her hair and I draw her screaming to the surface. She clings to my neck.

Small, soft bodies bumped against my arm. Drowned rats' corpses. Unable to escape the flood, they perished. We are all equal in God's eyes. I will not let the same fate befall Molly.

My feet lift from the sandy floor with each wave's pulse and I struggle to keep our heads above the surface. I search the horizon. A sign of land, a palm we can cling to. Debris from the house. But there is only water and cresting waves, forcing us under.

Rain beats down on my scalp, unrelenting. We will drown above water as well as below. Still, I keep us afloat. Molly coughs, spasming in my arms, vomiting seawater. Her body surrenders to fatigue and she floats. I cradle her head, despite exhaustion causing my arms to shake.

My vision dims as black clouds meet black water.

Molly is almost lost to me once more, but I catch her at the last moment by the wrist before she slips away. I am powerless, a mere human speck, crushed by God's will.

An undertow pulls me down and I am overtaken by an oncoming wave.

Water fills my lungs until my chest feels like it will burst.

Down we sink, into the pitch. I dig my fingers into Molly's wrist and wait for death. The last bubble of air in my lungs erupts from my open mouth. Mother and Father flash in my mind's eye, their arms open, ready to receive Molly and me alongside them in Heaven.

Molly tugs on my wrist. I open my eyes to see her treading water. Alive.

Above us, the ocean surface swirls with a dizzying pattern of raindrops and lightning flashes. Muffled thunder booms.

Far below, stars twinkle in a scattered cluster. Molly swims ahead, gesturing for me to follow. I dive after her. Dolphins swim with us, jubilant and ecstatic, guiding us deeper.

The stars multiply as we draw nearer; an entire galaxy along the ocean floor. The same blue-green shimmer I'd seen below the surface, before the storm. No illusion, but the leathery hide of an enormous creature, larger than any whale. A sliver of light like a seam opens along its body, brighter and more intense than the sun after a storm.

An immense iris, as large and gibbous as the full moon, shines upon Molly and me. We dive deeper and deeper until the eye encompasses all.

God is not man, aloft in the heavens. *She* is here, beneath the ocean, all along, mistress of the storms.

Like Ants We March

Jorja Osha

His parents had insisted they weren't running but at age six he knew that's exactly what they were doing. Back then he had two older brothers, ten and fourteen. 444. Angel numbers his mother explained when he'd lay upon her chest as she watched TV. He liked to listen to her heartbeat, the steady ba-dum, ba-dum, ba-dum as each of her breaths sounded like the ocean. Strong and unwavering up until the day the police showed up at their door, their hats in hand. His mother couldn't seem to catch her breath. Something wasn't right about having a white man tell you that another officer mistook your eldest for a 37-year-old robber in a camo-printed jacket. Not when Philip had been wearing his favorite hoodie, a pastiche of Van Gogh's *Starry Night* but with tentacles.

They'd learn later on the 37-year-old had been a five-foot-nine Caucasian with flaming red hair and not the six-foot-three Black man with a beard as reported. Philip had been five-foot-five with a smooth face and an infectious smile. Running to Renton seemed like the only option afterward. If the world wanted to implode on itself making a disproportionate amount of casualties out of anyone *the wrong shade* then it was going to do it without them. Or at least that's what Reece's father had said before his wife caught his skin between her french-tipped nails.

"Don't you start that again," she said. "Things are going to work. I feel it."

She looked back to Reece and his brother Malcolm; even though she wasn't smiling he saw hope in her eyes. He also saw how she avoided looking out the back window as if afraid she'd catch sight of Philip standing in the middle of the road dressed in his favorite hoodie now riddled with holes where the suckers of each tentacle had been. At least that's what Reece assumed after seeing that very thing himself.

Renton took them north, far north through a stretch of country with a strange name and people friendlier than they had any right to be. They'd stopped at a small diner where the owners treated them like family, feeding them well and showing them on an honest-to-God map which roads to take. The GPS had gone on the fritz eighteen miles back the moment they started up the mountain. The radio too had lost signal, distorting the oldies into a constant stream of white noise that Malcolm complained about. Reece on the other hand swore something was trying to talk to him through it. Being the youngest he'd won out, the radio remained on before the issue eventually resolved itself.

Their new home, though a simple town, was a bright and sprawling place with architecture they had only ever seen in larger cities. The lack of sirens as they drove had Reece's father releasing a breath like he could finally breathe. His square shoulders had rounded and he openly reached for his wife's hand, the action saying what he couldn't fix his mouth to say. They were safe now.

Getting settled had been easier than expected on account of the helpful inhabitants. *Colorful*, was the way his mother described a number of them, especially after a few of their neighbors had passed on Renton's lore. But those were just stories, old folktales and urban legends that Reece's parents easily dismissed up until they couldn't. He still remembered the terrified looks his parents had as they rushed towards him and Malcolm fresh home from school. Had it not been for the fact his brother was standing beside him Reece would have panicked at his otherwise calm parents' uncharacteristic agitation.

Apparently, knowing how to handle yourself around authorities and anyone who looked at them a little too long would only keep them so safe considering Renton had its own set of rules. At the time Reece hadn't truly grasped what his folks were saying but he'd been sensitive enough to read the room; it told him his parents had been wrong.

"I thought you said this place was safe," his mother's voice came from the kitchen, thinking him asleep. He had been until he got the odd feeling of being watched and startled awake.

"It was. *Is.* Look, I don't know what that was on the radio but it's stopped now. We're not living in a damn Shirley Jackson story, Anette." his father's voice was much louder.

Frankly, he didn't know why they were so upset. Who cared about blue tickets appearing out of nowhere? Malcolm had shrugged it off, joking about it now and again just to scare him until their father caught him one time with that wide palm and those thick-ass fingers of his. One swat to the ear and that man could make even the Devil apologize.

Despite all the talk about innocuous tickets and radio broadcasts, Renton stood as a bastion from all the outside insanity. Even without making any friends, Reece liked the town well enough. He'd found something fascinating about radios kicking on by themselves and listening to the torrent of static on air before The Caller's voice filtered out, distorted and nearly indecipherable save for the numbers they rattled off. But then the thing with Marcel Wooten happened.

In hindsight, it was only a matter of time before he heard something himself. While most of the residents repeated a set of rules and warnings, not many of them seemed to believe them, often citing the issues with the radios and the screaming as some type of hoax meant to keep the town in line. Reece Blackwell didn't believe that for a second, not when there had been those willing to talk to a now 12-year-old boy. The man from San Perlita whispered about people jumping down a 40 foot wide black pit during thunderstorms because something told them to. Others didn't hear whatever it was growling under the static like Reece did so of course they paid little mind. Of course, someone would get curious or worse, bold. Apparently, it wasn't the first time either. When he heard Marcel Wooten bragging about owning a stolen ticket outside of the bodega on the corner of Locust and Maple he kept his mouth shut.

Why? Because according to the news, the horrific cries of beloved 17-year-old boys with flawless caramel skin, hazel eyes, and a full head of curls don't get aired across every radio in town on a Thursday night while your parents try to cheat each other at go-fish.

When the hideous wails died off, absorbed in a symphony of static no one said anything. No one in Renton spoke about Marcel either as if it had never happened just like with all those that came before him. Reece himself was met with radio silence whenever he broached the subject. Only Malcolm responded though with a breezy indifference.

"It was probably the government," he said.

Reece wanted to punch him. Had Philip been alive he would have given a different answer. Philip would have cared.

"That could have been you."

"But it wasn't."

His father had been more animated about the matter, a dark shadow stretching across already dark features. "Mind your business, boy. That has nothing to do with you so you best keep it that way. Got enough to worry about as it is."

Only later would Reece realize it wasn't anger but fear, ripe and stinking, that spurred his father's outburst. He'd never been an angry man after all, the only thing to ever truly set him off were the red and white chyrons scrolling across the bottom of a news program.

"Goddammit, they got another one of us," the man would lament almost every other week, sucking his teeth as he sunk deeper into his recliner no doubt thinking of Philip.

It seemed as if Marcel Wooten had dredged up something from the depths that now sat there on the surface shining and persistent like oil on water. Something everyone seemed keen on navigating around with synchronized ignorance. Well, everyone except for Ms. Sharif that was.

Unsure of when or how the woman came into his life Reece only knew he'd follow the woman to the ends of the earth despite people calling her a witch. She was. She made no bones about it either as she watched the world as if knowing something no one else did.

"The smell of ozone is on the horizon and despite it sitting there festering we ants just keep marching," the woman said. She had a wrongness about her, her cadence off-putting because she spoke like someone capable of speech while not understanding how to project any emotion behind the words. That's how she sounded out on her porch drawing a long cigarette from a black metal case stored in the pocket of one of her many archaic-looking dresses she was fond of wearing. They were closer to cigarillos if anything, the cigarettes, all wrapped in black shiny paper with a blue stamp in the center.

Savoring a second slice of fresh lahmacun Reece looked over to the woman. "What do you mean by that?"

Ms. Sharif laid her bright honey eyes on him, the smoke filtering from her nose and mouth made her look like a pissed off bull though she was smiling. "You'll understand one of these days but until then let's just be patient."

That was Ms. Sharif, cryptic without meaning to be but because she was willing to acknowledge the things everyone kept ignoring Reece didn't mind. Better to think about all the queer things the woman said than be faced with the echoes of that horrific Thursday night whenever his mind stopped wandering. Better to remember that despite Renton's welcoming aura, Reece Blackwell would always sit on the wrong shade of white. As his father had said he had enough to worry about as it was and it came in the form of store employees asking him every two minutes if he needed any help. Once it was a man who likely meant no harm by calling him *boy* and waving him over to ask what he was doing walking alone. Most times though it was the occupants in their black and white vehicles who stared a little too long, and drove a little too slow as he waited at the crosswalk. He tried to ignore it though, and had success for the most part too until he started smelling the faint hints of ozone at fifteen.

Of course, he had to look it up to confirm his suspicions when the scent continued to linger. His parents had given him the side eye when he mentioned it but Ms. Sharif on the other hand had fixed him with this curious stare and cocked her head as if listening though he'd been silent for some time now. For a good five minutes, her chest didn't budge an inch before she finally blinked and smiled.

"Do you have your own radio?" she asked.

"No, but I can use the one in the kitchen," Reece replied.

Ms. Sharif shook her head before jerking her chin towards her altar room, her hands too busy with that case of hers. "There should be one in my trunk. Take it home with you tonight and keep it in your room. Nowhere else."

The first time Reece had stepped into the small room he found it dizzying, appearing endless under flickering candlelight. A disconcerting noise flowed from every corner giving the impression he'd been shoved headfirst into a tub of water while someone screamed from above. The memory made him hurry to the black trunk that sat against the far wall just below a large bone-colored sculpture that appeared to extend out from nothing. Conical in shape Reece didn't dare to stare for too long, not with the too many limbs and bony parts and winding bits that he could see. The minute he found the radio he rushed out only to find Ms. Sharif gone, the front door of her house open. Even the scent of her cigarettes refused to betray the woman's whereabouts though on his way home he'd swear he'd seen her watching him from the window of a nearby building with a dark shadow looming over her shoulder. He thought he'd seen Philip too just one window over but when he looked again he was alone.

Despite its antiquated look, the radio had all the clarity of a modern-day device, if not better, making Reece all the more willing to abandon his phone, he just needed to be mindful of the volume after seven. With his parents at work and Malcolm living the university life two cities over he mostly had free reign and indulged. He couldn't explain it but whenever he listened, sound seemed to be transmitted from within his head, the music swimming through his veins as if blood itself. That was before he felt himself falling at an undetermined velocity that had his skin rippling. Somewhere along the way, the music had devolved into a blizzard of noise that pushed its way inside his skull reaching a deafening crescendo while notes of ozone bloomed and festered setting his insides alight with unseen fire. In the midst of it all, he heard himself screaming. Marcel Wooten was screaming too, shrieking an orchestra of terror in a way the human vocal cords weren't meant to. Beneath the screams, a low din like a whale song pitched down to an almost numbing degree swelled. Whatever was making that noise was much larger than a whale, Reece felt it in his gut, felt it under him. Waiting. That's when he heard Philip's voice. Wrong and angry.

How much longer?

"Jesus Christ, he's bleeding!" his mother's voice was loud in his ear, her arms so tight around him that he could feel her heartbeat. *Ba-dum, ba-dum, ba-dum.* "Don't just stand there Samuel, go get the car!"

Reece couldn't explain just why his nose had bled enough to stain the whole of his shirt or why he'd been on his bedroom floor screaming, he only knew he was now in a hospital bed with his mother gripping his hand. An officer with puppy dog eyes stood at the foot of his bed watching him with a look he didn't care for. Reece knew what he was thinking before he even said it.

"While we're waiting on toxicology I just want you to know that I'm on your side. Whether this is drug or gang related I'll do whatever I can to help you," the officer said.

Had he not felt like something had been severed within him Reece might have laughed. Instead, he met the officer's gaze squarely.

"I heard a dead boy screaming in my room. How're you going to help with that?"

It was only because his parents didn't know about the radio or Ms. Sharif that Reece had been able to keep the former and visit the latter. His behavior after all was only a symptom of stress and not the fact something wasn't right about Renton. Ms. Sharif however thought otherwise as she presented him with his first cigarette and encouraged him to keep listening. Each time she told him he was almost there. Where exactly? He didn't know only that for the next five years the static spoke to him in his dreams using Philip's voice while he remained in an endless free fall towards whatever lurked just out of view. When conscious, he felt entrenched in molasses seeing everything in black and white aside from the red and white chyrons that zigged and zagged across his father's brand new television. The stench of ozone was all he ever smelled now even as he moved to the opposite side of town.

Unlike Malcolm, Reece didn't go to university, and by twenty he was a shell of himself going from job to job until landing a gig hosting at some underground club that looked like it had been uprooted from the 1950s where Dominique, an off and on again boyfriend, worked as a bartender. Admittedly he only stayed for the exceptional PA system, he liked the way the vibrations ran up from his soles and into his mouth when he clenched his teeth. He did that a lot these days, clenching his teeth until he felt the ground disappear beneath him. This time however he tasted blood as he pressed the phone against his ear.

On the other end, his mother was wailing but Reece had gone deaf to what she was saying as he fumbled his way out of bed, kicking at a pair of legs. He thought he'd never hear anything more terrible than Marcel Wooten's cries but his mother proved him wrong, his father joining somewhere in the background accompanied by breaking glass. Stumbling to the toilet in time Reece heaved out whatever had been left of his soul.

Malcom was dead.

Killed. The usual suspect. Traffic stop and an overzealous cop with a gun. Malcolm had seizures.

Reece must have hit his head and passed out because there was Philip crouched beside him, the tentacles on his hoodie outstretched and caressing his back with their bullet hole suckers. He leaned over him, his smiling mouth splitting until only a gaping maw of nothingness stared back, blanketing Reece with the acrid fetor of ozone. It burned his flesh as his brother gripped the back of his neck.

You angry enough yet?

He'd woken up to his boyfriend on the phone with Reece's mother. Philip was gone.

A week after the funeral Reece found the blue ticket on the front passenger's seat of his car as he got off work. He couldn't recall as he turned over the engine if he'd been the one to turn on the radio but the static washed over him regardless just before the chittering of The Caller came over the air reading off the six digit number stamped in black across the edge of blue paper.

0.4.7.1.3.9.

Instinct took him to Ms. Sharif and the way he found her waiting on her porch made him believe she'd been expecting him as she came down the steps dressed in cerulean puffing on her cigarette.

"Now it's time for you to see," she said.

They drove to the far east side of Renton where a stretch of buildings stood derelict before Ms. Sharif guided him into the old union station. They went down stairs that shouldn't have existed and yet further down they descended until the air was stinking and humid. From somewhere in the dark Ms. Sharif produced an electric lamp before seemingly gliding along uneven ground as if beneath that curtain of blue hid a battalion of skittering legs. Reece stumbled after her.

"Why are we here?" he asked.

"Because this is where He lives, has lived long before Renton's inception, and will continue to live." She didn't look back at him.

Before Reece could ask anything else they came to a stop in front of what could only be described as a wall of infinite blackness. It reminded him of Philip's face. In the dark something began towards them sending quake after quake through his frame as that familiar whale song came crashing down around him. Aided by the unnatural brightness of the electric lamp Reece Blackwell finally saw what had been lurking below.

This wasn't the sculpture in Ms. Sharif's altar, this was swollen and undulating with too many limbs with too many bony fingers that dragged the behemoth forward as fat tendrils slithered like headless snakes. Those glassy eyes, a halo of them blinked in unnerving intervals staring them down. God how they shined, revolving in their wet sockets in the palette of Starry Night. Had Reece eaten he would have spilled his guts out before him. Instead he gasped for air while his legs buckled beneath him and sent his knees cracking against hard dirt. He must have been screaming because Ms. Sharif had sidled up to him, placed a hand over his mouth, and shushed him.

"There, there now you're alright. You've been seen, Reece Blackwell," she cooed, dropping her hand. "He's seen your pain and now offers you the chance to put it back on the world if only you let him in and then let him out."

"I don't understand," Reece croaked. He touched his face, his fingers came away wet. When had he started crying? "I thought you said we're ants."

Ms. Sharif laughed. "Oh, we are. Pests exist just to exist but that doesn't mean some of us don't have our usefulness, not unlike spiders." She motioned up towards the horror that remained watching them, panting from its cavernous mouth. "Even gods need a few spiders, us callers, to maintain the garden before the harvest."

"So Marcel Wooten? Was he a pest?"

"He needed to be made an example of."

Reece gave a humorless smile. "No one cared. They all moved on just like they did with Philip."

A hand found his cheek, gentle and warm. "Then why not show them in kind?"

For a moment Reece was silent. Contemplative. "Is it just you?"

"Here in Renton? Yes."

"So what happens now?"

With a smile, the woman pulled out her cigarette case and handed it to him. "You don't have to be an ant."

As he carefully took to his feet, his eyes locked upon the creature Reece felt the familiar sensation he'd gotten whenever he listened to the static. And somewhere lost in the feeling, deep within this beast, he heard not only Philip's voice but Malcolm's as well.

Are you angry enough now?

Slipping out a cigarette Reece started laughing.

Burning Slumber

Jessica L. Sparrow

Late one evening, a vast ship invaded our crystalline waters. Dread threatened to rise like bile from my stomach and fill my throat as the massive hull swallowed the moonlight. Nothing but flickering gas lamps appeared on board, illuminating the portholes. No ensigns flew upon its giant wooden masts, and silence lay over the deck like a fog. The cryptic vessel vexed us all, as it pulled into port.

The coquis ceased their evening concert as the gangplank fell and ghostly forms stepped wearily onto our shores. Haunted spirits with blank, colorless faces rattled chains that tethered them through their stomachs. Dead eyes full of loss stared out from beneath thin wisps of hair as they marched.

Curiosity pulled at me—a horrific need to watch the damned men, but fear demanded I look away. Lifting my hands to my face, the way my people do in the face of bad omens, I shielded myself from the ghoulish sight.

I wish I could have covered my ears as well.

Torturous screams rang out from those around me who did not protect their eyes. Other sounds, wet and crunchy, followed, ending the cries. They were the sounds of Grandmother preparing fish before a meal.

"During the preparation," she had said, "one must thank the fish and the Mother for granting us sustenance and wisdom."

"Wisdom?" I'd asked.

"Wisdom." Grandmother repeated back to me as she gouged out the fish's eyes and popped them into her mouth. It was the same sound. The sound of flesh tearing away from its socket, the liquid burst as she bit into the gelatinous orb.

My hands shook as I lowered them from my face. All around, my people were ripping out their eyes with whatever object they could find. Some just used their fingers. I wanted to stop them, but it was too late; they were as blind and haunted as the pale invaders.

I quickly returned my attention to the ship. The wooden gangway planked itself yet still no Captain in sight, only the pale prisoners who rattled and moaned. Ice pricked my skin at the thought of someone unseen at the vessel's helm, waiting to give the order to annihilate us all. My breath hitched on the intrusive thought, causing the blind demons to turn in my direction. They jostled aimlessly, incoherently trying to out mutter one another, replacing the beautiful nightly noises of the island's insects with their chatter. The sound was maddening, but still I wondered what they were saying. I moved closer, my chest tight with anxiety, to better hear their words, luckily Grandmother was by my side and managed to pull me back. The ship's lanterns snuffed out, offended by her action.

She dug her nails into my arm, breaking the invisible thread that tethered my thoughts to the ship's force, "Keep your wits about you."

Out of the darkness, a flame emerged, lighting the steps of a blurry figure. Terrible longing sunk sharp teeth into the pit of my stomach as the figure materialized. My skin grew cold, even as sweat poured down my body.

I needed to touch the figure.

The feeling grew as it approached Grandmother and me; with each step it became more human. A man, but not a man. I fought, with every fiber of my being, against dropping to my knees. I wanted to *worship* Him. I wanted to be at His mercy. My life was wrong without Him.

He watched me with contemptuous eyes, his hair changing from deep brown to pale yellow to colors I couldn't comprehend. Finally, the ringlets in His hair uncoiled themselves and fell flat upon his shoulders. He ran a hand over his face, revealing his pale, poisoned sea-colored eyes. His jagged teeth cracked through a grin, as he relished the ramblings of his muttering marionettes. His amusement burrowed into my bones and made itself at home in my marrow. Panic urged me to excavate this sinister squatter. I dug my fingernails into the flesh of my arm to wake me from the feverish nightmare.

Stealthily, I reached for my macana strapped to my back. I gripped it tightly, readying to fight him all the way back to where he hailed from. Something I'd done many times before to drive back other invaders who came to our land with ill intent. But today, as I drew closer, His breath of death and decay filled my lungs and settled on my teeth like a poisonous film.

I couldn't move, and my hands trembled as my body demanded I drop to my knees and worship at His feet, so that the others would follow.

He will be your salvation.

"No." I backed away from Him, tripping over something in the process.

Not something, someone: Grandmother. She was bowing to Him.

I scraped my knees as I crawled towards her, "Grandmother, please get up."

She didn't move.

I watched in horror as the others began to tear off their necklaces and feathers and fall to their knees. The being cocked His head, watching me with sordid amusement.

"*Cacique*," I screamed, "rise!"

She didn't budge. She couldn't. My heart shattered in my chest.

The agonized cries of my tribespeople told me he plagued them as their souls fought to be released. The pallid ghouls rattled their chains—mocking the wails of despair. The sounds melted into a hellish cacophony. I knew that if I stayed any longer, I would fall into their trance. Instinct told me that deciphering their song would mean death.

I grabbed Grandmother's headdress and guanín necklace and ran into the forest. The incessant whispers followed, no matter how deep I plumbed. Coupled with the taste of rot still upon my lips, I could feel Him burrowing deeper into my brain. My entire body itched, as if tiny insects crawled beneath my skin, lighting up every sensitive nerve ending. I banged my fists hard against my temples to stop the spread of His influence, but it refused to stop.

I didn't know where I was running. Childlike panic raged as my home grew ever more foreign to me. This island was all I'd ever known. As children, we were taught that some trees bend towards the sun as it rises, while others bend towards the moonlight instead. We could forge our path by the way their branches bent. But now, I couldn't make sense of my surroundings.

The stars. I should look to the stars.

I struggled against a malevolent gravity to raise my head. No matter how hard I tried, I could not look up. Exhausted, I flopped to the frigid grass. My body welcomed this moment of rest as the Earth hugged me tight. Or was it crushing me?

Get up. I beg of you, get up!

I tried to roll over, but the ground curved against my back, pressing my chest to the sky. The stars rushed down until they were mere inches away from me, scorching my flesh with their unforgiving heat. I grit my teeth and writhed in a desperate attempt to alleviate the pain, but the burning would not subside. Fighting it was pointless. My body and soul lay there, two separate entities at war. My body, the betrayer, waited for Him to claim me.

Just sleep. My eyelids grew heavy.

"Specks of dust." A chilling, gravelly voice sounded around me. "Say it."

Tears blurred my vision. This is what the horde had chanted. Nihilistic words that made my people believe that we are nothing.

His voice boomed again, like thunder in the night sky, "Say it!"

Fire and ice twisted inside me, searing my soul. I tried to scream, but no sound escaped me.

He chuckled. "Very well, I will show you."

The Earth had not bent nor had the sky fallen upon my chest.

It was Him all along.

He was stretched above me beyond the limits of the world, while I was trapped in the palm of His hand. The final strand of sanity holding me together threatened to snap, when I noticed a bright light behind his giant pupils. Many colors slithered and twined around each other like squelching worms burning and lulling me all at once.

My view shifted, and I saw what he wanted me to see.

Three other ships arrived on my island, bearing the names of Rape, Greed, and Santa Genocidio Masivo. I watched the men from these ships savage my people in the name of their red and gray gods. They enslaved them to find gold, raped our sisters, and cut the hands from our brothers' arms. Fathers died protecting their children as their mothers were burned alive. Others still took refuge in the xaweye of the mountains, inscribing their stories on those limestone walls. Some believed it to be better to gain their freedom as spirits and leapt out of the caves.

"Like specks of dust." My words were not my own, and I clamped my hands over my mouth as the phrase threatened to emerge from my throat once more.

"Still don't believe me?" His rasping voice echoed hypnotically in my head.

I saw myself as He saw me no more than a speck in His hand. My grip tightened around my grandmother's necklace until the shells cut deep, and I bled. Like fingernails digging beneath skin to wake me. As my blood spilled, her spirit, and those of all the Caciques that came before coursed through me, pouring out from the guanín as I tied it around my neck.

His one red eye watched balefully as I crowned myself with the sacred headdress. I dared not speak—or even think—afraid that I might betray myself against my will. My body moved on instinct alone as it squatted in his palm.

An enormous burst of adrenaline woke my sixth sense, granting my soul freedom from its corporeal cage. Free of my flesh, my soul could jump from one body to the next, once more hidden from his gaze amongst a sea of others.

Once more? Have I done this before?

His thoughts emanated like heat from a fire—a noxious mixture of panic and rekindled frustration, answering my internal thoughts. Faces of men, women, and children of many colors flashed before me, my reflection in their glistening eyes. These descendants of *caciques*, warriors, *curanderos, brujas y brujeros,* of kings, and queens from far-off lands, all rebelling together against that which seeks to destroy them. They were not of my blood, but our spirits were the same.

The hope of their rebellion urged my soul to leap and gain its freedom.

My body remained, crouching down—an eternal reminder that I will always ascend.

Generations upon generations will give offerings to clay statues of me. They will light candles and pray to me as Mother of All Mothers. He has tricked many into thinking I am the evil to his benevolent God, but that is not true. I am nature, I am creation, and for the love of my people, I am the ancestral spirit that digs her phantom nails into our children's shackled arms and cries out, "Rise, Cacique. Rise!"

Passage

Cyrus Amelia Fisher

Cutting into the frozen earth would have killed two men more, so they buried Edward Jeffries under a cairn of loose stone. It was never long before all things in this place were devoured.

But it wasn't the threat of bears that kept Altan watching over the grave, long after the gaunt specters of her crew dragged their aching bones back to camp. They'd seen no living things since they crossed the southern threshold two years ago. All they had now was their hunger.

"A fine service, Captain," Paulson said in the silence. Her last surviving lieutenant looked little better than a corpse himself.

Altan's tongue scraped across chapped lips. "I didn't have the songs."

"I'm sure Jeffries wouldn't have minded." A blatant lie. They'd both seen the man fondling his sailor's phylactery on the endless days of the march, praying to a god of hearth and soil who certainly couldn't hear him here. But Altan had no chosen patron, and no funerary hymns to sing.

Perhaps it didn't matter. She was starting to doubt that even their souls could find their way out of this wretched place.

"What he would mind," Paulson continued, "is knowing his friends were suffering without reason. With all due respect, Captain, we aren't all holding up as well as you."

Altan shifted. Muscle, fat, and skin unbroken by scurvy all shifted with her. The weight of her body's betrayal, a vitality she hadn't chosen. It wasn't fair. And so she would be unfair.

"Did he leave you his will and testament, Paulson?"

"No."

"Then we best not assume what a dead man would have wanted."

Paulson left her then. Sound retreated with him, a long clinking slog back to camp. The air sang thin beneath the distant snap of sailcloth, their makeshift tents sun-bleached as bone. Even death was small out here, lost in the impersonal sweep of the landscape. It was her duty to ensure they were not entirely swallowed. This realm held all the sympathy for its ragged invaders as a stomach for a piece of meat. Privately Altan found it beautiful still, even as it dissolved them. Another self-betrayal.

"I know this won't comfort you," said a voice out of nothing, "but he's in a place of honor now."

Altan didn't raise her head from its contemplation of the death-stones. If she did, she doubted there would be anything to see. "And what honors does your patron dispense onto its food?"

"Do you really want to know?"

Altan said nothing. She heard the woman sigh; could perfectly imagine that mournful expression that had won so many indulgences on the ship. Gods, Altan had been blind.

"It doesn't have to be this way." The insinuation in Nazaire's voice was the warmest thing Altan had felt for a while, nauseating as its implications were.

"Yes," Altan said, her voice as hard as her captain's brass. "It does."

After that there was silence. Alone again, among the dead and the hungry living.

A proper captain might have prayed.

Two years earlier.

Nights were hard to catch during their first summer in the unseasonable ice, fleeting as they were. But Nazaire's rituals required the flavor of darkness, and so Altan had ordered the crew to gather on the main deck when the shadows of the seracs dipped the sun briefly into twilight.

Altan watched as Nazaire knelt in the runic circle wrought in iron on the ship's deck with a knife pressed to her palm. Each of Altan's officers carried such a knife and made their sacrifices during their morning ablutions with mechanical devotion. A few drops from the thumb: the gentleman's oblation.

Rote or not, Altan envied them their belief. The certainty, and sense of belonging. Of being held and kept by something that wanted them, and which they wanted in return. She had cut her thumb into a hundred silver bowls and felt nothing deeper than pain.

Nazaire's voice rose against the raw edge of the wind, speaking words that made the roots of Altan's teeth ache. Around the ship the ice groaned and shifted. Whether or not it was at the beck of Nazaire's patron, Altan could not be sure. Certainly, these rituals, though they had increased in frequency, had done nothing to release the ship from the unnatural ice.

As if sensing Altan's thoughts, Nazaire's eyes shifted to hers. A smile hooked at the edge of her thin lips; she did not falter in the words that traced a writhing euphoria over the surface of Altan's mind.

"We're close to breaking through," Nazaire said much later, after Altan had removed her smart dress jacket and then everything else, crammed into her narrow one-man berth with Nazaire snug against her side. Sometimes Altan wondered if she'd taken Nazaire to bed for her connection to the god alone; if Nazaire was her personal idolatry. Altan was better suited to worship than love.

"It certainly doesn't seem like it." Altan ran her fingers idly through Nazaire's black, short-cut hair. The low rumble of ice pressed around the ship. Some of the crew found it claustrophobic; to Altan it was like the tight embrace of a lover. She never slept so well at home as she did with the ice locked around her.

"I feel it." Nazaire caught her hand, and pulled it beneath the blanket where it could work to more productive ends. "My patron hears me. It just isn't responding."

"Why wouldn't it respond?" Altan said, already caring much less. A cold summer was not so strange; far less interesting than the slow expansion of Nazaire's pupils.

Nazaire's breath caught, and then she grinned. "Relax, Captain. You're in the center of my patron's power; we'll take care of you."

After that, the questions Altan asked were matters for the flesh alone.

The leather of the sled harness bit deep into Altan's shoulders and chest, layers of padding little use but to quicken the sweat that poured down her skin. The boat sleds scraped on the shale, containing the sum total of their lives: tents, blankets, those too weak to walk. By Altan's reckoning, they had only made four miles since leaving

Jeffries' cairn behind them that morning. Space did not behave the way it ought to, so close to the center of the god's own realm. It wanted to keep them close.

"I didn't know," Nazaire said.

This was the most common of themes between them now. She walked at Altan's side, her uniform robes spotless, the seal-fur ruff around her neck so soft Altan almost reached out to touch it, knowing it wasn't truly there.

"I don't believe you," Altan mumbled through chapped lips. She hadn't believed the grand visions the Navarchy painted to their investors, either of trade routes and maritime domination, of a new vast god to be appeased, tamed. But Altan had always known this god couldn't be placated. It merely *was*, sitting at the bottom of the world in the center of a labyrinth of ice, unmoved by human ambition, stirring only to the taste of human blood.

She hadn't believed. But she had led her crew into its maw all the same.

Nazaire's hand settled on her shoulder, light against the bone-cutting ache of the sled harness. "You can't blame a thing for following its nature. Not a god, and not yourself."

Behind her, the cry went up: another man had fallen.

They stopped there for the darkless night after just four miles of hauling. By evening there was another grave, and Altan drifted at its head like a living marker.

"We were provisioned for three winters at full rations," Altan said. "It shouldn't have come to this so soon."

Around the heavy oak table of her captain's cabin, her officers' faces were drawn. Nazaire sat far to the back, turned away from the table entirely; her dark eyes were fixed on windows cataracted with frost.

Doctor Makae stood up. They held a can from their stocks; the label read *lamb stew with vegetable*, but it had split where the metal had bulged outward from within. From their pocket they withdrew the bloodletting knife that all officers carried; its edge gleamed sharp in the lantern light.

"I apologize for the theatrics," they said, and began to work the blade into the solder. "But I believe the best explanation is example."

The lid sprang open, and from beneath it something pushed free. A few of the officers drew away from the table in disgust as the long, white-bodied worms drooled from the can's edge, probing blindly with their glossy black heads.

"The contents of at least half the cans have putrefied," Doctor Makae said, setting the can down on top of the inventory papers. "It appears our patron is displeased."

"It's forgotten us here," Paulson muttered darkly. Altan's sharp look was lost on him; his eyes remained fixed on the papers with their neat rows of numbers adding up to catastrophe, and the swaying dance of the worms.

"And what does our witch have to say?" Altan said, struggling to contain the anger in her voice. Nazaire was meant to be her ally, an advocate in the realm of her terrible patron. It had occurred to Altan long before that Nazaire was not quite human, in that way particular to all who served the gods. You gave your god enough of yourself, and eventually, it gave something back. Altan couldn't pinpoint when she'd stopped thinking of that as an advantage.

Nazaire turned back to the table, her eyebrows raised vaguely. "Ah. Yes. I can perform another ritual, of course. Something to improve the luck of our hunting parties, perhaps?"

Beneath the table, Altan's fingers clenched into a fist. "I expect a divination on how to assuage your patron," she said. Though it made her skin crawl, she reached out to pick up the can of worms before any could succeed in their frantic attempts to squirm onto the table. Walking briskly, she opened the hidden cover of the head and dropped the loathsome can into the ice-crusted void below. The smile on her face may as well have been embossed on stiff leather. None of her officers returned it.

"If we regain its favor, all will be well," Altan said.

They shook her awake at the gravesite in the dimmest part of night. At some point, Altan had slumped over her rifle with her brow to its barrel and a piece of her skin stayed frozen to its metal as the hands jostled her awake. Blood ran down into her eye as she stared into the faces of the near-dead, gray and sagging and without sympathy. She knew them all by name.

"Sorry, Captain," Paulson said. Already two of the sailors he'd gathered were beginning to pull away the gravestones, clinking and scraping in the brief twilight that was dusk and dawn.

"Didn't think it would be you to break first, Paulson," Altan mumbled. Exhaustion and pain were making her slow.

"Not just me," Paulson said. "We all agreed. We need the supplies." *The food.* Altan's stomach turned over, and she wasn't certain whether it was disgust or hunger.

"There's no uncrossing this line, Paulson."

"It's all well and good for you to cling to your principles when you're the only one among us not wasting away." Paulson spoke with holes, flashes of black where his teeth had begun to fall out. With brittle care, he knelt to her eye level. "You could tell us what you promised it," he said in a low voice. His eyes raked the planes of her face, still curved with muscle and fat. "Call back your witch. We'd make our offerings—whatever it took."

"I didn't promise anything," Altan said, the truth as bitter as blood. "I never wanted this."

Paulson's face twisted into a patchwork of stretched skin and void, hollowed eye sockets, a snarl of teeth. "Liar," he hissed, and slammed the stock of his rifle into her temple.

"It won't let you leave."

Nazaire faced her from across the table, the lantern light dripping shadows down her face. Of the entire crew and its officers, her cheeks were the only ones not hollowed out by hunger. Altan didn't ask where she was getting the food; she didn't go down to the room on the orlop deck where they'd stacked the contaminated cans, to check if any were missing.

"What are you talking about?" Altan said. She barely glanced up from the papers on the table before her: lists of remaining provisions, schematics, maps. Their third spring in the south was slipping away, and soon it would be too late to even attempt a march out. In the morning, Altan would call a meeting of her officers to begin the preparations. She had come to Nazaire for support, advice. Now when she looked up, Nazaire's eyes were pitying.

"It wants you here," she said. "All of you. As sacrifice."

Outside the ship, the ice groaned torturously. "I don't," Altan began, and then stopped. "You said we had lost its favor."

"I was wrong."

"You—you lied."

"No. Not at first. Altan, I—"

"*How long?*" Altan's voice remained level, and low. As long as she kept asking questions and gathering information, she could rise with the tide of horror in her chest. "How long have you known?"

Nazaire took a slow breath. She could be so dreadfully still. "Since last winter."

"Good *god*—" Altan cut herself off, turning away and pressing her knuckles to her cold-chapped lips so hard she tasted iron. "You have to intercede on our behalf. Beg your patron to reconsider. We can offer it—"

"It already has what it wants." Nazaire sounded very tired. "There's nothing more you or I can give it."

"Then we'll walk out," Altan snarled, whirling around to face her. "Your god's will be damned, I'll get my crew out of here."

"Altan, listen," Nazaire said. She took a step closer, her hands raised as if calming a horse. "You don't need to worry. You and I, we're safe. You have always honored it, knowingly or not. All you have to do is join us."

Altan thought of her reflection, staying fleshed and full while her crews' grew narrow with hunger. She'd cut her rations more than the lowest seaman, and still, she didn't starve. The horror deepened into revulsion.

"You fucking traitor," Altan said, her voice almost conversational but for the tremor of raw fury in it. "You said nothing, you sat through those meetings and you knew, you knew you had *fed* us to it—"

"And who led us here?" Nazaire's face changed: like the light shifting on the seracs, deepening their ragged shadows and lengthening their teeth. "Who returned, again and again, despite the agony and failure and the string of bones behind you? It's had its hooks in you for *years*, Altan, and you've been nothing but a loyal servant. Don't think you can turn away from it now."

In the silence, the wind whipped crystals of ice against the windows. The world itself seemed to strain, ready to splinter.

"I'm going to load my pistol," Altan said. "I suggest you get off my ship before I'm finished."

Nazaire hesitated long enough that Altan thought she was going to have to take the shot. But by the time she'd cocked the pistol and turned around, she was alone.

"Altan."

Warmth. In the darkness of her vision she felt it blooming from the top of her head. *This is death*, she thought with tender joy, and opened her eyes; Nazaire stared down at her. After so long staring into the skeletal faces of her crew, the smooth fatty curve of Nazaire's cheeks was grotesque. The empty grave lay beside her, torn open to the sky.

"It's over," Nazaire said softly. "Your crew have abandoned you. Even now they're roasting chunks of that poor boy over a spit."

Altan closed her eyes. She was so very tired; tired of the weight of that old life, its intricate, interlocking pieces of obligation that surrounded her like a cage. A part of her wanted nothing more than to let go. There was no one here to hear her; no one here to know.

"What was it like?" Altan whispered. "To join it."

Nazaire smiled down at her with terrible kindness. "Are you ready to find out?"

Altan's tears were warm on her cheeks for only a moment before they were ice. "My duty is to my crew."

"Fuck your duty." Nazaire's voice remained sweet. "Their world has taken enough of you. All those little bites, chewing off more and more, until one day there won't be anything left."

Altan managed a laugh. "Not like your patron. It swallows its prey whole."

"Yes." Nazaire's eyes were bright. "It wants all of you, Altan. Every piece."

"And if I'd rather be more than a meal?"

"We're all devoured by something, darling," Nazaire said. "Shouldn't it at least be something that loves you back?"

For a long while Altan was silent. Her body drank in the warmth of Nazaire's closeness even as her mind rejected it. Somewhere ahead, close or impossibly far, her crew were waiting for her. She felt them, drawing her inevitably on. The iron pull of duty she'd felt all her life. An anchor that had kept her moored, and now dragged her down.

"Then let me choose," Altan said.

Altan walked.

Paulson and his mutineers had taken her boots and her coat, but she no longer felt the cold. Bloody footprints trailed behind her as she limped, and stopped only long enough to pick herself up when she fell.

At a certain point, she must have closed her eyes. The air grew colder; far too cold for even a bitter southern summer. Her bloodied feet slipped on the shale, sending her stumbling—but when her knees hit the ground, they crunched into a layer of frozen snow.

Slowly, Altan raised her head. The plain of loose gray stone was gone. Now she knelt on the ice, seracs looming over her like an archway against a sky darker than any arctic summer. Far above, the rippling witchlights wheeled and undulated, throwing off spokes of colors Altan had no name for. Other shapes rippled behind the curtain of lights; trying to see them drove a wedge of pain into Altan's brain like a cleaver. Towering against that frenzied backdrop, its matrix of ragged spindles rising among the spires of ice, was her ship.

Altan pulled herself up the icy formations with fingers tinted gray by the light until she stood with the ruined deck beneath her feet. In the clenched fist of the ice the wood had buckled and then splintered, throwing up compound fractures of shattered boards. The sastrugi loomed over the deck like the walls of a blue-black cathedral, the sky a dome of living color above the ritual circle at its center.

As Altan saw it, she understood. It wanted this: wanted her duty and her pain and her principles. It wanted her worship almost as much as she wanted to give it.

But its teeth weren't in her yet.

For all the times that Altan's gaze had wandered during Nazaire's rituals, she knew what to do. Her bloodletting knife hung on her belt; the crew hadn't dared touch it. She began the cut on her thumb and watched dispassionately as the blood ran towards her palm. On further consideration, she let the blade follow that path, carving through the meat of her hand and then down into the tender divot of her wrist. The blood flowed like icemelt, and she reached out to press it to the hungry ice.

A lightning strike of cold locked her hand to the altar. It tore the breath out of her in a sharp hiss as her blood veined the ice, sinking deeper and deeper. Nazaire had kept her strong. Now she would spend that strength down to the last drop.

"Come on," she choked out through gritted teeth. "Isn't this what you wanted?"

What you wanted. An echo—an accusation. She found she could no longer deny it.

The silence shifted, deepening like the cold. Altan looked up.

The lights above had frozen in place, their edges rippling as if with the constant stirring of cilia. And when she lowered her eyes to the white slab of the altar stone she could see a reflection of those pale tendrils spreading from the ice into her flesh, tunneling through the open wound and down her arm until their dark heads bloomed against the bone.

"I was beginning to doubt you'd come."

Nazaire. The relief of footsteps creaking on the boards behind her was enough to make Altan's stomach twist. The god's power was still inside her, tunneling curiously, rippling worms of light tracing the path of her veins. Up to her shoulder now, pulsing deep in its sheath of blood and tendon and meat. She couldn't pull back.

"You have to be wholly willing. Or else it will destroy you utterly." A hand entered Altan's frame of vision, picking up the knife where it lay fallen at Altan's feet. "I can still cut you free."

Altan could feel it. It was growing into her, pulling her apart the way the ice had torn its way into the ship. But there was power there too, cold and crushing and vast. "Let them go," Altan said through chattering teeth. "My life for theirs."

Slim fingers touched Altan's chin, cold as ice. She looked up into Nazaire's dark gaze, reflecting that frozen nimbus of light.

"You can't bargain with it," Nazaire said. "It's not that kind of god. What you offer, it will only consume."

"I'm bargaining with *you*." Altan bared her teeth in a grin that was half-madness, half-joy. "You want me? Free my crew."

Nazaire laughed. It was not a wholly joyless sound. "There's no coming back from this, Altan. Once it has you, it—*we*—won't ever let you go."

"I know." Altan held her gaze, shuddering at the breeding ecstasies within her. "You were right, Nazaire. This is what I wanted." Belonging. Belief. And Nazaire at her side.

At some point Nazaire's fingers had shifted to her cheek, cupping it as once they had in the warm closeness of Altan's bunk. The tendrils burrowed deeper, curling around the bend of her shoulder and pushing up the column of her neck. One hooked over the shelf of her jaw and nestled against Nazaire's palm from within her flesh; she watched the shudder of disgusted rapture travel through Nazaire's body. The hollow shell of the world caved in. At last, she could let it go; she could be consumed.

Nazaire lowered the knife. The worms of light boiled into the base of her skull, and she screamed as they pushed out through her eyes with a vision that splintered through her mind like the altar through her ship's deck; on the wave of that power it was nothing at all to find the distant, pulsing lives of her crew, and gently disentangle them from the curls of spectral intent which held them back.

The god barely felt them go; it was too intent on claiming her. In a flash of agony, the ice around her went clear as water, and she saw in the wild plain around them a dozen ships, a hundred, of every nation and every era, all crushed in the jaws of the terrible cold, their marrow sucked dry. And above them, all the lights heaved and rippled their colossal bodies like a plain of shining viscera spread across the heavens. They poured into Altan's skull, too large and glorious for that fragile shell of bone to contain it.

As it burst free into its terrible becoming, Nazaire stroked her hair. It felt incredible; it felt like coming home. Altan opened her eyes to stare, smiling, into Nazaire's luminous face; and their god was present in all things, seething within them both.

The Comfort of a Cold Pit

Michelle Tang

The deep pit pulsed with malignancy: it rose from the cold dirt up to the rafters and pressed against neatly-polished windows on every wall. Its presence filled the large house with a ringing silence that echoed in one's ears like a dirge.

Eliza warmed her hands on a gold-rimmed cup of Oolong tea, and watched red-yellow leaves pirouette in the brisk autumn wind, a *pas de deux* between the short-lived and the immortal. This was the way of things: summer's lushness faded, became desiccated corpses that crumbled back into the dirt.

She shifted her mind away from dirt: the heavy, uncaring blanket that eventually covered everyone the way dreary, tedious life smothered childhood innocence. There was work yet to be done.

Eliza groaned as she descended three stories to reach the bottom of the pit, her knees creaking like the stairs underfoot. Her heart fluttered like butterfly wings, and combined with her breathlessness, reaching the pit always evoked the heady feeling of falling in love.

These days, the only thing that still worked properly were her eyes—and they weren't even hers. She didn't remember much of the ones she'd been born with, but she didn't miss 'em: if eyes were the window to the soul, Eliza preferred to keep the shutters closed. She set her steaming cup of tea on a small antique table beside her stool and turned the space heater on. Here, in the deepest part of the pit, the cold numbed, and she needed to keep her fingers nimble, or as nimble as they could be these days.

Above, the doorbell rang. Its insistent melody thrummed through the house, echoing in the mostly empty space, distorting as it reached her ears. It wasn't her weekly delivery of groceries, and her assortment of staff knew never to bother her in person. Eliza ignored it. Surely the visitor, whoever it was, would go away.

They did not.

The doorbell rang again and again, until Eliza rued the day she'd opted for a fifteen-second sample of Bach's *Toccata and Fugue in D Minor* instead of a half-second chime. The visitor began knocking: heavy thumping impacts that rattled the locks.

"Can't an old woman die in peace?" Eliza muttered, and hurried back up the steep staircase. Her time was running out to finish what she'd started, and the sense of failure would surely follow her into the afterlife.

The knocking and bell-ringing hadn't stopped by the time she reached the main floor, something she was both grateful and annoyed about: imagine climbing all those steps at her age just to find an empty front porch!

Her hands were slick with sweat and trembling as she drew back the deadbolt and yanked the door open. It was a young Chinese woman she didn't know, vibrant and healthy. The stranger took a step back when the evil power emanating from the pit escaped through the entrance, but she did not run. She cowered under Eliza's glare—Eliza well-knew how terrifying her large, pearlescent irises were. It felt like falling endlessly through the sky, never knowing when the ground would rise up to obliterate you. She felt it herself, even after all these decades, each time she gazed into the mirror.

"What do you want?" she spit out, as venomously as she could while huffing and puffing.

"I…don't know." The stranger's voice wavered, but her shoulders were squared and her lower jaw jutted out. Not just with determination, Eliza noted. One side was bruised and swollen, and the purple around her dark eyes wasn't from eye shadow alone. "Something called me here."

Eliza felt a rush of heartbreak and relief all at once. This young thing was here to replace her. To replace *her,* after sixty years of faithful service. A newer model, who could no doubt skip up and down those flights of stairs without breaking a sweat and could eat anything she wanted without breaking a wind.

"It's *my* house," Eliza protested. She hadn't even been asked. Still, she stepped aside to let the woman in.

"It's wonderful," the stranger took in the sparse, sheet-covered furniture, and stared at the gaping hole cut into the floor, ringed by tiny rooms and banisters as if it were a center stage.

"It was…once." But then other things had not been so good. Eliza tried to remember how to smile. "What's your name, dear?"

"Sam."

"You've come at the right time, Sam. I suspect you're going to be the one to inherit this house." Eliza's voice wobbled. Again, she wasn't sure what emotion filled her: Maybe, like a stew, it was any number of things.

Sam's eyes widened—brown, though that wouldn't remain the case for long. "Oh, I couldn't possibly…"

Eliza shook her head to cut off the argument. "You arrived here empty-handed, and wouldn't leave when no one answered the door. You haven't been driven mad by the pit's energy, and you're clearly running from someone who means you no good. This house, and what lives below, happens to need a care-taker. It's not giving you a choice." Eliza always thought she chose this life, but Sam's arrival made everything less clear.

"You want me to take care of you?" Sam asked. "I can do that. I used to take care of my mum, see, and—"

Eliza sighed. "Not me. It." The young thing didn't understand, and why would she? "Come with me. I'll show you."

The stairs creaked louder with twice the weight on them, but even Eliza's failing ears heard Sam's gasp of delight.

"It's gorgeous! Did you make that?"

A strange little feather of pride tickled inside Eliza's chest. "I did. It's taken me my whole life."

A life full of luxury and freedom, thanks to her god.

They reached the packed dirt at the bottom of the pit, and Sam reached out to stroke the giant quilt that lay over most of the floor. "My mum used to sew. Just clothing for us, though. Never something like this." Sam's eyes narrowed as she examined each quilt square. "What are these pictures?"

The little feather of pride fanned into a peacock's tail. Eliza grinned, genuinely this time, excited to share her secret with another person. "They're pictures I've sewn…of *It.*"

"It?" Sam's forehead creased with confusion.

Eliza grasped the edge of the heavy quilt and pulled. Sam bent down to help her. It took several arm lengths of material before the edge of it appeared, and at last Eliza's god was uncovered. She gazed at it with a mixture of terror and love. "This used to be my father's house, you see. My brother was the favorite, and I was locked here in the basement, where my screams would not be heard. I pried up wooden floorboards, seeking escape, and instead found salvation."

She pointed at a pair of eyes amidst the thousands, the only pair open, dark brown pupils, sclera blackened with congealed blood. "These were my eyes, melted at the mere sight of Its glory." Eliza turned to Sam and gestured to the pearly orbs on her face. "But my god was merciful and gave me a pair of its own. When it awakens, it's going to do the same for you, I wager. It will be an agony beyond comprehension. Until then, you will care for it as I do."

Eliza showed Sam the cloths and equipment she used to keep her god clean of dust and dirt, and keep its multitude of eyelashes neatly brushed. "It seems to like the cold, so make sure the space heater is pointed away from it. And it doesn't seem to eat, or poo."

"Will it… will it wake soon?" Sam didn't seem eager. Not like Eliza had been, but that was the younger generation for you.

"I've no idea. It's at least somewhat aware—It replaced my eyes and killed my family for me." Eliza shivered at the memory. It had been impossible to clean the teeth and bone shards from the carpet, let alone the blood and bile. She still had nightmares, both of her father and her god. "And now, It has called you here."

"You can stay in one of the bedrooms, and help yourself to whatever food is in the kitchen. New groceries come every Tuesday." She scrawled a hasty note for her lawyer, signed it with a flourish, and handed the paper to Sam to place with the other important documents upstairs. Eliza had no family left, no one to contest this last-minute change.

She waited until Sam had reached the main floor, envious of how easily the woman's long, slim legs carried her.

Eliza groaned herself onto her stool and picked up the last square of her quilt. "I should have trusted you'd take care of yourself," she muttered to the sleeping mass of leathery skin and twitching eyelids beside her. "Couldn't have summoned her a bit earlier to help when my arthritis got bad though, I see."

Eliza sewed carefully, hands weak, heart skipping beats. But her eyesight, as always, remained keen: Eliza wondered if they would continue to see long after she died. It was a strange, uncomfortable thought, but that wasn't unusual given the life she'd led. And it had been a much better life than she'd expected. Her god's presence granted her an aura of power, and people treated her with respect, or fear, far beyond what a single Chinese woman in a large town might otherwise have been granted.

"We're the same, you and I," Eliza bit off the excess thread. "All the power in the world, and yet here we are, vulnerable as newborn kittens."

The quilt was large enough for both Eliza and the entity—a giant marriage bed where neither side would need to fight for the covers. Eliza skimmed her borrowed eyes fondly along the images she'd sewn: the entity in various states of repose, a pair of its eyes up close, a handful of tentacles, and a rat that got too close to its malevolent power and exploded.

The tea had cooled: She finished it anyway, savoring the last, earthy sip before setting the delicate gold-rimmed cup back on the table. Eliza lay flat on the packed dirt, so close that long eyelashes tickled butterfly kisses along her skin, so close the entity's chill raised gooseflesh beneath her bright orange knit sweater.

She pulled her handiwork over her legs, her body…her face—a brightly-colored burial shroud to shield her from the cold, uncaring world. Like she had done for her god.

Eliza closed her borrowed eyes.

Gyges

Vaughn A. Jackson

Whiskey bites harder when you're the only one drinking. The bronze liquid burns hotter when it's stoked by the tobacco fumes of a black and mild and the roar of a wood-burning fireplace. Words swim across the translucent flesh of The Bible's pages: "*And I stood upon the sand of the sea, and saw a beast rise up out of the sea, having seven heads and ten horns, and upon his horns ten crowns, and upon his heads the name of Blasphemy.*"

Philomena scoffs and tosses the black, leatherbound book back onto the coffee table beside her charred shirt. "Exorcisms used to be simple: learn the name, say a prayer, order the damn thing out in the name of Jesus Christ, profit."

"You and I have very different definitions of 'simple,' Phil." Thaddeus fastens the highest button on his coat and rubs his arms for warmth. He's been pacing back and forth for over an hour. "But I will admit it was never this cold before."

Phil nods. Her breath comes out as gray vapor in the air as she sighs, blending with the puff of smoke from the cigarette. "The cold isn't—"

A choir of shrieking voices start a chant with growing fervor. The pounding from the neighboring room kicks up again, held at bay by nothing more than a flimsy wooden door and a painted sigil resembling a crooked and upturned crow's foot. It was a hasty replica from a wrinkled handful of loose pages that had been tucked away in the back of one of the books they brought with them.

"So what are we going to do about that...*thing?*" Thaddeus stops pacing, and the two lock eyes. He shifts from rubbing his arms to wringing his hands.

Phil mutters the word "demon" under her breath.

Thaddeus slams his fist against the wall. "I have seen demons! *We* have seen demons. That...I'm not even sure if it's *there* half the time. Demons are real—"

"So is it." Philomena exhales a cloud of smoke. "Real enough to toss us around like fucking ragdolls and leave me with one less shirt to cover up this ratty-ass tank top."

"We could just leave." Thaddeus' pleads, but his heart isn't in it.

"We could," Philomena nods, "the family did already pay us. Do you want to?"

"God, yes."

"Are we going to?"

Thaddeus' jaw shifts visibly behind tight lips, his teeth grinding in the way they always do when he thinks hard. He casts a longing glance out of the window at their black sedan. "No. Of course not."

"Right." Philomena stretches her arms over her head, crossing them at the wrist until something in her spine pops, and a wave of relief washes over her body. She cracks her neck, and turns to her partner. "You still got those pages we found?"

"The ones neither of us can read?" Thaddeus reaches into his coat pocket and pulls out a handful of yellowing, dulled pieces of parchment. He unfolds the pages and flicks them with his finger. "They're here. Glad we both realized the fire was getting low."

Philomena stands and snatches them from his hand. She gestures at the spray painted symbol on the door. "The only thing that even remotely worked, we found in these pages. They're more than fucking kindling—we just haven't figured out their secrets yet."

"Maybe if they were in English, or Latin, or—or Japanese, and not some made up shit that looks more like chemical bond diagrams than actual letters." Thaddeus shakes his head. "It's esoteric even for occult texts."

"Something is *always* better than nothing in these situations." Even as she says it, Philomena can't help but feel disheartened, staring down at the cryptic script surrounding the original version of the ward.

The letters—at least she assumes they're letters—wind in towards the central image like they're being sucked down a drain. No character appears more than once, making any kind of pattern recognition impossible, and Philomena knows that they are never in the same order after she looks away and looks back. Trying to make sense of it causes a sensation akin to the starting edge of migraine—nausea, vertigo, and the distant drumbeat of a brutal headache. Her mind rejects the potential of understanding what lay before it.

Philomena tips the ashes from her cigarette onto the carpeted floor before flicking the butt into the open flame. She watches the tip catch and join the crumbling logs. "Okay, from the top—what do we know?"

"Those tentacles are not consentacles," Thaddeus deadpans. "And no one can ever say that centipedes have too many legs ever again. Or do millipedes have more?"

"I'm serious." Philomena rifles through the pages, frowning at her partner's joke.

"And I'm seriously regretting my sobriety, but still…" Thaddeus recounts their sparse knowledge of the situation. "None of the classics work—holy water, crosses, Jesus' name, Jesus' name in vain—they're all bunk. The possession—if we can call it that—is both physical and spiritual, as usual, and the longer we stay here, the colder it gets. Oh, and we don't know its name. That's all I've got." The sound of a shrug lilts in his voice.

"And we know that it can't—or refuses to—speak."

"It just kind of…gurgles, yeah."

The shapes on the page wander before Philomena's eyes, locking themselves together in strange and discordant patterns spiraling in a vortex all leading down to the strange sigil. They slide and adjust, pieces of a puzzle arranging themselves into a pictogram that reveals no more information than they do as separate entities. Pain throbs at the base of Phiolmena's skull and burns behind her eyes like crimson flames. Tears trickle down her face. She wipes them away, staining the back of her hand red. Panic lances at her heart. She checks to see if Thaddeus notices—he doesn't—and dries her eyes on the ravaged t-shirt, staring back into the fire again. The burning cracks wind through the black-charred wood like hellish lightning that swirls into the same archaic pattern as on the pages. She blinks, and the logs are just logs once more.

"You okay?" Thaddeus asks. "Your eyes—"

"I'm going in." Phil folds the pages into a tight square and shoves them deep into her pants pocket. She pushes past Thaddeus and heads towards the door. "I have an idea."

"Finally manage to translate those?" Thaddeus juts his chin in the direction of the concealed pages then pauses, scrutinizing her face. "Wait, you're not going to use—

"No." Philomena rubs her eyes again. "Or at least, I don't think so. I'm hoping this works."

"Ah," Thaddeus absentmindedly dusts at the breast of his coat and flashes a snarky grin, "the great detective's hunch."

"Hasn't gotten us killed yet."

Thaddeus let out a heavy sigh. "Why'd you have to say 'yet?'"

The knob is cold as ice despite the roaring flame to her back. Frost crystals cover the door frame and creep along the walls like tiny snow spiders. Phil shivers as she slides the key into the lock and turns. Hinges creak as the door swings inward. The burning smell of hydrochloric acid rakes her nostrils and brings fresh saline tears to her eyes. She grits her teeth as the pounding on the door shifts to the front of her skull, beating behind her eyes with a vengeance. All the chanting voices fade, replaced by an undulating moan like the waves of a tarry sea burbling against a stony shore. The room is dark as pitch, but it doesn't take long for her eyes to adjust—for her to see the *thing-that-is-not-a-demon*—in the low light of the room.

A sliver of moonlight lances through the window. Thaddeus calls the appendages tentacles, but as she sees them again, Philomena thinks of them more as the branching limbs of an old and crooked tree, knotted and gnarled with age. There are at times hundreds of them, at other times thousands, and then sometimes none. They reach, and grasp, and claw.

Its body—if it can be called that—is a series of planes and curves overlapping and threading through each other at fractal, non-Euclidean angles that grow and shrink arrhythmically; the breathing of a broken beast.

A broken beast that had once been—and Phil hopes still is—a child. The gray light reveals a pallid face, eerily serene despite the predicament. The girl's eyes are open, staring up at the ceiling, but not seeing it. Phil shudders, wondering if she's aware of what's transpiring.

Six months ago, Allie was an orphan at St. Augustus' Home for Lost Souls. The Levantes adopted her—brought her into their happy little family—only to find themselves trapped in a living Hell. The parents told of whispering shadows, rooms out of order, and an omnipresent voyeurism lingering over their every action. In the hours she and Thaddeus stayed in the house all of those—and more—have been confirmed. Behind her eyes—when she dares close them—she can still see the twisted alien images the thing showed her the one time she accidentally touched it. It was a world where cancerous growths sprouted from the ground, and horrific creatures roamed like tyrant lizards; a world of monsters.

Philomena couldn't imagine suffering through that kind of nightmare day after day. It was a testament to their strength, and their love for the daughter they took in. She pulls up a chair and sits in it backward, draping her arms over the back and rummaging through her pockets. Her pack of Black and Milds is empty, so she tosses it at the entity. It's petty, but it feels good. "You've had this girl in your grips for almost five months, and you've done nothing but cause terror. Don't you think that's long enough? I do."

The creature purrs, its fuzzy planes shifting in what might be acknowledgement. Or maybe agitation. Phil looks away, afraid to let her eyes linger on its shifting form for too long lest she lose her nerve. She sucks in a deep breath.

"Look, I can't say I have the slightest idea what you are, but I get the feeling you aren't supposed to be stuck like this. You tried to use Allie as an anchor, but it didn't work. So I did some thinking on that. God I wish I had another smoke—"

Thaddeus leans against the door frame. "You're gonna talk it to death?"

"Better," Philomena flashes a wry smile, "I'm gonna name it." She stands suddenly, toppling the chair, and points at the writhing mass of creature spilling from Allie's mouth and onto the floor of her room. "I dub thee 'Gyges,' abomination, and I know you!"

At first, nothing happens, but then the low groaning grows louder, and the branching limbs shudder as if caught in a violent wind. The creature lurches upward, shattering into mirrored shards of existence, and shrieks.

"Oh great, you pissed it off!" Thaddeus inches back out of the room.

"I don't think so." Philomena's heart races in her chest, hoping her hunch is right. "I think—"

Her words disappear as the creature's planes shuffle around—something out of Escher's worst nightmares—unfurling into an open void.

The void speaks.

The words are alien, all consonants and howling screams, an eldritch opera sung from a thousand-throated abomination. Thaddeus sprints from the room, hands clasped over his ears. Philomena grits her teeth until she feels a molar crack, the pain lost amongst the tidal wave of sensation brought to bear by the god-awful sound. It's the sound of a storm, and a trumpet, and the death of a thousand men—the end of the world rattling a little girl's bedroom.

Beneath Gyges' shifting form, Philomena sees Allie's body rise as though lighter than air, then lock in place; frozen in the creature's pulsing form. Her mouth is open wide in a silent scream, her eyes rolling back into her skull until the last bit of the creature evacuates her body, dropping the girl back onto her bed in a heap. Now free from the girl's body, Gyges begins to actualize; the ever-shifting planes become a stark undulating blob, its branching limbs solidifying into something akin to fossilized bone.

"What the fuck did you do?" Thaddeus screams.

Philomena ignores his question and rushes towards the bed. She scoops Allie into her arms and shoves her at Thaddeus. "Take her!"

Thaddeus fumbles with Allie's limp form and hurries into the living room. Philomena follows, stopping at the table to grab her shirt. Wrapping it around her hand in tight layers, she reaches into the fire.

"What are you doing?" Thaddeus' eyes widen as Phil turns with the burning log in hand.

"Get her outside." Philomena hurls the burning wood into the girl's room as bony appendages scrape along the floor, dragging an impossible bulk toward the open door. She repeats the process until there are no logs left in the fire, and the skin on her hand begins to crisp and burn as flame eats through the layers of the shirt. She chokes on the smell of her own cooking flesh, equal parts nauseating and hunger-inducing.

The house is ablaze. Smoke clogs the air and blurs Philomena's vision as the abomination approaches.

Gyges was horrible to look at before, but now, as its oily flesh piled like molded taffy throbs forward on gnarled joints of fossilized bone, the fear in her heart confirms one thing: the fire won't burn fast enough.

Eyes—bulging and inflamed like cystic acne ready to burst—shlick on Gyge's surface as they turn to look at her. They flare with rage, and it lurches forward, writhing tendrils reaching, grasping. One slips over the threshold, and narrowly misses brushing her leg.

Phil jerks away with a hiss. "Shit."

She searches for the can of spray paint, hoping it won't burst in the heat before she finds it. Dropping to her knees, she squints beneath the smoke and sees the tell-tale yellow cap peeking out from under the coffee table. Phil scurries on all fours, cringing at the burning sensation afflicting her hands. Her body comes to a rough stop against the corner of the table. She clamps down on her tongue to keep from crying out in pain, pulls the spray can out, and gives it a good shake. Pages of research flicker through her mind's eyes, but she only needs one thing: quick as she can she clears the rest of the coffee table and in one quick motion sprays a golden triangle on the glossy black surface.

"Sorry, I know you don't like me using alchemy, Thad, but desperate times and all that…"

The creature's cry is a thousand foghorns lost at sea. Endless hands pull at the warping frame of the bedroom door as its ophidian form oozes into the light.

There are teeth in all the wrong places, protruding like sharpened ribs or clawing talons—it hurts to look at it.

Philomena clamps her eyes shut.

Whatever it is, this creature is something new to her, but she was going to introduce it, face-to-face with one of the oldest things known to man: The Promethean Flame.

Alchemy is a dangerous gambit, especially under duress, but it's all she can think to do.

The paint bubbles and boils like lava on the wooden surface, reacting quicker than Philomena expects. She curses under her breath and scrambles for the exit, hurling the can of paint at Gyges for good measure. She leaps across the threshold as the house erupts in volcanic flames, consumed in an instant by the ancient roaring fire.

Inside, Gyges screams—a howling whine of rattling chains and tormented voices—and then falls silent.

The crackle of the flame fills the night as Philomena climbs to her feet. She opens stinging eyes and glances down at the burned fabric of her tank top, blackened to crumbling ash up to her midriff. "Fucking kidding me." She coughs up a glob of ash laden phlegm and spits it to the ground. "You know what, I think I'm done smoking...for real this time."

"Sixteenth time's the charm," Thaddeus taunts.

"How's the girl?"

"She's in the car...resting." Thaddeus' gaze shifts between her and the burning house, back and forth as he processes the last few minutes. "Alchemy?"

"Can't I get a shower before you start chiding me?"

"Damn your shower, Phil, you know there's always a cost."

Philomena shrugs. "Saved the girl."

"What the hell, Phil? How did you even know that would work?"

"Had a hunch." Phil coughs again, this time into her hand, revealing a splatter of sticky red. She clenched her fist, hiding the blood from Thaddeus. "You said that the creature wasn't always there, and everything about it seemed out of place."

"So you burned down our clients' house?"

"Let me finish," Philomena snaps. "Despite its size and everything, after five months it had never harmed anyone. Plus there was the ward..."

"What about it?" Thaddeus raises an eyebrow.

"Sure, *it* couldn't be broken, but that thing easily could have torn through that door and shattered the sigil in the process. It didn't." Philomena pauses, letting Thaddeus catch up with her train of thought. "Because it *couldn't*. We were just dealing with a projection of the entity—maybe psychic or spiritual, since it was affecting the girl—until *I* made it real."

"You said its name."

"I *gave* it a name," Philomena corrects him. "I doubt something like that even had the concept of names. Gyges is a hundred-handed monster from Greek myth, so it kind of fit—and I believed it enough that the creature felt the reality of it and was able to self-actualize."

Thaddeus blinks. "And if that hadn't worked?"

"We'd have figured something out." Phil grins.

"And the fire?"

"Historically used for cleansing evil and other infections. Figured it was our best shot." Philomena rubs the back of her head. "Thank fuck we added that collateral damage and incidentals clause to our contract."

"No, I mean," Thaddeus narrows his eyes, "the alchemy."

"I decided it was worth the cost." Phil stumbles to the sedan and presses her back to the cool metal door. She slides down to a sitting position. "That girl deserves to have her life."

"And you don't?"

"Not what I meant," Philomena grumbles.

Thaddeus sniffs. "Well, you've always been the braver of us."

"That almost sounds like a compliment, Thad," Phil smirks up at him.

"My point is," Thaddeus says, waving away her statement, "without you, so many horrible things would run amok in this world."

Philomena laughs a deep, belly laugh and extends her hand. "Now you're just flattering me."

"Don't get used to it." Thaddeus clasps her wrist and pulls her to her feet. "Now, can we go get paid?"

Beggars Can't be Choosers

L. Marie Wood

INT. MONTE'S APARTMENT—DAY

The apartment was dimly lit. Potted plants with green and brown leaves populate the windowsill so much that light is not shining into the house well. The walls are a dirty tan covered with a gloss that makes the wall look like it is sweating. There is a sofa, a coffee table, a chair, and a huge entertainment center full of modern acoustic equipment and a 20-inch television. Thick bars adorn the window. The furniture in the room is covered with plastic.

Monte walks into the kitchen while Kyle is standing at the door.

>   MONTE
>   (looking at Kyle)
>   What's up, man? Take your coat off.
>   Get comfortable.
>   (beat)
>   You want somethin' to drink?

>   KYLE
>   Yeah. What you got?

Monte opens the refrigerator.

                    MONTE
                (not looking up)
            Bud, OJ, Kool-Aid.

                    KYLE
            What color?

                    MONTE
            Red.

                    KYLE
            That's me.

Laying his coat gingerly on the sofa, he surveys the room.

                    KYLE (CONT.)
            Looks like…

A roach scampers along the wall leading to the kitchen.
Kyle looks away from it.

                    KYLE (CONT.)
            Nothing has changed.

Monte joins him in the living room. He hands Kyle the
Kool-Aid as he turns on the television then drinks a sip
of his beer. Kyle sits in a chair. An awkward silence.

                    MONTE
                (beat)
            So, what's been goin' on, man? I
            Hear you doin' real well out in DC.

                    KYLE
                (shrugging)
            I guess you could say that.

                    MONTE

                    (nostalgically)
          Chocolate City.

                    KYLE
          More like Dodge City if you ask me.
          I moved to Virginia last year.

                    MONTE
          Really?
                    (sipping)
          Can't be worse than here. Folks
          turnin' up dead left and right. Moms
          got mugged on her way back from the store
          one day.

                    KYLE
          What?

Monte nods his head.

                    MONTE
          But it's cool.
                    (beat)
          So what's the dealio? Tell me about the
          phat crib, the honey, I wanna hear it all.

                    KYLE
          You need to come down and see for
          yourself.
                    (beat)
          When are you plannin' on coming to my place?

                    MONTE
          When you invite me, nigga!

Monte laughs and takes another swig of beer. Kyle has an
artificial smile on his face—

"Good God! This is so... stereotypical," Wayne said, letting the bradded screenplay fall to the floor.

"Please tell me there's something else."

Another script was pressed into his hands and he hummed in response. He read the front page, frowned at the title, and sighed as he cracked it open somewhere in the middle.

EXT. BACK OF MALL—NIGHT

Greg makes his way to the back of the mall. There are policemen with chest protectors milling around the area. Greg SEES a fireman's coat hanging from a hook on the side of the fire truck. He LOOKS to the left of the truck and SEES the owner of the coat. Firefighter #2 is wiping his brow with a paper towel.

Greg sneaks to the fire truck. He lifts the coat gingerly off the hook and tries to back away from the fireman. Firefighter #2 turns and sees Greg trying to sneak away.

                    FIREFIGHTER #2
          Hey! What the hell are you doin'?

                    GREG
          I just need to borrow this.

                    FIREFIGHTER #2
                    (approaching)
          What? You can't use that!

SERIES OF SHOTS

     A) Firefighter #2 reaches to grab the coat out
        of Greg's hands.

     B) Greg blocks his reach and punches Firefighter
        #2 in the mouth.

     C) Firefighter #2 stumbles back but then

lunges angrily at Greg, grabbing at him.

    D) Greg, looking frantic, swings the ladder away from the truck and slams it into Firefighter #2's head.

    E) Firefighter #2 crashes to the ground. He is unconscious.

BACK TO SCENE

Greg stands over the downed man.

                GREG
    Sorry.

Greg quickly puts on Firefighter #2's coat and the hard hat and runs toward the mall doors.

INT. CAL'S APARTMENT—NIGHT

Molly walks into the hallway quietly. She LOOKS into Joe's room and SEES him bobbing his head to the music while he pecks away at the computer. She turns her head away from Joe's room and turns toward the linen closet. Opening it slowly and quietly so that Joe doesn't hear her, Molly REVEALS shelves crowded with towels and bedsheets. The top shelf houses only a GRAY LOCK BOX.

We SEE Molly take a deep breath. She TAKES the box off the shelf. When she feels how light it is, her face crumbles. She cringes as she opens the box and SEES the empty box of bullets. She picks up the empty box and stares at it in disbelief.

              MOLLY
    Oh my God, Cal.
      (beat)

What have you done?

INT. THE MALL—LEFT WING—NIGHT

Greg enters the mall crouching. The damage is minimal
on this end. The doors to the stores are all open,
as everyone evacuated before the security doors were
activated. Greg sheds the hard hat and coat as he slips
into a sports store and searches for a weapon. We SEE Greg
walking through the corridor, looking for something for
protection. He stops in front of the bats.

Greg exits the store with the bat and runs cautiously up
the hall.

INT. SECURITY ROOM—NIGHT

Cal is sitting in a chair looking at the screens. He is
watching the festivities below as the police search for
the bomb. Kerry is sitting on a chair beside him, her
hands and mouth taped up. The gun sits on the table next
to Cal's restless hand.

On one screen we SEE Greg crouching around in the corridor,
trying to advance. Cal SMIRKS at Greg.

On another screen, we SEE five policemen approaching the
corridor that leads to the security room.

                    CAL
            We've got company.

Wayne shook his head, unable to form words at first.

"It's like something out of the 90s. I mean, they're in the *mall*, of all places. I
liked to hang out there too… when I was a kid, but duh, progress."

He held up his cellphone to illustrate even though there was nothing on the
screen. The battery had died long ago.

"Who would we even get to play the lead? Paging Michael Keaton…"

He chuckled: he always did find himself amusing.

They did not.

"Look, give me something contemporary. Something that screams post dial-up."

Another screenplay magically appeared and he was happy for it, but he didn't let on… couldn't. A gnarled finger tapped the front page leaving a reddish-brown smear in its wake. He didn't want to think about what the viscous liquid left behind might be.

Wayne cleared his throat and read the title.

Christmas Eve.

Ok.

He turned the page and started from the beginning this time.

FADE IN:

INT. LIVING ROOM - CHRISTMAS EVE - NIGHT

WE SEE MICHELLE walking up the stairwell into the living room. She is exasperated. WE HEAR muted sounds of several people arguing: chattering at the same time coming from the basement.

Michelle (28), an African American woman with short cut hair, walks into the kitchen and tosses the plates into the sink. Standing over the sink, she SIGHS. WE SEE CLIFF (30), an African American man with a broad-shouldered build, comes into the kitchen exasperated. They look at each other and shake their heads slightly.

WE HEAR bustling from the basement and coming up the stairwell. There is a mixture of loud and muted arguing erupting from the basement. There is STOMPING in the stairwell. Michelle and Cliff run into the living room to see what is happening.

BEN (30), a Caucasian, slight man, stomps up the stairs. He is covered with punch and small pieces of potato chips. He proceeds through the living room and out the front door, SLAMMING it.

WE SEE Michelle and Cliff staring at the door in amazement.

BEN opens the door, yanks his wet shirt over his head, wipes his face and neck with the dry area of the shirt, and throws it into the living room. WE SEE the shirt land in front of Michelle and Cliff's feet. They LOOK down at the shirt and then back up at Ben with the same look of amazement. Ben's hair is sticking up all over his head and his skin is streaked pink, the color of the punch.

                    BEN
              (shifting his feet)
        Hell, I don't even like that shirt.

Ben slams the door. Michelle and Cliff look at each other in surprise. We still HEAR the muted sounds of arguing coming from the basement.

FADE TO BLACK

RUN CREDITS

EXT. OFFICE BUILDING - ESTABLISHING SHOT - DAY

Michelle's office building is a 30-story office complex. People are going in and out of the office. Display type

INSERT

which reads

Two Weeks before Christmas

BACK TO SCENE

INT. MICHELLE'S OFFICE - DAY

Wayne gasped involuntarily and heard a knife being unsheathed. Strange the things he could identify now, sounds, gestures, vibes he wouldn't have recognized before were it not for the occupation. His ability to pick things up quickly, to watch what was happening around him and adjust had helped when the orbs descended from the sky and the visitors stepped on land. When Wayne saw them coming toward the studio, gliding more than walking, their ships digging divots into the ground—when he only had a few seconds between life or death, he pivoted. Marlene, the secretary? She was suddenly his wife. The picture of her niece and nephew framed on her desk were now their children and Wayne was at the office to pick up a script because he just so happened to be in the neighborhood. He didn't do that kind of thing often, in fact, this was his first time—and that part was true—because he was a "big deal" director after all, and usually had "his people" do those kinds of things. Bullshit, all of it, but they took him at his word and the woman he had been hitting on for weeks was suddenly his. The screenplay he held in his hand the moment the people from the sky took over had been his own. Wayne had been dropping off a physical copy in the hopes of getting someone's attention. Again. Somewhere deep down inside he knew he wasn't making any headway, not really, but he had to do something, or else he'd go fucking crazy. So, he kept coming. And then they showed up. Now he had someone's attention—a lot of someones—and, well, he was up shit's creek.

He had filmed his own movie for them and it was a disaster.

They wanted better.

They wanted more.

They had Marlene dig out scripts from the slush pile (Wayne couldn't help but chuckle at the fact that there actually *was* a slush pile and that it really was like he imagined it would be, a huge, overflowing bin of spec scripts collecting dust in a forgotten room at the back of the office), and give them to Wayne to read. It was where dreams came to die, but for Wayne, it was the goldmine that could save his skin.

They told him to shoot something and do it fast.

He said he needed a bigger crew, so they gave it to him.

He said he needed state-of-the-art equipment. They gave him that too.

Now all he needed was a good story.

Wayne filmed one, two, three of the scripts from the slush pile, scripts that looked decent on paper but didn't translate well to the screen. Either that or he was just a shitty director. He was inclined to believe the latter. He had never wanted to direct, never wanted to produce. All he wanted to do was write. And now, instead of wearing one hat, he wore all the hats.

"Ok," Wayne started, afraid to look any of them in the eye. "It's—there's a lot of words on the page, but I think I can work with it. There's potential here," he said, failing to see how he was going to make a Christmas Eve party exciting. They had already seen the movies that tried and succeeded or tried but crashed and burned. They had consumed Earth's media before they stepped foot on the soil, gobbling it up like candy. Or popcorn. Wayne knew they wouldn't hesitate to gobble him up too, use the screenplays he had thrown aside as kindling, and roast him there, on the spot. But there wasn't enough of a story there, not in that script… not in any of the ones he'd read thus far. He couldn't start shooting it—not the way it was.

Wayne knew if he didn't start shooting something soon, he wouldn't be able to shoot anything ever again.

Wayne felt the nail as it pierced the base of his neck, felt the blood run down his back in a sure and steady stream.

Monte and Kyle.

Molly and Cal.

Michelle and Cliff.

Mmmmm and *Kkkkk*… Wayne hadn't noticed that before.

A thump at his side, the sound of dead weight hitting the floor, made him jump in his seat.

The last cameraman.

Blood pooling where his head had fallen dark red staining the worn tan carpet.

They had gotten antsy.

Wayne was on his own.

He picked up the handheld that lay on its side on the floor just beyond the stiffened hand of the first cameraman to fall all those years ago, bones so white they seemed to glow under the overhead fluorescents, and whispered sharply to his "wife" the weight of their eyes on him nearly driving him to his knees.

"Wipe your face, honey. Get ready for Molly's cameo."

Editor Bios

Vaughn A. Jackson is an author and editor of dark speculative fiction and the occasional poem. His published works include *Up from the Deep*, a kaiju thriller, and *Touched by Shadows*, a novel of cosmic horror. He is a member of the Horror Writers' Association, and can usually be found cracking jokes and trying to make H.P. Lovecraft roll over in his grave. You can find Vaughn screaming into the void @Blaximillion on Twitter and BlueSky or posting photos/videos of whatever tickles his fancy on Instagram and TikTok @blaximillon_author.

Stephanie Pearre is the co-chair of the HWA Maryland Chapter and is an affiliate member of the Horror Writers Association. While she is currently working on her first novella, she also enjoys writing short stories and poetry. Her true passion is in supporting independent authors and publishers, and hopes to become a consistent editor in the future. She lives with her fiancé, two adorable cats, and an equally adorable dog.

Author Bios

Timaeus Bloom is a black author of speculative fiction from Alabama. A fan of the strange and fantastical, he spends his free time laboring over just what to do with his free time. You can find his words in *Howls from the Wreckage,* and in *Nightlight Podcast, Cosmic Horror Magazine.* He is also the co-editor of the upcoming *Howls from the Scene of the Crime: an Anthology of Crime Horror* in 2024.

Amanda Headlee has spent her entire life crafting works of dark fiction. She has a fascination with the emotion of fear and believes it is the first emotion humans feel at the moment they are born. Most of her work focuses on dark fiction associated with folklore and cosmic horror. By day Amanda is a Program Manager; by night she is a wandering wonderer. When she isn't writing or working, she can be found logging insane miles on her bike or running the backcountry of Eastern Pennsylvania. She's one of those crazy people who compete in long-distance endurance races. You can follow Amanda on Facebook, Instagram, Twitter, and at her website: www.amandaheadlee.com.

Danny Brzozowski (they/them) grew up feral, between the woods of North Eastern Pennsylvania and the decaying skeletons of industry in Upstate New York. They were dubiously domesticated by the promise of unlimited books at public libraries. As a biology teacher, writer, and grassroots community organizer, Danny's work reflects a life in dynamic equilibrium between modern empirical science and traditional ways of knowing. Tiny acts of resistance are their self-care. After sampling every biome, they have settled in central Vermont because it feels like home but the weather is better.

Chris Nelson lives in Seattle, where he teaches at a Montessori school, sometimes tries to be funny, is learning American Sign Language, and has recently become convinced of an idealist metaphysical ontology. His short fiction has appeared in *Andromeda Spaceways, Speculative North, Spectrum: A Queer Neurodivergent Horror Anthology*, and elsewhere.

Pedro Iniguez is a Mexican-American horror and science-fiction writer from Los Angeles, California. He is a Rhysling Award finalist and a Best of the Net and Pushcart nominee. His writing has appeared in *Nightmare Magazine, Never Wake: An Anthology of Dream Horror, Shadows Over Main Street Volume 3, A Night of Screams: Latino Horror Stories, Speculative Fiction for Dreamers, Worlds of Possibility, Infinite Constellations*, and *Star*Line*, among others. He can be found at www.pedroiniguezauthor.com.

Vicky Velvet is a transfem author whose favorite genres are mystery, horror, and paranormal action, all centering around strong characters. Her writing is often interconnected within her own urban fantasy-horror setting, of which "Six Underground" is the first to see light of day. Vicky is also a poet and digital artist, and can be found at @velvetvexations on Instagram.

Jessica McHugh is a novelist, a 2x Bram Stoker Award-nominated poet, & an internationally-produced playwright running amok in the fields of horror, sci-fi, young adult, and wherever else her peculiar mind leads. She's had twenty-seven books published in fourteen years, including her bizarro romp, *The Green Kangaroos*, her YA series, The Darla Decker Diaries, and her Elgin Award nominated blackout poetry collection, *A Complex Accident of Life*. For more info about publications and blackout poetry commissions, please visit McHughniverse.com.

Mary SanGiovanni is an award-winning American horror and thriller writer of over a dozen novels, including The Hollower trilogy, *Thrall, Chaos*, The Kathy Ryan series, and others, as well as numerous novellas, short stories, comics, and non-fiction. Her work as been translated internationally. She has a Masters degree in Writing Popular Fiction from Seton Hill University, Pittsburgh, and is currently a member of The Authors Guild, The

International Thriller Writers, and Penn Writers. She was a co-host on the popular podcast *The Horror Show* with Brian Keene and her own podcast-turned-blog on cosmic horror, *Cosmic Shenanigans*, and is currently a co-host of *The Ghost Writers Podcast*. She has the distinction of being one of the first women to speak about writing at the CIA Headquarters in Langley, VA, and offers talks and workshops on writing around the country. Born and raised in New Jersey, she currently resides in Pennsylvania.

Julia Darcey writes sci-fi and fantasy novels and short stories. Born and raised in Colorado, she now lives in Kenya with her partner and two rescue mutts.

Ichabod Cassius Kilroy (Ick, to its friends, fans, and haters alike), is a transsexual pile of mostly-real guts that could probably pass the Turing test, were the Turing test given to gutspills rather than to computers. It is a graduate of the 2023 Clarion workshop, enjoyer of iced coffee, and running out of cute little witticisms for this author bio. In case of emergency or boredom, it can be reached at: mx.sickilroy@gmail.com

Chris Hann hails from New Zealand—a distant yet charming pair of islands on the far side of the globe. He is of Korean descent (a "Kiwi-Korean," so to speak) and hasn't thought twice about his love for horror since reading "The Black Cat" by Poe.

S. A. Cosby is an Anthony Award-winning writer from Southeastern Virginia. He is the author of the New York Times bestseller *Razorblade Tears* and *Blacktop Wasteland*, which won the *Los Angeles Times* Book Prize, was a *New York Times* Notable Book, and was named a best book of the year by *NPR*, *The Guardian*, and *Library Journal*, among others. When not writing, he is an avid hiker and chess player.

Marnie Desdemona is a self-taught writer who has been honing her craft since her awkward, angsty teenage years when she filled up her first novel in a bundle of notebooks, believing it would be her big break as an author. A little over a decade later, Marnie still believes that each year will be her chance to be in the spotlight on the stage of literature.

Specializing in the sapphic, surreal, and self-reflecting, she likes to intimately examine the more broken and vulnerable sides of humanity. Despite suffering enough trauma at a young age to become the protagonist of the kinds of books she writes, as well as having enough physical and mental illnesses to fill a small ledger, she still remains an optimist and believes that life can be good and that love wins in the end.

Once from Massachusetts, she became a U-Haul lesbian a while ago when she moved in with her then girlfriend of two months. These days she is joined in her little apartment in Virginia by three cats of varying temperance, a very sleepy girlfriend, and one well-worn typewriter.

Rachel Searcey is a filmmaker and writer living in the Florida panhandle with her husband, two children, and three cats (2 black, 1 torti). She's bi-racial—Indian and white—and has recently ventured into prose after over two decades of producing indie horror films. Her work has been published in *Cosmic Horror Monthly, Diet Milk Magazine, Flash Point SF, Aphotic Realm, Dark Void Magazine*, and *Collage Macabre: An Exhibition of Art Horror*. To view Rachel's films and news on published works, visit agirlandhergoldfish.com

Jorja Osha is a speculative fiction writer living on the East Coast. When not writing about otherworldly beings, troubled characters and everything else in between she can usually be found playing video games, listening to music/creepy narrations or partaking in her current pastime of binging old classic films with either a crochet hook or knitting needles close at hand. Her short stories have previously appeared in *The Dark, A Coup of Owls* and *Martian* under the pen name Bibi Osha.

Jessica L. Sparrow writes Gothic fiction, supernatural thrillers, and ethereal poetry that can save or damn your soul. Sparrow's writing is heavily influenced by her Taino & bruja Puerto Rican roots embodied by the matriarchs in her family. This is evident in her debut Gothic novel, *Blood Behind the Walls*, a 19th century supernatural thriller spiced up with Puerto Rican witchcraft, love, and matriarchal power.

When not writing or teaching about writing, Sparrow is usually cooking up delicious spells in the kitchen. Or playing with her shorkie, Yoshi, while binge-watching horror movies with her husband, Jason.

Cyrus Amelia Fisher writes queer tales of shipwrecks, mycelium, and horrors of the flesh. After years of driving around the United States in a beat-up minivan, they finally returned to the mossy fens of their birth in the Pacific Northwest. Now they while away the hours communing with their fungal hivemind and writing about cannibalism. Naturally, they also love to cook. Find their work at cyrusameliafisher.com or Twitter at @hubristicfool.

Michelle Tang writes speculative fiction from Canada, where she lives with her husband and children. Her short stories have been published by Cemetery Gates, Escape Pod, and Flame Tree Publishing, among others. When she's not writing, Michelle enjoys watching horror movies, playing video games, and lurking on social media.

L. Marie Wood is a Golden Stake Award-winning author, a MICO Award-winning screenwriter, a two-time Bram Stoker Award® Finalist, a Rhysling nominated poet, and an accomplished essayist. She writes high concept fiction that includes elements of psychological horror, mystery, dark fantasy, thriller, and romance. Wood has won over 50 national and international screenplay and film awards. She is also part of the 2022 Bookfest Book Award-winning poetry anthology, *Under Her Skin*. Wood has penned short fiction that has been published in groundbreaking works, including the anthologies *Sycorax's Daughters* and *Slay: Stories of the Vampire Noire*. Her nonfiction has been published in *Nightmare Magazine* and academic textbooks such as the cross-curricular, *Conjuring Worlds: An Afrofuturist Textbook*. Wood is the founder of the Speculative Fiction Academy, an English and Creative Writing professor, a horror scholar, and a frequent contributor to the conversation around the evolution of genre fiction. Learn more about L. Marie Wood at www.lmariewood.com.

Acknowledgments

No one is truly "self-made". We all have people who guide us, teach us, mentor us, or offer a kindly word that alters our trajectory forever. Neither Vaughn nor I would have been able to produce this book were it not for the dedication of parents and teachers who taught us how to read and write…along with many other important things. Likewise, an anthology like the one you've just read (or, we hope you read it, and didn't just skip to the end) isn't just the work of the editors and authors you see credited—those are just the names that fit—but of countless individuals who put their time and effort into making something wonderful. We'd like to thank as many of them as we can here:

First, we are endlessly grateful to Raw Dog Screaming Press' Jennifer Barnes who not only took Vaughn's idea of "making Lovecraft roll over in his grave" and gave it a home, but also acted as a mentor for two new editors who had almost no idea what they were doing. None of this could have happened without her, and honestly this small paragraph at the back of the book doesn't feel like quite enough.

Thank you to Lynne Hansen for her beautiful cover art. You were the first person we thought of when we were thinking of who we would get to decorate the front of this amazing anthology.

If you've been following the anthology, you know that it was crowdfunded via Kickstarter, a first for RDSP and for us! We want to thank Mikah Meyers—who put his artistic skills to work in designing our logos and stickers for the campaign—and everyone else who helped us run, manage, spread the word, and fund the project. While this was a nail-biting adventure we were fortunate that the horror community was incredibly supportive, and because of you, everyone got paid! This was especially important to us since so many times artists are asked to work for free and knowing historically marginalized people are not always paid equally. So, thank you, to all of our backers.

Thank you to our guest authors: L. Marie Wood, S.A. Cosby, Mary SanGiovanni, and Jessica McHugh. And no less important, thank you to our chosen authors, whose wonderful words are printed within this book; your names are already in the Table of Contents, so people know who you are! Thank you for trusting us with your phenomenal stories. We literally needed them for this anthology to exist.

It was an honor to work with you all. You made the editing process a pleasure.

Thank you to everyone who submitted to us. We were shocked by how many we received and you did not make the selection process easy for us.

And last, but certainly not least: Thank you, dear reader, for picking up this anthology and joining us on this wild ride *Beyond the Bounds of Infinity*. I hope you enjoyed the madness, and maybe we'll meet again beneath the acknowledgments of a future book.

—Stephanie Pearre